Born
TONG
est an
natura
life du... .... protound social change.
Namesake of the prestigious Dong-in Literary Award, Kim Tongin's succinct writing
style, complex psychological portraits, and
detached point of view provide insight into
early 20th century Korea.

GRACE JUNG is a writer, translator, and film-
maker from New York. She is the author of
Deli Ideology and producer of the feature
documentary *A-Town Boyz*. She is currently a
PhD candidate in Cinema and Media Studies
at the University of Los Angeles, California.
She is a former Fulbright scholar.

YOUNGMIN KWON is a professor of Korean
literature at Seoul National University and
former dean of the College of Humanities.
He is currently a visiting professor at the
University of California, Berkeley. He has
written and edited numerous volumes of literary history, literary criticism, and reference
works on modern Korean literature, and is
the current president of the International
Association of Comparative Korean Studies.

SWEET POTATO

COLLECTED SHORT STORIES
BY KIM TONGIN

Translated by GRACE JUNG
Introduced by YOUNGMIN KWON

HONFORD STAR

This translation first published by Honford Star 2017
honfordstar.com
Translation copyright © Grace Jung 2017
Introduction copyright © Youngmin Kwon 2017
All rights reserved
The moral right of the translator and editors has been asserted

ISBN (paperback): 978-1-9997912-0-9
ISBN (ebook): 978-1-9997912-1-6
A catalogue record for this book is available from the British Library
Cover illustration by Jee-ook Choi
Book cover and interior design by Jon Gomez

Printed and bound by CPI Group (UK) Ltd, Croydon, CR0 4YY

This book is published with the support of the
Literature Translation Institute of Korea (LTI Korea).

CONTENTS

INTRODUCTION

Style and Technique in
Kim Tongin's Fiction

1

Kim Tongin was born on 2 October 1900 in P'yŏngyang, South P'yŏngan Province, in the north-western area of the Korean peninsula. His father, Kim Taeyun, a local magnate in P'yŏngyang, recognized the importance of Enlightenment thought, became a Christian and eventually a Protestant elder. After finishing elementary school in P'yŏngyang, Tongin moved to Japan at the urging of his father. There he graduated from Meiji Gakuin University's Middle School and later took courses at the Kawabata Art School.

In 1919, Tongin started the first literary magazine in the Korean language. *Creation* (*Ch'angjo*) was published in Tokyo, and included works contributed by Chu Yohan, Chŏn Yŏngt'aek and Ch'oe Sŭngman. In the magazine, Tongin emphasized literature as an autonomous art form and championed 'art for art's sake'. *Creation* was an important medium for popularizing modern writing styles among Korean intellectuals in the early part of the twentieth century.

Tongin's short story 'The Sorrows of the Weak' (*yakhanchaŭi sŭlp'ŭm*, 1919) featured in *Creation*'s inaugural issue, establishing him as a serious writer and he forthwith poured his energies into writing fiction in the Korean language. Other stories of his such as 'Boat Song' (*paettaragi*, 1921) were early templates for Korean writers interested in modern literary techniques.

After the successful publication of *Creation*'s first issue, Kim left school and returned to Korea. In March 1919, the Japanese colonial police discovered from Tongin's younger brother, Tongp'yŏng, that Tongin had penned a memorandum for the anti-colonial March First Movement, and they jailed Tongin for four months on charges of violating publication law. Tongin recounted his prison experiences in his short story 'Flogging' (*t'aehyŏng*, 1922–1923).

When *Creation* was discontinued in 1921, Tongin started a second literary magazine called *Spirit Altar* (*yŏngdae*), which was contributed to by the writers from *Creation* magazine along with new talents such as Kim Yŏje and Kim Sowŏl. In 1923, he published a collection of original short stories under the title of his 1921 story, 'The Life in One's Hands' (*moksum,* literal translation 'Life').

Tongin then published a series of works expounding a Zola-esque, naturalistic view of life, including 'Sweet Potato' (*kamja,* 1925). Following this, he published works such as 'Fire Sonata' (*kwangyŏm sonat'a,* 1929) and 'The Mad Painter' (*kwanghwasa,* 1935) in a sharply aestheticist vein employing the themes of artistic madness and aestheticist desire.

In the 1930s, Tongin tried his hand at long historical novels published serially in newspapers. These colourful historical novels flesh out the individual character and inner psyche of historical personages poised at the centre of well-known historical events, presenting new interpretations of their human side. This approach was a major break from the experimentality of Tongin's earlier short stories.

In the final years of the Japanese colonial rule, Tongin could not but conform to the ruling policies of the Japanese imperialists. He visited war areas in the Manchurian region at the behest of the Chosŏn Governor General of Japan, and published articles in line with Japanese colonial directives. As Korean writers were divided into left and right political camps, Tongin chose to criticize the political partisanship of the leftists and organized the Association of Pan-Korean Writers in 1946, a right-wing nationalist group of Korean writers. In addition, he published short stories such as 'The Traitor' (*panyŏkcha,* 1946), critically depicting the pro-Japanese activities of literary figures at the end of Japanese colonial rule. He died on 5 January 1951, during the Korean War, at his home in Seoul.

No clear-cut determinations have been made as to why Tongin chose to become a literary artist. But something of his philosophy can be gleaned from his first work of literary theory, 'On the Korean Conception of the Novel' (*sosŏre taehan josŏn sarame sasangŭl*) in the journal Light of Learning (*hakchikwang*) No. 18, 1919. His worldview defines the novel as 'a world expressing the human spirit' and the literary world as 'an expression of the individual's inner consciousness'. His definitions are comprehensive and general but reveal Tongin's attitude to literature, an attitude placing the highest value on the personal nature of literature and art. Tongin's perception of literature as foremost a medium for individual expression essentially reduces art to the expression of individual emotions and desires.

Tongin's literary philosophy was further expounded in his essay 'The world of his own creation: comparing Tolstoy and Dostoevsky' (*chagiŭi ch'angjohan segye: t'olsŭt'oiwa tosŭt'oyep'ŭsŭk'irŭl pigyohayŏ*) (*Creation*, No. 7, July 1920). This early editorial encapsulates his judgment on the fictitious nature of the novel and elucidates his awareness of the essence of art.

> What is art? [...] the legitimate answer is 'the world man creates by breathing life into his shadow' – that is, the world that man himself controls. This reveals why art came into being and by what need. Man is not satisfied with the world God created. The world that pleases Man is created by the great creativity of his life, the world that comes into being only after it has been built up by his own energies and powers, even though it be an imperfect world [...] The art produced from his great need is a

shadow of life, a unique bible of life, the vitality of a love on which human life depends.

Tongin held up literature and art as the work of man's towering creative mind, emphasizing the connection between artistic creation and the artist's individual talent. Art, in so far as it relates to life, can only be achieved by the inner demands of the self. The truth to be embodied through art – namely, beauty – is closely linked to actual human life, and personal desires and creative intuition constitutes the principle of all artistic choice. Tongin viewed art as life created by an artist, not real life. The artist must dominate his art as a world of his own creation, and it is this mastery that determines the author's greatness. For Tongin, art is a new creation of perfect life, wholly self-sufficient because its meaning exists independently of actuality.

This attitude is reflected in his fiction. Creating a truthful life is the fundamental task of fiction. For Tongin, the problem of life is the essence of existence and it is in fiction that life can achieve completed meaning. The aim of literature is to create a life that the artist can manipulate like a marionette. In most of Tongin's short stories, the plots and characters occupy a fictional space quite unlike the realities of life in Tongin's day. He affirms only pure artistic values and rejects all others, finding a space within the novelistic world where literature can exist in complete autonomy. This space is fictional, created by the artist outside the realm of real life. The problems of life that Tongin depicts in his fiction correspond to essential aspects of human existence largely independent of historical and social reality. Tongin was in pursuit of an artistic value that is both timeless and constant through these essential aspects of the human being. Of course, that artistic value derives from the completeness of the work's internal structure. From the outset of his career as a writer, Tongin was obsessed with the form of the short story in serving a

kind of functionality with regard to life and the possibility of
its completed meaning.

3

Tongin's early short stories 'Boat Song' and 'Sweet Potato' are
fine examples of his narrative focus and style. The two works
limit their focus to one aspect of life in order to show the
contrasting destinies of the main characters. The characters'
personalities are created through the narrative technique.
  'Boat Song' has a 'story within a story' narrative structure.
This structure has the formal advantage of securing completeness of the inner story by dint of an outer story that enhances
the credibility of the inner story. 'Boat Song' recounts the
destruction of the relationship between two brothers following a misunderstanding by the hero who is trapped in his own
feelings of inferiority. The older brother's uncontrollable feeling of inferiority leads to the breakdown of the relationship
between 1) himself, a man of gentle but honest character, 2)
his sociable, pretty wife, and 3) his reliable, warm-hearted
younger brother. Ultimately, the work shows that human
destiny is defined by the 'demands' residing within each man.
The tragic destiny playing out in the inner structure becomes
intertwined with the experience of the narrator, 'I', existing
in the outer frame. 'Boat Song' is less about describing the
tragedy of a human life as inducing people to rethink the
problem of life through the machinations of an inescapable
tragic destiny.
  The case of 'Sweet Potato' is different. This work follows
the tragic fall of the heroine, Pongnyŏ, ending in the loss of
her moral will amidst a life of extreme privation. At the root
of the heroine's dramatic downfall (that is, her death) is the
external social factor of poverty. Prior to her fall, Pongnyŏ
enjoyed a normative home education and was possessed of
an intact ethical sense. But when her family falls into penury

she is sold for 80 *wŏn* and weds a man twenty years her senior. Her husband's laziness results in her becoming a slum dweller outside the Ch'ilsŏng Gate. Condemned to slum life, she goes and finds a job as a 'worker who doesn't work but is amply paid' by selling her body to the supervisor. When she is caught stealing sweet potatoes from Mister Wang, she escapes certain doom by offering him her body, and maintains a relationship with him while taking money for her favours. Notable in this process is the way Pongnyŏ's character rapidly devolves and the devolution's fatalistic meaning. Also of importance is how external conditions of poverty can corrupt a human being. Unlike 'Boat Song', 'Sweet Potato' does not contain subjective commentary, and the work's concise style reinforces the impression of objectivity. This contrast in attitude between 'Boat Song' and 'Sweet Potato' points to modern narrative techniques emphasizing balance between objective and subjective description in an array of fictional works.

Other short stories by Kim Tongin such as 'Flogging' and 'Red Mountain' foreground the contradiction and pain of Japanese colonial rule. Based on his own experience of imprisonment in a detention centre for violating the publishing law immediately after the March First Independence Movement in 1919, 'Flogging' is a detailed depiction of major and minor events taking place in a cramped prison cell. The work suggests that the circumstances of Japan's oppressive reign over colonial period Koreans can be understood by reference to the scenes in the cell, but rather than expressing resistance to Japan, the story focuses on the ugly, egoistic instinct of those anxious to find comfort against their painful reality. 'Red Mountain' relates the pain, sorrow and patriotism of Koreans who, unable to survive the severe plunder of the Japanese Colonial period, went to live in Manchuria.

Tongin's 'Fire Sonata' and 'The Mad Painter' are unconventional works written from unusual perspectives of the fierce desire to create art, and madness in the obsessed artist. The two stories are representative examples of Tongin 's aestheticist literature. 'Fire Sonata' expresses the author's extreme advocacy of aestheticism. Aestheticism is the core philosophy of the artist in the story, a musician named Paek Sŏng-su who commits murder, arson and other crimes to transgress social taboos and thereby draw inspiration as a composer. Utilizing the 'story within a story' technique, the work appropriately adjusts narrative distance to achieve the compositional completeness that Tongin admired. 'The Mad Painter' also takes the form of a 'story within a story'. The hero, Solgŏ, attempts to depict supreme beauty, the beauty of a beautiful woman's face, with his brush. But supreme beauty does not exist in the real world, so he chases after fantasy instead, perpetrating acts of near insanity for the goal of enhancing his artistic achievement. Tongin pursues the tragedy of the artist because he is unable to achieve absolute beauty. The pursuit and inevitable frustration of failing to grasp through art the pure, transcendent beauty of life is at once the dream pursued by the painter within the story's frame and the novelistic aesthetic of Tongin. Tongin's obsession with the lives of artists striving to overcome the tragedy of their life derives from his own extreme distrust of reality.

The immensely popular historical novels published by Tongin in the 1930s reflect his escape from problems of colonial day-to-day reality and his conscious return to the historical past. His historical novels consist of historical material reworked using fictional narrative principles. The combination of historical fact and fictional elements opened up the possibility of employing aesthetics to view historical problems with an eye to contemporary reality.

4

Kim Tongin's literary achievements had important literary

historical significance, leading to the establishment of modern Korean fiction and its rapid popularization. From Yi Injik to Yi Kwang-su, Korean fiction before Tongin had been based on the full-length novel and was characterized by a broad historical pursuit of life as a whole and exploration of life's meaning. However, Tongin was interested in the short story, where narrative could attain dramatic completeness by isolating and presenting a single section of human life for analysis.

Through the establishment and diffusion of the short story, Tongin made possible the advancement of modern novelistic techniques in Korean literature. One advance was the method of personifying characters in stories. Although not the case in all short stories, limiting the central characters to one or two people is a common feature of the form. This is shown in Tongin's 'Boat Song', where the main character is described as a man who drifts around singing the '*paettaragi*' tune. Since the number of important characters in the story are limited to one or two, the story's attention can be focused on the protagonist. The character's personality can be portrayed by drawing out particular aspects of the character's life.

In Korean classical fiction, the narrative point of view was not clearly defined. Narrative distance was not maintained, as the narrator narrated everything with absolute authority. The lack of distance between subject and object means that maintaining narrative tension is made difficult, and suggests that people living in the era of classical novels did not have objective and rational perceptions and views. The rational subject was not properly established until the 'New Novel' (*sinsosŏl*) movement at the end of the nineteenth century, but vestiges from the classical period continued right up until Yi Kwang-su's novel *Mujŏng* (1917). The narrator was given an omniscient role that completely dominated the narrative's internal space.

However, Tongin's narrative method included use of the

past tense verb ending as an aspect of his literary style, and generalizing the third person pronoun *kŭ* (he) in the narrative. These developments helped the introduction of a narrative point of view that understands the aesthetic potential. A change of the narrator's position in the story now meant that a clear line had been drawn with the world qua object, and the narrator has learned to place themselves at a distance from it. The 'narrator' gained the ability to view the outside world from a certain angle, define their own categories and establish their own status as a subject. Angle and distance for seeing the object became clear in Korean literature, as had the focus of description.

Thanks to stories such as 'Boat Song', 'Red Mountain' and 'The Mad Painter', the first-person narrator would become a standard literary technique in Korean fiction. Tongin incorporated the narrative past tense to maintain a strict distance between the narrative subject and object. He used the past tense ending to secure narrative distance, thereby enabling objective descriptions of objects through literary style. It is no exaggeration to say that the Korean literary establishment's use of the narrative past tense in the novel originated with Tongin.

Kwon, Youngmin
Emeritus Professor of Seoul National University
Adjunct Professor of Korean Literature at UC Berkeley

TRANSLATOR'S NOTE

*The Melodramatic, Meta and Impaired
Stories of Kim Tongin*

I noticed several patterns while translating this collection of Kim Tongin's short stories: the first is the author's gift at weaving melodrama; the second is his habit of meta-storytelling; the third is his obsession with the physically or mentally challenged. These three things pave a way into the author's inner world as well as the significance of the period in which modern Korean literature began to take shape.

Scholars generally point to Kim's realist/naturalist tendencies, and while this may be, what I discern the most is his love for melodrama. Quite a few of his stories include the trope of the fastidious young woman who tries and tries but can never make it out of poverty due to social constraints. A character such as this is a staple of classic melodrama, and although scholars generally pit Kim against Yi Kwang-su and his didactic literary tendencies, an argument can be made for Kim's own knack for didacticism via melodrama – a form of storytelling that gives readers a clear sense of who is morally upright and who is not. Recurrent techniques of melodrama visible in Kim's stories are certainly apparent in films and serialized dramas produced in contemporary Korea, particularly emotional excess such as tearfulness.[1] Many of Kim's characters suffer from a helplessness due to their *p'al-ja* – the circumstances they were born into but cannot change – and this often lends to moments of rage, madness or crying. Stories like 'Sweet Potato' shift more towards the 'fallen woman' category; in fact, a number of Kim's stories fall under this genre. The misogynistic trope of punishing the woman who isn't 'virtuous' is apparent in Kim's work; female characters who don't retain their virginity wind up dead or lost, whereas those who keep it are shrouded by an untouchable other-worldliness, giving us a glimpse into Kim's patriarchal

---

[1] For more on melodrama, see John G. Cawelti, 'The Evolution of Social Melodrama' Imitations of Life: A Reader on Film and Television Melodrama, (Detroit: Wayne State University Press, 1991), 33-49.

preoccupation with female chastity.[2]

In 1915, after transferring out of the Tokyo Institute, Kim became a student at the Meiji Institute in Japan where he developed not only an interest in literature but also film; thirteen years later, he and his brother tried to establish a film production company in occupied Korea but failed – a fate that other modernist writers have also succumbed to while chasing the romantic prospects of cinema (consider F. Scott Fitzgerald's history with Hollywood).[3] Reading Kim's works, it is apparent why he would gravitate towards the visual medium. His stories read like screenplays; they contain the rhythm of a film with cutaways and close-ups to facial reactions, buildups to an explosive climax, a frightening horror that either looms or bares its face, intense emotionality and heavy sorrow. It's no wonder that so many of Kim's stories were adapted into films in the 1950s through the 1980s, including but not limited to 'Sweet Potato', 'Fire Sonata', 'Like Father Like Son' and 'The Mad Painter'. 'Sweet Potato' also influenced *Bedevilled* (2010), directed by Jang Cheol-soo and written by Choi Kwang-young.[4] Kim's skill with dramatization, however, does not discount his sense of humour. 'The Life in One's Hands' has some comical moments, as does

[2] What's interesting (and troubling) is just how frequently this trope is used in popular works of contemporary literature and cinema by male writers and filmmakers (see essay by Gina Yu, 'Images of Women in Korean Movies', Korean Cinema: From Origins to Renaissance, (Seoul: CommBooks, 2007), 261-268). The trope of the female body as a symbol for masculinist-nationalist anxieties continue in these spheres, and the only way to move past this and discover new horizons is by creating more opportunities of media expression for women who have different ideas and understandings of the female body and its potentials.

[3] Hyunsue Kim, Naturalistic Sensibility and Modern Korean Literature: Kim Tongin, (Florida State University, PhD diss., 2008), vi.

[4] See Michelle Cho, 'Beyond Vengeance: Landscapes of Violence in Jang Chul-soo's Bedevilled', (Acta Koreana, 17:1, 2014), 137-162.

'Flogging', which contains instances of tenderness, although both stories are generally of a dark disposition. This balancing act is a testament to Kim's versatility, and as Youngmin Kwon notes in the introduction, his colourful writing.

As Kwon mentions, Kim often creates 'a story within a story'. Beyond this, however, Kim is a highly self-reflexive writer. In 'Notes on Darkness and Loss', the author refers to himself by his own name and writes in the first person, making the story closer to a personal essay than a work of fiction. In the case with 'The Mad Painter', the protagonist waits around for a story to come to him as he lounges around in the mountains before bringing another character to life. Although the transference is spelled out for the reader, the general feeling isn't too far from Virginia Woolf's style in texts like *To the Lighthouse* and *Mrs Dalloway* where the reader gets carried from one character's interior into another's. In 'Barely Opened Its Eyes', Kim demonstrates meta-storytelling by outright telling the reader that he is tired of writing this piece and would like to move on to another. In 'Fire Sonata', Kim preps the reader with a setting, and the rest of the story reads very much like a chamber play. In 'The Mad Painter', the narrator deliberates openly as to how he should end the story, a bit like a choose-your-own-adventure piece. In 'The Old Taet'angji Lady', Kim starts out by wondering aloud if his stories don't sound hackneyed at this point in his career. These examples of bold self-reflexivity make Kim all the more interesting as not just a writer but as a character himself, unafraid to immerse his readers while also dialoguing with them directly while hovering above the story-world.

Returning to *p'al-ja*, I earlier noted Kim's fixation on the physically or mentally challenged. In the cases with 'The Old Taet'angji Lady', 'The Mad Painter', 'A Photograph and a Letter' and 'Mother Bear', Kim delights in creating characters who are social rejects due to their physical appearance. In 'Fire Sonata' and 'The Mad Painter', characters suffer from impairments such as mental disturbances and blindness. In 'Notes on Darkness and Loss', 'The Life in One's Hands' and 'Like Father Like Son', characters are invalids. In 'Barely Opened Its Eyes', there is a character with a deformed ear. Kyeong-hee Choi observes that many modernists during the colonial era had an 'interest in bodily anomaly' due to the colonial government's censorship – a form of literary impairment. Choi argues that the authors of this period transgressed colonial censorship through their own form of 'self-censorship' in the form of impaired literary bodies by 'amputating actions of the external censor'.[5] Although Kim is often championed as an 'art-for-art's sake' writer, his works demonstrate a clear political interest through literary transgressions with the bodily impaired, complicating his oeuvre's 'pure art' status that scholars often cite. Kim was political, and in stories like 'Flogging', 'The Traitor' and 'Red Mountain', his activism shines through.

Kim produced stories that generate a vivid visual world through melodrama, suspense and humour, while maintaining a vision for modern Korean literature during the occupation through political rigour both as a writer and activist. This collection exhibits just some of the rich layers that this author possessed.

Because Kim was a writer from P'yŏngyang, many of the stories are set in places that remain largely inaccessible to the world. The beauty that Kim paints of North Korea produces a deep longing for these settings, while current events remind us of the national divide. Kim's works contain many idiosyncratic words and expressions that are native to the P'yŏngan dialect or simply no longer in mode. Certain

[5] Kyeong-Hee Choi, 'Impaired Body as Colonial Trope: Kang Kyŏng'ae's Underground Village', (Public Culture, 13:3), 431-458; Choi references Kim's 'The Mad Painter' in her footnote (432n).

words and expressions, although Korean, are not necessarily native to everyone who is familiar with the language; dialects in Korean are diverse and can be drastically different from one another. Working around this, in addition to outdated terms and Japanese expressions, was challenging, but I had a good community of people to rely on with questions as they came and general support as I needed. For this, I'd like to thank Bruce Fulton, Ju-Chan Fulton, Dr Young Ae Choi, Todd Kushigemachi, John Jung, Tam Quach and Miru Kim.

Grace Jung
Translator

SWEET POTATO

*Collected Short Stories
by Kim Tongin*

THE LIFE IN ONE'S HANDS

I thought he was dead. He'd contracted a strange illness five months ago. At first, his appetite disappeared and he couldn't eat. Then his belly gradually bloated. In fact, his entire body swelled. It looked like three or four bowls of water could pour out of his jaundiced face if someone pricked it with a needle. He said that his belly was in about the same condition. When asked if he was in any pain, he said that he wasn't. He only complained of dizziness and the occasional nausea. He went to S Hospital and began to take medication, but his condition only worsened. He eventually checked into S Hospital as a patient. I went to see him every day. He was always lounging on an easy chair, and when I arrived, he greeted me happily, asking for a cigarette. It's a Christian hospital, so they ban cigarettes among patients; he could only smoke when I paid a visit. He and the nurse were on familiar terms, so when she witnessed this transaction, she'd just give a knowing grin and leave it at that. Given his active nature, sitting still within hospital confines appeared to be a struggle for him. Then I took a trip for a couple of days to prepare for a job out of town. When I returned after two or three days to say goodbye, his health had changed drastically and he refused any visitors. I heard that the chief of medical staff had delivered some bad news, telling him that he was dying. When I heard this, I just turned around and went home.

He's dying. This fellow, whose voice was once so full of energy that the power overflowed and flew in all directions around him, is dying. A person's life is ... unpredictable.

I don't know when our relationship began, but it runs deep. While I was researching as an entomologist, he was writing brilliant poetry that was printed in newspapers and magazines here and there. Despite this, he and I had something in common. While I, on the one hand, had the scientist's determination to dig out every part of the earth in order to find a way to live in a world that relies on human strength, he, on the other hand, had the artist's determination to leave behind his imprint in some shape or form. Our point of commonality was a desire for expression. Our relationship doesn't have an official starting point, but as I mentioned, it runs deep. So the moment must've been when we first declared our dreams to each other, which became our point of commonality.

When I heard that they had given him a death sentence, I wanted to rationalize my sadness on behalf of society: *It is losing a talented and promising young man.* But the surprising truth is that I was sad on my own behalf for losing a friend to have frank conversations with (I never had a friend who understood me as well as M). The next day, I left behind my ailing friend and took my long-awaited trip to the vast plains of Kangwŏn Province to collect insects. I took a butterfly net and insecticide to the field and wandered for two months collecting beetles, butterflies, and caddisfly.[1] I put my dying friend M out of my mind during this time.

---

[1] *ŭnojŏllyu* (隱五節類) – an insect with five joints; *hojŏmnyu* (胡蝶類) – a species of butterfly; *mosiryu* (毛翅類) – a type of moth.

When I returned, my desk had a pile of letters. Among them was a letter from M:

> *I'm dying. Even the chief can't help me now. I hate everyone who goes on living. I can't wait for what I'm going through to happen to everyone else. Even you. But before I die, even though I dictate this letter, I just had to write a note of farewell to you. Although I hate you for being one of the 'living people', I also love you as a friend and will never forget you – not till death. I believe you'll forgive me for these conflicting feelings.*

This was written in another's handwriting on hospital stationery. I was struck with the kind of loneliness that hits a child after losing its beloved dog to a beating. I imagined what he must have looked like while writing this letter to me: M forces his swollen body to sit upright with one arm, but only makes it up halfway. He summons the ghostwriter and begins to dictate his letter. When the ghostwriter reaches the line 'I hate everyone who goes on living', the ghostwriter suggests not putting in such a sentence. M frowns and shouts in a raspy voice:

'How dare you discount a dying man's last words!' The ghostwriter, shocked, continues to write. M plops his ailing body back down on the hospital bed and closes his eyes. He no longer thinks about death but becomes obsessed with all kinds of life's concerns.

'Why am I dying?! People – not just people but animals, plants even, fish, the stream, even the ocean – are alive. Why do *I* have to die? There goes the tram. Damn it! I'm pissed. Die – all you who live on this earth. Disappear. Let's all just disappear together!' He bolts straight up on his bed in anger. His jaundiced face flushes bright red.

Ah. M's dead. Whether it was me thinking back on our

friendship or pitying a fellow man, my eyes welled up with hot tears. Without a doubt, M was the kind of person who was twice as obsessed with life and hated death just as much. So why should it be strange for someone like M to scream with all his might for everything to disappear? I called S Hospital to enquire the whereabouts of M's grave. I wanted to go more to restore my own conscience than to comfort M's resting soul. I just had to pay a visit to his grave and offer him a drink, but I couldn't get any information from the hospital. They said that a person named M did check into the hospital but that he was discharged upon recovery. I thought it might've been someone with the same name as him so I enquired once more, but the nurse replied that she was a new nurse currently on her probationary period so she wasn't sure. I asked for the chief, but she said that he was away. The resident physician was on call, and Nurse S, who looked after M, was no longer working there. I turned and sat at the table, laughing.

'Ha ha ha ha! M is alive! M practically died then came back to life! Does this mean that life overcomes death? Ha ha ha ha.'

So a month's time passed. This was four days ago. All I did for that month was think about M's hometown, which is in North P'yŏng'an Province. This was all I knew about his hometown, but it was on my mind. Then the servant came to me and said that someone who looked just like M paid a visit.

M isn't dead! But would something like this happen? Who could have saved the patient that the doctor had dismissed? He's alive! According to the nurse-in-training, if M was dead, his news would be in the papers, but she hasn't seen anything. He's alive. I took a moment to put the pieces together in my head. I brought my scattered thoughts back in order as I bolted for the door. When I reached the door, I couldn't see M's body but I could sense his presence nearby. As soon as I rushed outside, I grabbed hold of every person I ran into.

He's back. He's back. He isn't dead. He regained his strength ...

'I didn't die after all.' It was M's voice. I looked up and saw M. His face glowed with strength and its expression read, *Whoever told you I was sick?* He gave me a friendly smile while peering back at me.

'Come. Let's go inside.' I put my arm over his shoulders and led us both into the living room.

'What on earth happened?' I asked. He looked back at me blankly. I couldn't explain my question.

'A dead person coming back to life, I mean ...'

'A person's life ought to have a price tag of one *chŏn* and five *li*.'[2]

It was my turn to stare back blankly.

He explained, 'You'll understand if you read my thought journal. In any case, I've come back to life. I left the hospital a month ago, and during that time I took a pleasant trip for myself. And I've appeared before you with twice the strength and energy as before, have I not? Even so, the price of my recovery is one *chŏn* and five *li* ...' He handed over a unique-looking manuscript – a collection of scrap paper with poorly scripted handwriting. I was eager to know what he meant by 'one *chŏn*, five *li*', so I snatched the manuscript and began to read.

Me and Life: M's Thought Journal

Thought Piece One

I was at my wits' end. My family continued to nag me even though I didn't feel particularly ill. But my stomach did ache and sent faint waves of nausea, so I hauled my body by force onto a rickshaw and headed for the hospital to check in, which appeared before me like a structure of hell on earth. Each time the black rickshaw tires ran over rocks, the awfully

[2] One *li* is approximately 0.5 kilometers.

bumpy ride relieved the extreme pain in my stomach with a cramp that pushed vomit all the way up to my throat before going back down. The sky looked tiny as though I was staring at it through binoculars. Its light was yellow like pollen yet dark as ash. The yellow looked endless. At the same time, it looked like it was falling down from the top of my head. And there appeared a peculiar mustard yellow cloud picking up speed as though it was racing against the rickshaw, heading south. The bright yellow sun must've been right beside it, but no matter how much I stared, it hung darkly over me.

For a cloudy spring day, the weather was quite fair. But to my eyes, the day seemed darker than winter's. The sun was gloomy, but the inside of my head felt duskier. Murky and heavy. My skin was desensitized and felt as though it was completely separate from my body, and resting heavily on top of me. My body, having lost its connection to my head, stretched out idly. The nausea continued without fail. I would have been better off if my nausea turned to vomit, but for reasons beyond me, it stayed as nausea. It lingered inside my body. When I spat, saliva filled up inside my mouth within mere seconds. When I spat again, it came right back. When I swallowed the nausea back inside to hold it under my chest, it went down into my stomach, circled around then raced to my head, making me lose all my senses. Then it aimed for my fingers, producing spasms.

'Die,' I cursed, then shut my eyes. After my eyes closed and my sensation to the outer world reduced, the horrid spasm and nausea turned into pain. I'm not sure why pain is preferable over spasm. I could breathe.

This is it! A person experiences pleasure once he closes his eyes. After contemplating this thought that didn't even make sense to me, I took in a deep breath of dusty air. The rickshaw rang its bell lightly, jumping over the rough and rocky terrain, riding far away, perhaps all the way to India. I got on the rickshaw at eleven thirty in the morning, but hadn't heard the noon shots fired yet. For me, though, it felt like I'd entered tomorrow's eve. I wanted to know the time, but the space between my hand and pocket felt no different from several hundreds of *li*. I couldn't stand it any longer, and I opened my eyes. The people who hopped to the side of the kerb at the sound of the rickshaw bell looked like goblins you see dancing in hell for the god of the underworld.

'How fun,' I muttered to myself. I'm not sure why but it felt as though all the creatures in the heavens had come down to tickle me. Convulsions spread throughout my body. Every pore released nauseous sweat. The anxiety was overwhelming to the point where if I had a knife, I would've jumped out of the rickshaw to stab and kill a dozen people.

I came down with this illness (so mysterious not even the doctors have any answers) two months ago. At first, I didn't want to eat. My stomach was constantly bloated. I ate some bread that was supposedly full of nutrients but that eventually came right back out of my mouth. My stomach looked like it belonged to a pregnant woman, gradually swelling up within days. It looked like a polished red cherry, nice and ripe. It looked like, if someone pricked it with a needle, it would gather cherry juice like eyes gathering tears. But my face was completely drained of blood till it turned yellow and eventually blue, save for my bloodshot eyes. My head grew heavy. Eventually all the weight gathered up towards my head. *Right now, my head and body are two separate entities.* I occasionally wondered where I would dispose of my head. I lost my mind completely. I would indulge in moments of extreme happiness or upset myself with endless sorrow by mixing up the events of my daydreams with reality. I'd even befriended several important historical figures. Occasionally I would snap back to reality and the state of my illness. Goosebumps would cover me as if cold water was pouring down my head, and an inexplicably demonic fear would shatter my mind. The whoever-it-was doctor that diagnosed me would hand me some useless powder and water, calling it 'medicine'.

Hospitalization. I ultimately came to this unavoidable conclusion. The bright yellow sky shook before me as though my binoculars were shaking. The road looked muddied with death below the sky – no, from up above in the sky – and a thirsty voice cried out from an unknown place. I couldn't stand the nausea any longer, so I closed my eyes again. The rickshaw continued to run without stop. The sunlight pierced through my eyelids, turning orange, and travelled through my optic nerve towards the brain that stretched out my neck. It grabbed hold of my resisting brain and harassed it. I opened my eyes at the sound of the noon's gunfire. Bang! The rickshaw man set down the bar. Before me was S Hospital's hellish red light with two hands in its pocket, letting out a terrible laugh. By the power of absorption, I got sucked into the hospital. Slurp.

Thought Piece Two

This is practically hell. This terrible sadness. It is indescribable.

'*Uu-uu-uu* ...' A single cry following a groan.

'*Ayu, ayu, ayu* ...' A howling in the throes of death. The sound of the noisy tram disappears. When the whistle of the train goes off intermittently like an afterthought, it's like hearing shrill screams of ghosts reverberating towards me from ten *li* in all directions – above, below, next door, all around. Ah, if this isn't hell, I don't know what is. If these aren't the cries of invalids attacked by scorpions, what else could they be? Whether I'm scared or what, I can't say. I'm nervous. The train takes off violently. I can feel its tremors.

That's right. I'm taking off. Fiercely heading towards death. Off you go. Run with all your might. If you run into the devil, smack him. The devil is a blue light. With your red light erase his blue light. That'll turn into a purple light. It becomes a purple firework.

'*Ai*, save me ...' A shout from a room nearby.

'You idiot. Fight with that purple firework!'

'Hu ...' the person yells again.

There must be a cigarette. I bolt right up and roll off the bed. I raise my head towards the reflected light entering from outside. I bite on the end of the half-cigarette remaining from earlier and sit on an easy chair. Cigarettes are delicious. The doctors who say that cigarettes are unsanitary are idiots. They are the dumbest things on earth who can't decipher what's sanitary from what isn't. When it comes to sanitation, there are two kinds: the physiological sanitation and the psychological sanitation. There's the way to maintain one's bodily health through mental conditioning, and the way to maintain it through physical sanitation. Cigarettes represent mental sanitation, and they can't help but be that way. I inhale the cigarette smoke into my lungs and exhale it through my nose and mouth quietly, aiming for my cheeks. The train whistle blows sharply as though reacting to this with surprise. Someone yawns loudly. It's the kind of yawn that throws up the living spirit. Frightening sounds enter my ears.

'Ah, hey, ah, ah, ah, *ayu*, I'm gonna die ... Hu ...'

Terrifying objects appear before my eyes and inside my head. There's a person whose head is split open lying on the bed. The left cheek is dark, completely covered in blood. The skull and forehead are wrapped in gauze. Below the dark skin are bloodshot eyes glistening. There's no expression. The mouth is slightly parted. I fall in and disappear. I cry out but my mouth doesn't move. My tongue prances about like boiling oil. The pain in my head feels like my brain is wearing a hat made of tens of thousands of needles. My body shivers. Brrr. Next to that bed is a person with an amputated arm. He moves just enough to keep the tiny bit of remaining arm hidden beneath the gauze. Next to that bed is a person without a leg. Beside that person is someone with a stomach split open. All kinds of shouting can be heard here. The cries are cursing life and the living. We're been reduced to an intimate hell setting – no, we've expanded into one.

'Die!' someone cries out.

'I'm gonna die ...' another cries out as though in reply.

But what is death? I think. *Death is brown. Could it be anything else but that?*

Brown. It's brown. There's no way to know. I realize just how bad my head has become.

Death is brown. And ... I don't know what else.

'*Ai.* I'm gonna die, gonna die.' I hear this from quite afar. I could foresee a final, terrible act.

'I'll kill you. You just wait. That'll be more restful for you anyhow.' I hobble up from the easy chair thinking of the penknife sitting amongst the scrap paper that I brought with me. My vision is still blurry. The brown column. White walls. As the black – no, blue – atmosphere turns into a vast endlessness, I think, *I'm falling.*

Before I am able to complete that thought, a flash appears before my eyes, and bang! I fall right in place.

Thought Piece Three

I still recall vividly. It had been my tenth night at the hospital. I was watching W playing with a bug before falling asleep. It was probably around five in the morning.

'*Hyŏngnim, hyŏngnim,*' I heard my younger brother call me.[3] I was the designated owner of the house prior to my hospitalization. In the far room were my kid brother and my mother.

I eventually asked, 'What?'

There was no reply. I waited a while. Again,

'*Hyŏngnim. Hyŏngnim.*'

'What?' I repeated. I waited a while but, again, I heard nothing. I sat right up and pushed open the side door. There

---

[3] *Hyŏngnim* – how a younger brother addresses his older brother.

I found neither my brother nor my mother. Not only that but there wasn't a single stick of furniture inside. It was a completely empty room shining clear and bright under the light. I stood up straight. Goosebumps rose all over my body. I stood there for two or three seconds before swiftly turning around to lie back down in place. Right then from the empty space around the corner appeared a strange monster. It was a brown demon. Both sides of its cheeks drooped down. His eyes were blank and without life. He appeared to be hiding a ferocity as sharp as a needle's point.

'It's brown. It's brown,' I shouted from within.

As if it heard me, the demon started to laugh in a raspy voice, 'Ha ha ha ha.'

I suddenly grew bold and asked, 'What are you doing here?'

'What am I doing? Why? Can't I come here?'

'Of course you can't! You can't!'

'Come now. No need to be so angry. I was coming to get someone next door, and I stopped by to check in on you.'

'You have no reason to be here.'

'Well, you might become our henchman some day, so I stopped by to see you.'

'Not me. No. I won't be your henchman.'

'Ha ha ha ha.' Its raspy laughter was enough to break every object in the room.

'So you have intentions to get involved with us?'

'No involvement. I just won't go where you are.'

'For how many days ...?'

'How many? One month, two months, a year, five years, ten years, twenty years, fifty years, until I die ...'

'When do you think you'll die?'

'Only God knows that.'

'*Hǔng.* God? That's only something that *I* know.'

'That's a lie. That's a lie!'

'You'll come to know once time passes. Ha ha ha ha ha. Let's not do this. Let's compromise and ...'

'I don't need to compromise!'

'When you join us in our world, I'll grant you supreme power.'

'Are you seducing me?'

'Then what'll you have to envy?'

'A person can't live on bread alone.'

'Then what's he live on, eh?'

'With his vibrant strength! With life!'

'That vibrant strength, that vibrant life ... If you had "governing authority" don't you think you'd be happy?'

'I don't want my rights to be pinned down by you!'

'That's exactly it ... This is the weakness of you humans. Humans sacrifice their entire futures and lives fighting over their rights. You are indeed a weak item.'

'No. Humans are mighty because of that!'

'Ha ha ha ha. Humans are mighty, too? In our world, that's the concern of the weakest beings ...You wanna know?' The demon grinned.

'I don't wanna know. I don't wanna hear about it.'

'Then why ask?'

'I was just asking.'

'Then I don't need to explain?'

'Don't need? After I ask something I need to hear an answer.'

'Ha ha ha ha. Indeed, you want to hear, eh? In our world, the strongest proclaims, "I absolutely will do what my heart desires." Got it?'

'Well, there you go. I, too, don't want to go where you are, so I won't ever go.'

'That's just a human being's petty concern over what he doesn't want to do. Now, in your heart, you want to go, right?'

'I hate all of it. I'm just waiting for you to get out of here.'

'You really hate me being here?' the demon asked me, fuming in anger.

'That's right!'

'If you hate it then I'll just do this.' With that, it stretched its claw-like hands and approached me.

'Ah! Ah!' I let out small cries. At this point I realized that this was a dream. I used all my strength to open my eyes. They flashed open.

A dream, I told myself, and continued to tread the dark path. Up ahead, I saw a light. Without any hesitation, I walked towards the light. There was no end. There's no way to know where the end of the road is. I wasn't sure how many hours – no, how many days – I had been walking. I eventually reached the light. It was an enormous palace – enough for me to wonder how such a house could even exist. I went inside. There was no way to know where the main entrance was. I was an uninvited stranger just wandering into somebody's house. As soon as this occurred to me, I turned around to leave when suddenly I heard a voice say, 'M. Why are you leaving? Please come in.' I turned to look. It was a familiar face but a stranger's nonetheless.

'Who are you?'

'Me? You met me earlier. Where is your head?' I looked at him again. It was the demon. The brown demon. I turned and ran towards the darkness as the voice called after me, 'Where are you going?'

I ran twenty-three thousand *li*. There was a house across from the palace. I ran inside, crying out to be saved. The house was the palace from earlier. I'd somehow returned to where I started. I turned and ran away again. I'm not sure how many times I went through this. Every house I arrived at was the original place I'd started from. I didn't know what else to do so I ran away again. The eastern light gradually became brighter. From afar, a nasally voice cried out, 'Help me.' I ran towards the voice. It was an elderly man. He was also my younger brother.

'*Hyŏngnim*, what's wrong?'

'Help me.' He didn't wait for an explanation. Without

hesitation, he said that he knew of a being with infinite power and that we should go and request salvation. We ran together towards that direction. It was a magnificent home. After standing there for a bit, I went inside alone, found the owner and brought him out. Again – it was the brown demon.

'Why do you keep following me?' I shouted at him.

'Me? Follow you? Didn't *you* invade *my* home?' he replied. 'I shall end your life for you,' he said as he unsheathed a sword.

'Why are you doing this, sir?' my younger brother shouted.

'You bastard. You're this guy's henchman, aren't you?' the demon shouted as he aimed his sword at my brother and went after him. At some point, he grabbed my neck and started to shake me.

'Save me!' I screamed as I opened my eyes.

'What's wrong?' asked the nurse as she shook me. I glanced around with drunken eyes. I looked at S who'd just woken from a nap. His face was full of energy. My illness worsened severely from this day forward.

Thought Piece Four

I received an ultimatum from the chief of medical staff today. It was around two p.m. I was wrought with unbearable nausea. Every pore in my body sensed the sounds of slippers coming towards me as I slept. I caught a whiff of my mother, who'd come up from our hometown. I heard the sound of the resident physician's feet. Finally, I heard the clomp, drag, clomp, drag of the German biologist's feet. He had eyeglasses pasted onto the bridge of his nose, his head tilted forward slightly as if he was afraid that the glasses would fall from his face. He had one hand in the pocket of his white coat, while the other one dangled. My eyes narrowed at the sound of these footsteps, then I realized something: even footsteps can sound arrogant. I didn't even want to move. I just kept my eyes shut and continued to snore. The smell of limestone and alcohol invaded my senses. I felt a sudden grasp around my hand.

I kept snoring. Under my ear, I heard the tick, tick of a wristwatch. A moment later, he let go of my hand and raised the skirt of my nightgown and touched my belly. I hated the sensation but it was tickling and refreshing at the same time. After he took my temperature, he clicked his tongue.

'What's the matter? What's the matter?' I looked at the doctor with my eyes shut but through my mind's eye. He seemed to be frowning. His forehead seemed crinkled. He appeared to be twisting his beard.

What's the matter? I thought. The three people's footsteps headed back towards the door and stopped inside the frame. The long and consistent sound had suddenly changed. I gathered all of my focus with my ears and tried to listen in.

'That boy ... that boy M, who used to be so strong ...' I heard my mother's sharp tone.

'Now, now. It won't do to have an invalid hearing this.' The Westerner's awkward speech mixed in with my mother's words.

Ha ha ... I thought. I wasn't surprised. I didn't attack. *The chief's thoughts are probably that. My mother's surprise is probably from the same.*

Then gradually the heart's pitter patter grew louder. Gradually my anxiety rose.

My illness can't be cured? The revolting sounds of the doctor's slippers were the only response to this as they grew distant.

'That boy ...' When I heard my mother's voice, I heard the whispering of the resident physician – a friend from my elementary years – calming her down, not letting her finish her sentence.

'Mother, don't worry. They say that even in the darkest

hour, there's always a light of hope to be found somewhere. Not to worry ...' They came closer towards my bed. I flashed my eyes open. They looked surprised.

'How are you? Feeling a little better, right?' R, the resident doctor, smiled.

'All better,' I answered, staring at the ceiling. My voice quivered even though I didn't want it to. 'I'll be all better in just a few days.'

'Ha! How many days?' I ignored his remark without changing my expression in the least bit. My mother stood there without a word. R grew silent.

'R, tell me the truth. I'm dying, right? I'm not going to live, am I?'

I heard my mother crying and R denying my question. 'Not at all. If a fella as strong as yourself dies, who will be left alive on this earth?'

I began to calculate the ceiling. In order to break the rectangular shape of the ceiling that ran east to west into a square, I knew just exactly how many pieces I needed to break off and paste in the directions north and south. After pondering this for a while, I asked again, 'But ... that's what the chief said earlier. That I'm going to die ...'

There was no response. My mother's crying had turned into sobs. There was a long pause and R spoke.

'Did you hear everything?'

'I'd have to be deaf not to catch that.' I became needlessly angry, so I took it out on R. R spoke after a pause,

'Ah ... M. Don't worry. They say that even in the darkest hour, there's always a light of hope to be found somewhere. Do you think a person's life is that worthless?!'

'Do you think a person's life is that *valuable*?' He had no answer to this. I repeated my question. 'R! R! Tell me the truth. Consider this your way of saving a person's life. If I'm going to die, I should be able to prepare myself thoroughly before I go!'

'I don't have an answer. In my opinion, I'd say there's no need to worry, but in the chief's opinion, there is nothing more to be done, so I don't know.' He told me not to torture myself over this so much then escorted my mother out. I stared at the ceiling. The sound of the trolley in the distance, a rickshaw, the sound of cars passing, the chatter of people – they were all enjoying life. I could tell even without looking. But here on the other side of just a single wall, '*Ŭm – ŭm – uu – uu ...*'

I tried to admire their lives but I just couldn't, so my cries turned into damnation. Such irony. As a car passes, the rumbling shakes my room a bit.

That car probably has a person inside of it. He's someone who doesn't know how to enjoy life the way I can. Someone who is less obsessed with living than I am. Hm. This is no good. I'm someone who needs to be alive more so than he – someone who knows how to live better than he can. What a conflicting predicament. There's no need to think. I'm dying. Maybe in two or three days. Maybe even today ... I bounced up from my bed, took the ink bottle beside my headboard and threw it towards the door that led out into the street. The bottle hit the door, broke, and blue ink splashed in all directions.

'Ha ha ha ha,' I laughed. Then I suddenly grew anxious, so I gathered my body close together. From my dream four days ago, I heard that demon's laughter (a raspy voice, the kind that could shatter everything in sight) in my own. I lay back down. I slowly looked up at the ceiling. That weird and muddled item called death – no matter how much I tried, it just wouldn't enter my brain. It was so weird.

I'm dying? I put a question mark at the end and gave it a long thought. No matter how much I went over it in my head, it was weird. It was like a drop of water in oil. No – like a drop of oil in water.

I'm dying, I thought again. Gradually the heaviness of 'death' slowly entered my brain.

I'm dying. Why? I want to live so why should I die? Who the hell is killing me?! I said I want to live, so who the hell's trying to kill me?! Everyone dies. But I just want to live. My upbeat personality, strength, stamina – why should I die before I get to spread this all over the world?! I won't die. What the hell is the chief talking about?! Suddenly sadness, anger – a strange feeling – pressed against my brain.

'Dying!' I screamed. I shut my eyes in exhaustion.

Thought Piece Five

I want to smoke. The craving is unbearable. I could even inhale the sight of that cigarette smoke rising up ahead. Not even ash bits can be found. Matches are even harder to come by. Isn't there anybody who would give me a stick of cigarette? Ah – will I die without even having a smoke?

Thought Piece Six

I had surgery. They opened my stomach and took something out. Then they put some metal object inside and sewed me back up. The operation took place around ten in the morning. I climbed on top of the surgical bed like a sheep being lured by a butcher. The chief said that he couldn't guarantee my life. My friend R said that if I had nothing to lose, I might as well go through with abdominal surgery as a last resort. After R changed into his surgical uniform, he sterilized his scalpel, tongs, and some odd-looking hooks. My mind would not re-enter my body. At times, I looked at R sterilizing. At other times I floated over my body, peering down at myself. I looked down at my body for a long time and then returned to R. R turned his back to me and touched the tools with the nurse.

What's taking you so long? Nah – go on. Take your time. Take all the time you need, even if it takes you a whole year. My mind couldn't stand it any longer. It drifted away and stood before R. R was sterilizing the scalpel. It looked like it would handle well – like it would cut my belly open nice and easy. The thought scared me. It'll really handle well. If put to the test, it'll slice and dice anything it merely aims its blade at. My mind would not quit.

How many hours will it take? My mind, which had been lingering in front of R, played with such thoughts before circling back. But it did not re-enter my body. It just shivered strangely. I wondered if I should get up. My body wouldn't stay put on that surgical bed. About thirty minutes went by and several people entered. R and the nurse walked towards me. My mind scurried back into my body and hid. I shut my eyes with all my might. I heard some shuffling, then something covered my nose and mouth.

This is distressing, I thought, when the fragrant smell of ether suddenly pinched my nose. My mind grew slowly peaceful and floated out of my body. In my head a cool breeze blew. I gradually got high. I don't know what happened afterwards. As I fell asleep, I caught a whiff of something. It wasn't a doctor. It wasn't death. It wasn't life, either. It was the smell of cigarettes coming from a person's nose. I kept walking a dark path.

Where the hell am I headed? I wondered. *Right. I must've said I'm going to the demon.* I groped around in the dark yet light path towards the demon I recalled vividly. I somehow arrived at his enormous house. I was seated across from him in his grand living room. Today he was in human form (a young person), wearing shiny clothes. He wore a belt with a stone that was lit on fire around his waist.

'You've arrived.'

'I've arrived.'

'What did you come here for?'

'I came here to make a request.'

'What of?'

'You said last time that we ought to try and compromise, did you not?'

'Ha ha ha ha. Humans are unexpectedly honest things! That was all a lie ... all of that ...'

I wasn't even angry. I asked again, 'They were lies?'

'Sure. Is it bad to lie?'

'Of course it's bad!'

'That's the kind of thing people say in your society!'

I didn't even feel ashamed. 'Our society? The trickster is clever. The one who gets tricked is foolhardy.'

'The demon society is different.'

I laughed and said, 'Then I'll be going.'

'Why? Don't you have something to ask me?'

Upon hearing this, I felt like I did have something to ask him. 'Yeah, I do. Wait a minute. What could it have been ...'

'Think about it.'

I thought about it for a long time. Then I asked, 'When I die, what will I become?'

'Become? You just go onto the next world.'

'The next world? Heaven or hell?'

'Ha ha ha ha. You can interpret it however you like. Just think of your next life in the same terms as your past life.'

'Past life?' That sounded about right.

'Sure. The past life. The few months of a foetal life. Then the past life's few days as a sperm. And that life's previous life ...'

Sounded about right.

'When a sperm's life becomes a foetal life, the sperm dies and becomes a foetus, does it not? And that in turn dies as it becomes a human being, does it not? While taking on a soul ...? And that body becomes disposed while the soul continues on to the next life. This is a chosen path. After that, it enters the next life. Ha ha ha ha.'

'Is this the truth or a lie? I can't trust what you say to me.'

'Think of it whichever way you'd like!'

'Then what are you supposed to be? If there is no heaven or hell, why should you exist?'

'Me? We demons would be upset if we were interpreted in such a way. We demons are simply human affection and instinct.'

Sounded about right. Something slowly made me happy. That happiness gradually grew. I stood up and began dancing. My feet were off the ground. While I danced for a long time, someone suddenly grabbed my foot and pulled.

'Who is that?!'

'It's you, isn't it?' the demon replied.

'Have a drink first and dance.' I fed the demon drink after drink then headed towards the dark street. I was on some sort of battlefield. A vast and endless field. I heard gunshots but wasn't sure where they came from. My area was extremely bright. That other side up ahead looked just like night. A bullet struck my belly. I fell backwards. The place where the bullet entered began to itch. Someone pulled my foot. I bounced back up and headed into the darkness. I dreamt dozens of similar dreams before awakening. I found myself on my bed by nightfall.

Thought Piece Seven

After two months of checking into the hospital and a month after my surgery, I was finally discharged. I, the one who was given a death sentence by a supposedly distinguished doctor of Chosŏn, was able to come back to life and leave the hospital. I wore my undulating hanbok for the first time in four years and sat comfortably on an easy chair.

I lived. It felt like a lie. I've been discharged. It felt like an even bigger lie. My dead spirit still felt attached to human society and continued to wander. This finally felt true. A trolley went by. I can ride that again. People milled about. I am now just like those people. Ah, could this be true? I can smoke. I have nothing left to do but humbly celebrate this moment.

'Time for the train.'

'All right. Let's go.' R's voice and mother's voice struck my ears.

'I've come back to life, and I'm about to travel. It's a lie. It's a lie,' I said as I followed them. But as R and S made their fare-wells, and mother and I entered the large street, the sight of all the moving people on the other side slowly filled my head with joy, bit by bit.

'Wavering daily between life and death with frighten-ing clamours, I want nothing more than for that crowd to experience the kind of joy I am feeling now as soon as pos-sible.' Mother and I swayed amongst the crowd, and I lit my cigarette.

––––––––––––

I finished reading and caught sight of M. He was looking at a magazine on my desk.

What's the meaning of this? Can't a person's life be assured? The insects that I care for daily as well as the animals of this world can ensure their survival through their constitution, light, and skin. A person's life with an animal's soul cannot be assured without taking exhaustive measures. Running to the doctor without fail at every turn of danger. What's the meaning? What's the meaning? Had M not met his resident physician friend, would we have been able to meet again like this with M in such excellent condition? I walked over to M.

'M.'

'You finished reading?'

'Are you saying that a person's life cannot be assured?'

'If I think about how many hundreds of thousands of precious lives were thrown away just because of a doctor's diagnosis, I shiver.'

'I am so glad that you're alive!'

'That's right. Because I had a good friend named R ...'

'You lived,' I said, completing his sentence. 'You would have died otherwise.'

'That's right.'

I looked down at the town from our home, perched on hill. A mass of people wandered about like flecks of dust, expressing their joy for life. Ah, but who will assure them of their lives? A doctor's diagnosis could kill them in a year or even a month.

I look at M again. Health. The signs of health appeared in his round face, as his shining eyes looked back at me.

January 1921

BOAT SONG

A Brother's Lament

Fine weather we're having.

The kind of weather without a single cloud in the sky. It's not an arrogant sky that sneers, looking down at us little people who shouldn't dare look up at it. It's the kind of sky that appreciates us. It's the kind of sky that seems to want to come down and hold us by the wrists with its lumpy pink clouds.

It's a sky of love.

I don't stop for even a moment. I tumble around inside the bank of Moran Hill, which is headed for the Taedong River that eventually pours into the Yellow Sea. It's 3 March – the first day of the boat festival on the Taedong River. The blue boats glide over the dark water where the current sparkles. A colourful melody drunk on the season's fragrance comes drifting over, shaking the spring air, softer than velvet. Chosŏn court music sung by *kisaengs* flits over in a heartbreaking manner – long, slow, soft and flowing. The dark spring water flows through the Taedong River as if it's determined not to stop until it harmonizes with all the love of spring. The green shoots sprout from the Ch'ŏngnyu Wall. The fired-up blood streams inside the human heart. The humid spring air leaves nothing untouched.

Spring is here. Spring has come.

I hear music that starts out small, gently moving through threads of breeze in the dark Chosŏn pine and brushing past the freshly risen grass. It contains a beauty that can't be heard any other time.

Ah – the intoxicating beauty of green spring! I lived in Tong-gyŏng since age fourteen so I never enjoyed the season like this.[1] It's impossible for me not to have a greater impression than the others. Within the P'yŏngyang fortress are greens that just barely sprout through the ground, tossing the dirt aside, and new buds appear on the willow trees. It's not completely spring yet, but here in the entire vicinity of Moran Hill, up past the Taedong River to the rich forest reminiscent of the Canaan earth, spring and all its affections have arrived.

And the tall wheat and barley are decorated green. A farmer who looks out at the field with a smile is a sight I can imagine without seeing. The clouds seem to shoot through the sky. The shadow cast by the cloud right below it moves to the other side and, there, it spreads out as if it will create a new green world. Wherever the wind blows just a bit, the wheat falls then rises again like water currents. It dances like this whenever the day clears.

The black kites praise the lull of spring, drawing a circle high up in the sky, heightening the beautiful spring's intoxicating scent.

'It shall blossom in the warmth of spring. It shall blossom in the warmth of spring,' I recite twice as I light a cigarette. The cigarette smoke rises up and up into the sky. Spring has arrived in the sky, too. The sky hangs low. It's low enough that I could touch it from the top of Moran Hill. And the pink cloud that seemed to be up higher than the sky tangles into a knot before flying away. It's impossible for me not to think

[1] Tong-gyŏng – Tokyo.

of utopia whenever I look down at this gorgeous spring scenery, listening to the season's soft whispers. What's the point of all that hard effort we put in day in and day out? Isn't the answer within utopia? Whenever I think of utopia, I think of 'the man of great character' and 'the man who enjoyed his greatness till the end' – Qin Shi Huang. What must we do to keep from dying? Put three hundred young men on a boat in search of the elixir of life. He invested greatly in art to build a palace to feast and celebrate with thousands of servants. This Qin Shi Huang who attempted to erect a utopia, however, neglected the tens of thousands of years of history that would curse him. He was a hedonist. Even when history is over, he will be called a great man. Could there be anyone more purely courageous in the history of humanity? We can claim one.

'He was a great man,' I say as I raise my head.

Just then. Near Kija's Tomb, a sad song stirs the spring air. I unconsciously turn my ear towards it.

'Yŏngyu *paettaragi*.'[2] No *kwangdae* or *kisaeng* could match this singer.[3]

> *I pray, I pray*
> *I pray to the sky, the earth, the universe, to God*
> *Our lives that hang by a thread,*
> *I pray that you save us*
> E-eya, ŏgŭyŏjiya

Then, below on the water, the sound of drums along with a *kisaeng*'s voice takes over and I can't hear his song anymore. I had the opportunity to enjoy a summer all to myself a couple of years ago in Yŏngyu. Anyone who's lived there for several months would have a nostalgic attachment to the *paettaragi*,

[2] *paettaragi* – A folk song from P'yŏng'an Province of an unlucky fisherman who is the sole survivor after a storm out at sea; litterally means 'following the boat'.

[3] *kwangdae* – A performer.

which originates from Yŏngyu. I don't know the name of it, but from the top of X mountain looking down at Yŏngyu, one can see the endless Yellow Sea before him. Anyone who's seen that view in the evening will never be able to forget the sight. The sun, like a great ball of red fire, looks as though it might drown in the tumbling sea. At the same time, it looks as though it might rise right back up, dancing. On occasion, I would weep at the sound of the sad *paettaragi* that would come wailing towards me as I gazed out at the sea where no boats were in sight.

Considering this, if some administrator's wife gave up her entire life like some worn-out shoe and decided to go with a vagabond boatman, it wouldn't be an impossible story to believe. Even after my return from Yŏngyu, the *paettaragi* was etched deep inside my mind. The thought of returning to Yŏngyu just to hear it once more never left me. The sound of the drum and *kisaeng*'s singing stops and just the *paettaragi* comes flying plaintively towards me. Due to the wind, sometimes I can't hear it. When the *paettaragi* melody comes together with my memory, it turns into a celebration.

> *Came to the riverbank*
> *And took a look at me*
> *With one's heart in one's mouth*
> *A dream or a reality?*
> *Rushing over*
> *Grasping with slender hands*
> *Words containing the parents' grace*
> *boundless as the sky*
> *Fallen from the sky,*
> *Risen from the ground,*
> *Clinging to the wind*
> *Piled up among the clouds*
> *That's how it comes.*
> *Clutching on to one another like this, crying out*

All the many people
Friends and family, everyone gathered ...

I listen up until this point. I can't take it any more so I stand up abruptly and reach for the hat that I hung on a pine tree branch. I go to the top of Moran Hill, searching. There, I can hear the song a little better. The singer delivers the final stanza.

Stirring the rice
To turn into porridge
I plead
You not to become a fisherman
E-eya, ŏgŭyŏjiya

I find myself standing still, searching for the direction the sound is coming from. Where is it? Is it Kija's Tomb? Or perhaps Ŭlmil Pavilion? But I can't stand there for very long. I want to find it, no matter what it takes, so I go over to Hyŏnmu Gate and stand outside. The pine grove of Kija's Tomb spreads before me.

'Where is it?' I ask again. Then the opening of the *paet-taragi* starts. The sound appears to be coming from the left, so I wander through the pine trees for a long time until I finally come across the person rolling around alone on Kija's Tomb beneath the vast sky on the bright and spacious surface.

It's a face I wasn't expecting. His face, nose, lips, eyes and body are all square. His forehead has thick wrinkles and dark eyebrows, revealing the person's past sorrows and sincere character. He notices some gentleman staring and stops singing.

'Why did you stop? You should keep going,' I say, getting closer.

'Well ...' The man gazes up at the torn sky. They are good eyes. They contain no regrets. They are vast and wide like the ocean. I can tell he is a man of the sea.

'Is Yŏngyu your hometown?'

'Yes, well, I was born in Yŏngyu but I haven't been there in over twenty years.'

'Why wouldn't you go to your hometown for twenty years?'

'Does everything go as one pleases?' He lets out a deep sigh. 'Fate is much stronger.' The statement contains an unresolvable resentment and contrition.

'Is that so?' I simply look back at him. After remaining silent for a while I finally speak again. 'All right then. Let's hear your story. If there's nothing to hide, just let it out.'

'Well, there's nothing to hide …'

'Then let's hear it.'

He looks back up at the sky. After a little while he says, 'Okay. I'll tell it.' He sees me light a cigarette and lights his own before starting.

'It was a day I could never forget. One August day from nineteen years ago.' The story he tells goes more or less like this:

The place he lived in was a small fishing town facing the ocean, located about twenty *li* away from Yŏngyu Province. He was fairly well known in that tiny village (about thirty houses total). His parents passed away when he was fourteen. The only family he had left were his wife, his younger brother, and sister-in-law who lived next door. The two brothers were the wealthiest in that village, and caught the most fish. They were not only literate but also sang the *paettaragi* very well. In other words, the two brothers were the village's finest.

It was mid-August and the Ch'usŏk holiday.

On the 11 August, he headed to the market to purchase groceries for the holiday and a mirror for his wife.

'One that's bigger than the one at Tangson's house. Don't forget, okay?' His wife emphasized this to him as she followed him out into the street.

'I won't forget,' he said as he faced the red sunlight and headed out of his village. He (this is a bit funny) adored his wife. She was a rare beauty for a country girl, and quite affectionate (so he told me).

'It's hard to come across a girl like her in P'yŏngyang – even in the red-light district.' So, for a country couple, they were quite close – to the point of looking funny to onlookers. The elders around him always told him never to fall for the looks and charms of a woman. The couple had a good relationship – no. Because of their good relationship, he had a tendency to be overly jealous.

And his wife was constantly subject to his jealousy. It wasn't that she behaved poorly. She was incredibly naive and very bubbly, causing her to start up a conversation with just anyone with her charm.

Whenever there was a holiday, all the town's young men flocked over to that house, claiming it was the 'most pure'. The young folks called his wife 'Missus' and she called them back 'Mister', while laughing and enjoying their little game. Whenever they did, he'd sit in a corner and watch from the corner of his eye. After the young men left, he'd attack his wife, interrogating her behavior. Whenever a fight erupted, his younger brother and sister-in-law would come running over to stop it, and the boatman would give his brother a beating, too. He had a reason for treating the younger brother this way. His younger brother had a courageous dignity about him, and even though he'd been hit by the salt water winds, his face was still white. Perhaps this could've been enough to make the boatman jealous, but seeing his wife be good to his brother was a sight he could not stand.

It was about six months before he left Yŏngyu. It was also six months from when he left for the market – his birthday. He ate good meals at home, but he had a strange habit of saving good food for later. His wife was well aware of this habit of his, and yet when his brother came over around lunch time, she attempted to offer him the food that her husband had saved earlier. When he glared at her angrily, communicating, *No, don't give it to him*, she didn't take notice, and gave the meal to his brother anyhow. He felt a great discomfort inside. He promised himself internally, *As soon as this bitch gives me a reason, well, I'll* ... His wife prepared the meal for his brother then walked away. On her way over, she lightly stepped on her husband's foot by accident.

'You bitch!' He kicked his wife with all his might. His wife fell backwards over the *sang*, then got up.[4]

'You bitch. Where do you get off stepping on a man's foot?'

'So what? Did I break your foot or something?' His wife's face had turned bright red as she screamed at him with a quivering voice.

'You bitch! Talking back like ...'

He stood up and grabbed his wife by the hair.

'*Hyŏngnim*! Why are you doing this?' His brother stood up and grabbed him.

'Stay out of it, you bastard,' he said as he pushed his brother aside and pounded his wife however he could.

'Worthless bitch! Get out of here!'

'Just kill me! Kill me! I don't care if I die. I'm never leaving this house!'

'You're not leaving?'

'I'm not leaving. Whose house do you think this is ...?'

When the words 'I'm not leaving' hit home, he didn't want to hit her any more. While standing there in a daze for a moment, he said, 'Rotten bitch. Fine. Then I'll leave,' and ran out the door.

'*Hyŏngnim*, where are you going?' his younger brother asked, but the boatman didn't respond. He went to a bar in the next town over and sat at a table with a barmaid over a drink. That night, in his drunken stupor, he purchased some *ttŏk* for his

[4] *sang* – a small floor table.

wife and returned home.[5] And so peace was restored in the house for another three or four months. But this peace could not last for long. Thanks to his younger brother, the peace shattered once again.

The boatman's brother made trips to central Yŏngyu in early May, but towards the end of the month he would go and stay for several nights at a time. On top of this, a rumour went around claiming that he'd found a mistress there. Once this rumour began to spread, the boatman's wife hated seeing her brother-in-law go into town – more so than the sight of a bug. Upon his return, she went to his house and begged him to change his behaviour. She even went so far as to chastising his wife, who couldn't dissuade him from leaving. In early July, the boatman's brother left and didn't return for ten days straight. Just as she had last time, the boatman's wife went over to her brother-in-law's to pick a fight with him and his wife. Then she returned to the house to pick a fight with the boatman himself, saying he'd allowed his brother to go to a terrible place like that. The boatman couldn't stand the sight any longer, so he shouted, 'What's it to you? I don't want to hear about it.'

'You ugly man. Your brother goes to a place like that and you can't even stop him!' she shouted back in rage.

'You bitch. What did you say?' he said, jumping up.

'You ugly man!' Before she could finish the last word, she was already tumbled over on her back.

'You bitch! Where'd you learn to speak to a man like that?!'

'Where'd you learn to beat a wife like that? You ugly man!' his wife cried out.

'You fucking bitch. Why I ought to … Get out! You don't live here anymore. Get out!' he shouted as he pounded her down. He opened the door and shoved her out.

'As if I wouldn't leave,' she cried out before running off.

'Rotten bitch!' The boatman plopped down and mumbled

[5] *ttŏk* – rice cakes.

angrily to himself as though he were vomiting. The sun had set, but she did not return. Although it was he who'd kicked her out, he awaited her return. It had grown dark. but he did not turn on any lights. He shook with rage while he waited for his wife's return. Then he heard his wife's voice laughing with joy at his brother's house. This went on all night. He didn't budge and sat in place till the day broke. As the dawn's light began to break in the east, he went over to the kitchen and grabbed a knife, which he plotted to murder his brother and wife with. If it hadn't been for the sight of his anxious-looking wife standing outside the gate, he would've killed the both of them that day.

As soon as he saw his wife, his heart filled with realization of his love for her. He threw the knife aside, grabbed her by the hair, calling her 'bitch', and took her inside where he slapped her this way and that until they both fell to the floor and rolled about. If I should recite the whole story there would be no end to it. But what's clear is that there was a love triangle among them. It went something like this:

There was a mirror that she wanted from the market. It's the kind of mirror that makes your nose appear huge and your mouth look small, but at the time and especially in a country such as that, it was a rare and precious item. He finished his grocery shopping then purchased the mirror for his wife, imagining how happy she would be. He took in the sight of the evening sea soaked in red and headed straight for home. He even walked right past the bar that he usually frequented. But as soon as he stepped into his house, a sight he wasn't expecting appeared before his eyes. On the middle of the floor was a *sang* prepared with *ttŏk,* and his brother's shirt was draped over his neck. His clothes were completely loose, and a jacket was thrown aside into a corner. His wife's hair was dishevelled, and her skirt had dropped down past her navel. They were frozen completely still, unsure of what to do, staring back at the boatman. The three of people stood there for a long time like this without a word. Finally his brother spoke. 'Where's that bastard mouse?'

'Ha! Mouse? What a fine mouse you were going to catch!'

'*Hyŏngnim*! Really, there was a mouse and—'

Before his brother could even finish his sentence, he threw his bags aside and ran after his brother, grabbing him by the throat.

'Mouse? You bastard! Who the hell goes around catching mice like that with his sister-in-law?!' He slapped his brother's face several times then threw him out of his home. Shaking with rage, he then ran after his wife, who stood frozen.

'You bitch! What sort of wife goes catching a mouse like that with her brother-in-law?!' He threw his wife onto the ground and beat her this way and that.

'A mouse was really ... *ai,* I'm gonna die.'

'You bitch! You too? A mouse? Die!' His arms and legs flailed in all directions, aiming for his wife's body.

'*Ai,* I'm gonna die. Really. When I put out some *ttŏk* for him to have ...'

'I don't want to hear it! A bitch who sleeps with her brother-in-law. What right do you think you have to talk back?'

'*Ai, ai.* I'm telling you the truth. A mouse came and I ...'

'Just a mouse?'

'We were trying to catch a mouse and ...'

'Fucking bitch! Die! Go drown yourself in the water!' After beating her relentlessly, he finally threw her out just like he did with his brother.

'Go sell yourself on a fisherman's boat!' he spat. He did all he could to get vengeance, but his mind was still distressed. He leaned against a wall like a man who'd lost all his senses and stood there, staring vacantly down at the *ttŏk*.

One hour ... Two hours ... It was a village facing the ocean towards the west. It took a while for the sun to set, but between seven and nine o'clock, it grew quite dark. He went in search for some matches to turn on the light. But the matches that were always in the same spot were nowhere to be found. He dug around for them in the room. When he lifted some clothes off the ground, a mouse made a noise and ran out before disappearing.

'It really was a mouse!' he cried out in a small voice. Then he plopped down in place. The scenario he didn't witness himself earlier played inside his head like a moving image: his brother comes over. His wife, who's always good to his brother, sets down a *sang* with some *ttŏk* for him. At that point a mouse comes running out. The two of them (his wife and brother) run around trying to catch it. After chasing it for long time, the mouse suddenly disappears into a corner. They examine their room thoroughly in search of the mouse. That's when he arrives.

'Fucking bitch. She'll probably be home soon ...' He reassured himself the best he could and lay on his back. But as the night went on and morning came, even when the sun reached high noon, she did not return. His concern began to grow, and so he stepped out in search for her. His brother wasn't home either. He searched all over town, but no one had seen them. He walked about three or four *li* south of where they lived and finally found his wife by the sea, but she wasn't the same wife who was once full of life. Her body was swollen because of the water. Her lips, once beautiful and streaming with constant laughter, were full of foam. She was dead. He carried his wife on his back and returned home without a single thought inside his head. He spent a couple of days holding a simple funeral. His brother, who walked behind him, had a look of contempt that seemed to read, Hyŏngnim, *what is this?*

After the funeral, his brother disappeared from that small

town. He spent one or two days in wait but even after five days went by, his brother made no return. After enquiring here and there, someone said that a man that looked like his brother was found walking east as the red sun hit his back, carrying some luggage. And so ten days went by, then twenty days, but his brother, who went away once, had no path to return to. His sister-in-law, who was left behind to spend the rest of her days alone, let out a deep sigh. He couldn't stand the sight any longer. The blame for all of this tragedy fell onto him. He eventually became a fisherman, spending all his days on the sea that had swallowed his wife. He would hunt around for news of his younger brother wherever he went, and hopped onto any random boat he saw. Wherever he went, he gave his brother's name and a basic description of what he looked like, but he could find no news.

Ten years flew by as though on a dream's current. One autumn day, nine years ago to the day, the boat he boarded fought through a thick fog over the coast. Strong winds had brought on enormous waves. Several men died and he himself lost consciousness and floated out to sea. When he came to, it was night. He was on the shore somehow, and a bright red fire was going beside him, keeping him dry. And there was his brother nursing him. Strangely, he wasn't alarmed. He asked him in the most natural way, 'How did you get here?'

His brother stayed silent for a long time before finally replying, '*Hyŏngnim*, it's all fate.'

Sitting beside the warm fire, the boatman nearly fell asleep but to this he shook himself awake and said, 'Ten years went by but you've managed to stay young.'

'*Hyŏngnim*, I've changed, and you've certainly gotten older, too.'

He listened to these words as he fell asleep. He enjoyed two hours of honey-sweet rest before waking up. The red fire was still going but his brother was nowhere to be found.

He asked a man next to him where his brother went, and he responded that his brother had peered into his face for a long time while he slept, before walking away without a word as the red sunlight hit his back, and he disappeared into the darkness. He spent the next two days asking for his whereabouts, but he couldn't find a trace of his brother anywhere. He hopped another boat and sailed back out to sea. When his boat arrived at Haeju, he wandered the market looking to make a purchase. He looked over his shoulder; he saw a man that resembled his brother inside a store. As soon as he rushed over, however, he'd disappeared. The boat he took didn't stay in Haeju for long, so he left his heart behind and boarded the boat to take off again. He spent the next three years looking this way and that in search of his brother but couldn't find him. Three more years went by – six years ago from today. The boat passed Kanghwa-do. There, on a steep grave site, he heard the *paettaragi* flowing towards the ocean. The lyrics and melody were unique to his brother's. If it wasn't him singing it, it couldn't be anyone else – it was that kind of *paettaragi*. The boat did not stop at Kanghwa-do, and passed it. He spent ten days in Inchŏn then headed over to Kanghwa-do. He searched for his brother there, high and low. When he enquired at a local inn, he was told that someone who looked like his brother and shared the same name as him did stay there, but he left for Inchŏn four days ago. He hurried back to Inchŏn in search for him, but even in that small town, there was no way to find him. Rain came, then snow. Six years went by, but he never met his brother again. He didn't even know if he was dead or alive.

The man has finished his story. The evening sun reflects off his eyes, where some tears glisten. I wait for a long time before eventually asking, 'What about your sister-in-law?'

'I don't know. I haven't been back to Yŏngyu in twenty

years.'

'Where will you go now?'

'Don't know that, either. Do we have a fixed destination? I'm going to wander whichever way the wind pushes me.' He sings the *paettaragi* for me once more. Ah, a remorse locked inside that song that can't be tended to. A painful longing for the ocean. After the song ends, he stands up and turns. Soaking in the red evening's sun on his back, he walks towards Ŭlmil Pavilion. I don't have the strength to stop him, so I simply stare at his back and sit in place. I return home that night, but that *paettaragi* and that fatalist story keeps ringing inside my ears. I can't sleep. The next morning when I wake up, I don't even eat breakfast. I run over to Kija's Tomb in search for him. The grass he's been sitting on appears flattened, commemorating his last trip, but he himself is nowhere in sight. But – but the *paettaragi* rings over from some place as though to shake every pine tree.

'It's from Moran Hill. He's on Moran Hill,' I say, then rush over, but there is no one there.

He's not at Pubyŏngnu either.

'Ŭlmil Pavilion. That's where he must be.' I rush back to Ŭlmil Pavilion. From Ŭlmil Pavilion to Pubyŏngnu, perhaps even to hell, is a thicket of pine groves connecting them together. The *paettaragi* could be heard there, as if to shake every pine needle in the forest, but he can't be found. The millions of pine needles stretch out towards the sky on Kija's Tomb, the millions of grass blades, they all sing the sad *paettaragi*, but I can't find him anywhere on Moran Hill. When I go to the river and enquire on his whereabouts, I am told that he left at the crack of dawn on the morning boat.

Summer and autumn go by, and a year passes. Spring returns. That man left behind a fateful story and a *paettaragi*, but he himself does not return to Moran Hill. Spring has returned to Moran Hill and Kija's Tomb. The broken grass that he sat on has sprung back to life, and orange flowers appear to be blooming, but the man who sang the *paettaragi* cannot be found. All that can be found are the pine needles whispering as if to cherish the memory of the *paettaragi* that he left behind.

May 1921

FLOGGING

'*Kisho*!'[1]

I am deeply asleep, but this hasty sound can be heard faintly inside my mind. My sleep shatters for a full moment until I fall back into it again.

'Hey. It's *kisho*. Up and at it.'

The person next to me shakes me. I turn my back. As I enjoy my honey-sweet sleep for another couple of seconds, the person shakes me again.

'Wake up.'

'Where's the fire?' I ask. My head slips back down into the cavern.

'Come on. Get up. They're going to inspect room five now.'

'Look. Let me sleep for just ten more minutes.'

'You think that's up to me? If the guard catches you, you'll be in hot water.'

'*Ei*! What's it to him whether I sleep or not? I haven't even slept two hours yet. Come on ... just a little bit longer ...' Before I finish this sentence, I see a spacious bedroom, a

---

[1] 'Get up' in Japanese; a wake-up call.

cigarette by my head, and drift back into sleep. Someone is giving me a cigarette. As I go to smoke it, the person who shook me earlier shakes me again.

'They called *kisho*. They're going to start inspecting. Get up, for crying out loud ...'

'Hey! I just fell back asleep again. Why'd you wake me – why?'

'They're going to inspect.'

'So *what* if they inspect? What's it to you?'

'Forget it. Just get up.'

'I was just dreaming about noodles and cigarettes ...' As I am about to say this, I fall back asleep again. I fall into another sweet dream for a couple of seconds, when the sounds of swords and doors bursting open from next door make me jump right up. But the sleepiness that makes my whole body drunk blankets over my head again. I sit up and hold my knees together. After burying my head in between them, I snooze. One or two seconds pass. Bang! The sound of our door opening. I throw my hands up in the air and raise my head. It was obvious, but I anxiously try not to appear like someone who was fast asleep just a moment ago. The door bursts open and three or four officers rush in.

'Inspection!' The room is just under five *p'yŏng*.[2] When a loud noise reverberates inside of it, it's deafening. The sound of our numbers (our identification) is what I am used to being called by now. This and this number. The numbers that usually flow out suddenly have the head officer stuck.

'*Nanahyakunanajuuyongo.*'[3] No answer.

'*Nanahyakunanajuuyongo!*'

Your number. The poor thing who can't understand his number being called in Japanese – number seven hundred and seventy-four (the one sitting behind me) – does not

[2] Five *p'yŏng* is just under a hundred and seventy-eight square feet.

[3] 'Number seven hundred and seventy-four' in Japanese.

answer. I can't stand it any longer so I poke him. Shocked, the man barely speaks up.

'Yes, *hai*!'

'*Nango hayaku henjio shinai*?[4] This way!' the head officer shouts. But the old man sits still. He makes no sound.

'Come this way!' At the second command, the old man hunches over and walks towards the officer. A quick sound cuts through the air. That kind of movement clearly takes long practice. The officer's whip gets brought down against the old man's back. The old man stands still, but tears well up inside his eyes. After calling out all the numbers following number seven hundred and seventy-four, the officers shout at him to pay attention. He returns to the cell and the prison door slams shut.

It's strange how when one person gets disciplined, everyone else in the room shakes. (It's neither public rage nor camaraderie.) It's not just the body that shakes, but the heart shakes with it. The first time I experienced these shakes is when I got beaten up at the police station for three hours straight and shook like a poplar in the detention room for two hours. I figured I wouldn't die. (This is now something I deal with at least twice a day, every day.) The room is like a dead person's cell. Not a sound. I can't even breathe loudly. No one wants to look inside here for fear that they might encounter a ghost. *Are they even alive any more?* After a while, the inspection ends. The sounds of the officers go past our door. Then, the sound of that old man's voice breaks the silence.

'I have a son older than that officer bastard back home ...'

It's hot. I don't even know what degree it is. It must be at least a hundred and ten if not more ... Every morning I see the same thing – the sun rising in the east. At first, twenty people shared this room of five *p'yŏng* but it filled up to

---

[4] 'Why didn't you answer sooner?' in Japanese.

twenty-eight people. This troubled me. When the people from Chinnamp'o prison were moved over to the prosecution cells, that number expanded to thirty-four, and we all let out a frustrated sigh. But when prisoners from Sinŭiju and Haeju came over, that number became forty, and now we can't even exhale. We're crowded to the point of choking on our own tongues. The hot sun that seems to be caught on the edge of the eaves sends down its endless heat. Who knew that the body had so much water? Sweat has been pouring out of me nonstop since morning. After sitting still for a long time due to exhaustion, I finally gather the strength to slowly stand up, leaning against the cell wall. This is hell. The people sit jam-packed alongside one another with their heads tilted back and mouths open like corpses. No one thinks to wipe away their sweat and drool. They just sit in mute silence. Their rounded backs hunched, lifeless hands folded on top of their knees, faces swollen blue, lips slack, dull eyes, dishevelled hair and beards – everything about them suggest death.

Are these the same people who ran to the bathroom in the morning and moved about just two hours ago to have lunch? Even my weary senses can detect the stench powerful enough to make my eyes water. What did they come here for? Why leave behind the world where the wind blows and cigarettes abound, and come to a place like this? For what? I'm sure some of them have lovable grandchildren. I'm sure some of them have pretty wives, too. I'm sure they have a mother back home who'll starve to death if they don't provide for her. And I'm sure all of those people are eating, drinking and enjoying the breeze to their hearts' content. But what on earth did these men come here for?

In their minds, they have no liberty, no nationalist self-determination, no freedom, no loving wife, son or parent, and no consciousness to even comprehend this heat. They've been subject to suffering and abuse on top of this heavy air.

Somewhere deep inside their skulls, a tiny wish is crouching inside, and that is the wish for a cold sip of water. They'd trade in their nation, their homeland, their relatives and all their happiness for just a cold sip of water. What I mean is, a flowing stream of cold spring water and a dipping gourd flashes before their eyes (a phenomenon that happens every now and again).

'Give me a sip, please ...' I don't know who I implore but I do. I open my tired eyes again and see bodies among bodies, rubbing against one another, covered in boils. Seven out of them seem to suffer from an itch. Time passes in endless silence. I sit back down lifelessly.

'*Eh,* it's hot as hell!' At the end of my outcry, I hear someone vomit. Clear as a bell. But nobody has the energy to pay it any heed. The endless silence continues. If the mind and body do not work, a person is unable to live. How are they able to withstand spending the last several months without any brain activity in a space where they can barely move?

And in this heat, too ... The heat gets gradually worse in the evening. All my cells behave like they have their own body and expand in the heat. It's hard to think that they are a part of a single body. Whenever the heavy air fills my lungs and escapes, the heat gets worse. How could a person not catch a fever like this? A person fell ill five days ago, and another person left the day before yesterday. Another two got sick today. Whenever a guard takes a sick person away to a nurse's station, we look on with envy. They keep only about a dozen people there per room, and they give the patients liquid medication. Not only that but they get to breathe fresh air.

'Today is Sunday, right?' I sit on the toilet beneath a dim lightbulb, catching lice, and ask the person standing next to me. (We decided to divide the night into three parts and the group into three parts, and rotate. While one group sleeps, the other groups stand and wait their turn.)

'How should I know? The bell does ring, but I can't tell if it's a Wednesday or a Sunday ...' The bell sound goes *clang clang* and reverberates through the night sky. It's as if to tell us, *There's a person here who can freely drink cold water and sleep in a spacious spot.*

'I want to see a person's face ...'

'Yes. I really long to see a person's face.'

'There's probably water out there where the bell rings. Probably a lot of room, too. Wind ... the wind probably blows there, too.' So go the grumblings.

'Water? Water? Hey – don't even mention it. When I was living outside of this place, I, too, drank water when I grew thirsty, and slept on a roomy spot.' The person looks away in irritation. Come to think of it, I also used to drink water freely back then. I used to sprawl myself and sleep freely. But what remains of that memory all seem now like a distant dream.

'There was ice cream, too.' Now some young fella over on the other side brings up ice cream.

'Ice cream? That's it? Is that it, fella? I had a wife, okay? It's the season when that peach is the most ripe for plucking,' I reply.

At this, the old man turns to me with irritation and says, 'A wife? Listen to you. A man like yourself making such immature remarks. I have two sons. Back on the eighth of March, during the spring, when folks went running into the valley to cry *manse*, our household joined in.[5] As we were about to start, sounds of gunfire went off – bang, bang! And I see over there my older son bent over on the ground. I wanted to go over to him, but then I saw my younger son next to him fall over. They took away my boys all at once ... So I attacked without thinking twice about it. Hmph! But you're talking

[5] *manse* – A cry of celebration.

about your wife? What good is a wife anyhow?'

'So, what happened?' I ask while catching lice.

'How should I know? I was arrested since then. No one's sending any food or clothes so I assume they're dead.'

'What about me ...' This time a man just over forty years old, who attacked three or four people, began to speak up.

'I kept shouting out that day, so a couple of soldiers followed me. I ran and got all the way to the edge of a mountain cliff. When I turned around, I couldn't find any other place to run. Just like a trapped mouse. What good is a pickaxe in that situation? I jumped. When I did, they started shooting. One here, another there – bang bang! I crouched down behind a clay *toenjang* jar but then ...' He stops speaking at this point as though he were going back to that time. Then he continues.

'While we're sitting there, I saw that our younger brother was hit. When I threw him on my back and started running again, I was shot from behind and fell. When I came to, it was already night and very cold. I could barely move so the both of us crawled a bit when we heard the sound of people's murmurs. At the sound of people's voices, I felt relieved but I couldn't move anymore, and I collapsed again. I lay there panting when I heard the sound of footsteps approaching. A voice said, "There are two dead men here," and a foot kicked me. When I cried out in pain, the voice said that I wasn't dead. Then I realized they were officers. Even if a person is forced to the end of the valley, he'll survive. They didn't even treat my wounds but I'm all better now.' At the end of his sentence he raises his coat to reveal a bullet wound.

'My father (I'm from Maengsan) got shot at a military officer's detention house. Fifty men pushed me out then took a machine gun and ... those bastards!'

But quite a few of us (we the few standing and waiting our turn) are already asleep. The man sitting on top of the toilet with me nods off until he falls, then continues to sleep right where he fell. The only indication that the person smothered beneath him isn't a corpse is that he kicks his feet a couple of times then continues to sleep.

I'm not sure when I fell asleep. My chest feels uncomfortable so I wake up (something that happens to me multiple times throughout the night), and I see that my chest and head are jammed beneath the feet of several people (dozens). I barely free myself from them and push aside several more feet clinging on to my shoulders and exhale heavily. It is a showcase of legs. The heads and bodies are nowhere to be found and seem to have disappeared from the room. All I see are legs piled upon more legs. Over on that end one leg thrashes. Over on this side, two legs squirm about. The legs look blue like a dead person's. These people, who have left behind the world to dream just like people do (dreams about drinking cold water, possibly), occasionally make sounds that can be heard through the legs. The sounds of their dreams.

Ah – if they could only go back home. They'd live a poor life but at least have a roomy place to rest ... Over in the distance about seven or eight legs move about. A head appears among them, then lets out a deep sigh before disappearing into them again. After catching sight of this through a haze, I, too, let my lifeless body slip into the legs to fall asleep.

Whenever I wash my face in the morning, I realize that I haven't died. I might be swollen or fattened but after sitting all day in the sweltering heat, then suffering through a whole night of sleepiness and sweating, when I wash my face with refreshing cold water I realize this. There's no mirror, so I can't tell what my face looks like. It might be looking gradually like the others', but when I wash off that slippery sweat and touch my clean cheeks, I come to know that I am still alive. After I wash my face, we spend two or three hours doing household chores. The work is relatively valuable because we can at least live like people.

It's only at this time when the light returns to our eyes and we have the will to live. There are even instances when people nod their heads and crack jokes. It's a completely different sight of the same people who will become (in just a few hours) paralysed, with their heads drooped and eyes shut while panting as they were thrown in boiling oil.

'It'll get hot again later, won't it?' I ask the person next to me.

'Hot? Why would it be hot? Look at this. It's rather cold ...'

I shiver in exaggeration then laugh.

It's a chilly mid-June morning. We don't have a calendar so we don't know the precise date but it is definitely past the fifth of May according to the lunar calendar. The heat has diffused into this chilly morning.

'Hey. Did you go to yesterday's final hearing?' I ask the person.

'Yes.'

'What's the situation out there?'

'How should I know that? The poplar is a mean green, the clouds flit about violently – everything is alive. Even the ground appears to be moving. All the people's faces look dark. They looked like thieves to me.'

'If I could only see that just once ...' I let out a deep sigh. I got here on the last day of March when people were still wearing thick cotton clothes. I can't recall if the poplar was a bright green or a light green.

'You'll be going to trial in a few days, too.'

'Not sure. I'm sure I'll get there at some point. But did you hear any good news?'

'I don't know. From the talks the other day, it seems we'd be free in *swi*.'

'*Swi*?'

'In about ten or so days.' While I am talking to him, I

hear someone banging the wall beside us. It is morse code for ㄱㄴㄷ and ㅏㅑㅓㅕ.[6]

    What. Is. It. So it comes.

    Good. News. Independence. Is. Complete.

    Where. Did. You. Hear. This.

    This. Morning. Breakfast. Talk. This. Side. ㅈ. The code stops abruptly.

    'See? What did I tell ya?' the person from earlier says, proudly.

    'They're going to call a person to trial in that cell next door. Today ...'

    'You must go today.'

    'Not sure ... I need to go. See people, see some green trees, a wide space ...' But the only folks they call out from our cell today are the old man who took a beating the other day from the head officer, and two or three men from Maengsan. I do not get called.

    'I'll be called out some day.' My spirits fall, and my head starts to ache, so I mumble to myself. But when on earth is that 'some day'? I've been telling myself, *Today's the day*, and three months passed. The same me, stuck in the same place for three months straight, waiting for a trial every single morning. 'Some time soon' – what could this mean? These three months will repeat themselves ten times over and become thirty months ...

    'They left you out again.'

    'Tell them to screw it. Bastards!'

    'Isn't it about time?'

    'About time? When is this *time* you speak of? It'll be the same even if I wait ten years, twenty years ...'

    'But still. Isn't it about time?'

    'You mean after I die?' I vent my rage at him. Even up until a little while ago when I was eating breakfast I wasn't as

[6] ㄱㄴㄷㅏㅑㅓㅕ and ㅈ – hangŭl letters that don't formulate any coherent word or sentence.

anxious. This isn't so much due to the administration torturing us by delaying our opportunity to see the outside world. It was out of heavy jealousy against those who will experience joy when they get called out to trial.

At every lunch, after I finished eating, I would gulp down some reeking cold water. While avoiding the prison officer's attention, I'd pick off the remaining rice pieces stuck onto the bowl and begin kneading them.

It is stuffy and cramped. They don't let us speak to one another. Even if we want to daydream, we don't have the means to conjure any, and so this is the only game we can entertain ourselves with. When the grime turns the rice dough black, it becomes one lump of *ttŏk*. We knead that *ttŏk* into the shape of a dog or a pig – sometimes the shape of the prison officer – until we finally throw it into the toilet. The lump of *ttŏk* that had been moving between my fingers for a long time eventually turns into a docile cow with horns that are just a little too big for it, and stands on top of my knee. I raise my head. I was so absorbed in my little game that I didn't realize the sun starting to melt everything again. The shadows of the prison bars are clearly defined on the cement wall, splattered with sticky bits of blood. The scorching heat smacks against our backs turned towards the window. The rays bounce off the wall and smack us right in the chest, rotting away our bodies that are densely packed together. The ripe stench of shit and piss, the stink of rotting flesh, scabies, and the daily sweat all combine and turn into a poisonous gas that fills the room, which has no ventilation. It is the kind of stench that even our senses, dulled from fatigue, can detect. Of course, the prison officer never stops by to check on us.

Now that I think of it, it isn't just my body but everyone else's bodies that are covered in boils. The toilet is filled to the brim with waste which evaporates into the air. Whenever I sit upon it and look back, the powerfully angry humidity covers my ass. Boils spread over my body because of that and the bedbugs. Not a single one of us is exempt from this condition.

Sweat doesn't just drip down my body. It rushes down like a stream.

'Ye ... sweat,' I moan weakly. It's a strange game of hide-and-seek. After my meal, when I gulp down cold water, all of it turns into sweat and rises out of my pores. It's like a waterfall that falls down my chest and feels like bugs crawling all over my body. I can't even describe that awfulness. But no one washes away that sweat. No one bothers to wash off the sweat because it feels as though we might fall right into hell if we even lifted a finger.

Send me to the doctor this very instant, my tired head pleads with me. I can use the boils as an excuse this morning to wait in line for the doctor. There is nothing else I want more at the moment. The precious taste of fresh air and wide open space (even if it's just for ten or twenty minutes) can't be traded in for money or honour. Not only that, but ever since my imprisonment, sending any word of greeting is out of the question; I can't even find out which cell my younger brother is in, nor any news of his condition.

Things randomly appear before me without me meaning to. The cement wall that was once white but is now yellow bounces the sun's rays, and there I see cigarettes, cold water and a wide space reserved just for me. It appears (at first hazily) distinctly before me. A fly hops from the cigarette box to the matchbox and back. (I don't know how I am able to see these tiny details.)

'Shit!' I spit out all the hotness from within me. 'Even the fly roams around freely.' My mind hardly has the wherewithal to produce anger but I let it out anyhow, and try to remove that picture from my vision. The cigarettes and cold water soon disappear but that damned fly won't go away. I lift my hand (as though to swat it) and fan my face a couple of times. Without any focus in my eyes, I reach for the cow I made earlier.

Those who never experienced this could never understand the sweetness of air. After I exhale the hot stench and inhale fresh new air, I nearly faint from joy. It's a nice cool day. It was unbelievably hot earlier, but where has the heat gone to? On my way to the medic, it feels cool – almost chilly. It's great. But what makes me even happier is meeting my brother there.

'Which room are you in?' I ask him in a tiny voice, while facing the prison officer.

'Cell four, room two.'

I ask him again a little later, 'How many are in there? It's hot, isn't it?'

'Everybody's flesh is swollen thick.'

'Thieving bastards. Our room has over forty people in it. Their bodies are all rotting. Back home, there was almost too much room for us. Did you cry out in pain?'

'You need to cry out in prison in order to avoid illness. The heat gives me a headache.'

'How did you get here – the medical clinic?'

'I said I had a stomachache.'

'I'm covered in boils. Look at this,' I say, and raise my trouser legs, showing him my rash.

'Don't you have any scratchers in your room?'

'Of course we do ...'

My brother says that so and so is a scratcher, as is another so and so, and lists seven or eight names.

'But why isn't anyone coming to visit us from home ...?'

'Indeed. Did they all die ...?' A thought that hasn't even occurred to me suddenly erupts inside my mind. For three months, we've seen nothing but prison officers. We have no idea what state the world is in beyond this place. We've seen folks go to the court house every now and then, and the walkway over and back is outdoors. While we are wrapped up in our gloom inside the fortress, the marketplace is bustling with coin exchanges, and just like before, the streets are filled with bargaining, sounds of laughter can be heard inside homes, and the church conducts weddings. It's as though they've all forgotten the event that took place just three months ago, or don't even know of it.

What's going on with my friends and family is a complete mystery.

'Perhaps there was an accident.'

'I heard from some folks who went to the hearing that they'd seen our eldest brother in front of the courthouse,' my brother tells me with a worried expression. But just as he finishes his sentence, 'Number one thousand and seventeen!' rings inside our ears. It's my number.

'Here!'

'Examination.'

I quickly stand and hurry before the doctor.

'Where does it hurt?'

'Here,' I say, removing my trousers. The doctor takes a quick glance at my bare ass and legs, then wordlessly hands me over to the nurse. I am given some sticky ointment, which I slather on myself, then I sit in the line where those who have completed their checkup wait. I hear my younger brother speak to the person next to him (loud enough for me to hear). Shocked, I look up at the prison officer. My brother has the officer's attention. I raise my arms as though to stretch. My brother doesn't see me. I cough loudly this time. But he still doesn't hear me. My chest begins to tremble.

I need to let him know ... I shift my body around but he is completely absorbed in his conversation and keeps going without pause. When the officer takes a couple of steps towards him, he finally comes to his senses and stops, pretending as though he's been quiet all along. But the officer does not show any mercy. A sharp crack of the whip goes off. My brother puts his hand over his shoulder and falls onto the floor. My eyes grow wide as blood and fever rush into my face. As we return to our cells, I glance towards my brother. He looks back at me with his eyes filled with tears. What's made this pure young boy's eyes well up with such tears? I finally got a taste of that sweet, clean air that I wanted so badly but I return to the cell with my head a lot darker and heavier than before.

After finishing dinner, I take the chopsticks out of a bowl that they haven't cleared yet and stick them onto two ends of a handkerchief . I try fanning myself with it. The air is warm and entangled with a slight scent of sweat but I can sense a slight breeze from it. Why didn't this occur to me sooner? I flap my arm like an insane person. For the first time inside the cell, I feel a breeze – albeit smelly – that brings a honey-sweet coolness and helps fan away the sweat on my chest that crawls around like bugs. The ceiling light goes on, but the heat does not reduce. The rest of the room begins to copy my fan. The folks behind me fan my back. The rotten air moves. But our fanning stops because of the people who return from the courthouse. Three or four people who left our room come back. Even the old man returns with an expression that looks as dead as a corpse's.

Once the prison guard leaves, I search around for the old man with my hands.

'What's the situation like?'

'I don't know.'

'What's the verdict?'

The old man makes no reply. Have a needle and thread shut his lips up? But a while later, he just about responds. His voice trembles a great deal.

'Flogging. Ninety counts.'

'Well, that's good! Now after four days, you can smoke cigarettes, take in the fresh air ... I'm always—'

'Hello?! "Good"?! What do you mean, "good"? I'm over seventy years old and if I get beaten – I don't even want to talk about it. I don't want to die yet! I asked for an appeal!' He goes off on me, enraged. But my anger doesn't let him have the final word.

'Listen! Enough already. Have you gone senile? You're worried that you might die, so does that make you the only human being in here? This room with over forty-some-odd people will become just a little bit roomier once you get out. Don't you think about that? With both your sons shot to death, what good is it to go on living anyway, huh?!' I direct my voice to the others: 'There's a man here who's been sentenced to flogging.'

I start to laugh in a strange voice. The others do not show the old man any mercy either.

Old and useless.

Idiot.

Only thinks of himself.

Kick him out.

All kinds of disparaging comments start to erupt. The old man does not respond. A long sigh fills our ears. We, too, exhausted from all the jeering, finally calm down. A heavy and insufferable silence takes over. It grows dark outside. The sky with its Taedong River hues covers all the lands. We sit below it wordlessly as the heat and thirst drive us to madness. All of our lips have been sewn shut by a needle and thread. After a long while, the old man finally breaks the silence with his voice aimed towards me.

'Hey.'

'What?'

'Then what should I do?'

'You need to accept the sentence!'

The old man grows silent again. But after a little while, he speaks to me again.

'You're right. Both my sons are definitely dead. What good is it to go on living on my own? I'll accept the sentence.'

'You should've done it in the first place. Then let's call the prison guard.'

'Please do.' The old man's voice trembles.

I call for the prison guard. He arrives. As I interpret for the old man (more for us than for him, really), the prison guard grabs the old man and drags him away, as though he were made irate by my explanation. When I turn back towards the room, the people's faces shine with joy at the fact that the room has gotten just a little bit roomier.

Bath time. This is a joyous occasion that comes to us once every ten days or so.

'Bath time!' At the sound of the prison guard's call, we rush ourselves into a single file and run out. The cement ground, heated under the sun, sears our feet which have been resting for three months. But that's a part of our joy. After we cross that path, we go to the bath tub, throw aside our clothes and jump into the water. The happiness is indescribable.

There's a tap beside us. Fresh water flows from it. It has 'sweet, cold water' that never left our minds – not even for a second. After dipping myself in the bath tub for a second, I go to the tap and drink water like an elephant. I see all kinds of prisoners labouring outside. That, too, is an envious display (to those of us stuck inside the suffocating quarters). They can take in fresh air whenever they please. If they are thirsty, they can drink water after getting permission from the guard. Not only that, but they are not subject to any cramping.

The prison guard's call commands us to stop. Our twenty seconds of bathing has come to an end. We (to avoid a beating) quickly put our clothes back on and follow the guard to our cell. It is the hottest hour of the day, too. The moment the door closes, we are already buried under heat. The heat beats down as though to punish us for the joy we experienced earlier.

'It's already hot!' I grumble to myself.

'I should've taken a beating and stayed a little longer ...' somebody says. I can hear three or four people laughing but silence follows right thereafter. The silence continues for several more hours. Then a frightening sound makes us jump. It's the cry of death.

'*Hitotsu, futatsu.*'[7]

Along with the sound of the prison guard's voice we hear, '*Aigu*, I'm gonna die! *Aigu, aigu!*' The sounds pierce our ears that were numbed by the heat. We forget about the heat and raise our heads. We shake as though we are one body. The cries are coming from a man getting flogged. At thirty, the sound of the prison guard disappears. We only hear the sound of the man getting beaten. The second person in line for flogging seems to be up.

'*Hitotsu.*'

As soon as it comes down, a single cry, '*Ayu!*' follows.

'*Futatsu.*'

'*Ayu!*'

'*Mittsu.*'

'*Ayu!*'

We recognize the owner of that voice. It's the old man we kicked out the night before. The man taking the painful beating with no energy to let out a proper scream emits a single, 'Ayu!' It's the old man that we forced the flogging onto.

'*Yottsu.*'

'*Ayu!*'

'*Itsutsu.*'

'Hu ...'

My head hangs low. The sight of the man getting dragged

[7] 'One, two' in Japanese.

out from the room the other night appears before me.

'You expect an old man in his seventies to survive that beating? No matter what happens to me, you fellas ...' He couldn't complete his sentence as he got dragged away by the guard. And the ringleader who kicked him out is me. I hang my head even lower. My vacant eyes are about to tear up. I shut them to keep from crying. My tightly shut eyes tremble.

December 1922–April 1923

BARELY OPENED ITS EYES

1

This is a minor event that took place five years ago.

2

Up, down, east, west, south, north – lights everywhere. The light that hangs over the two hills on each side of the river, the thousands of glistening lights coming off the boats moving up and down the stream, the countless boats filled with rambling, the shining blue lights from the shores appearing between boats, the herd of chattering people on the hills and the boats, the sound of *kisaengs*' loud singing reverberating over such chatter when they are not contributing to it, the light reflecting from the darkness encapsulating all of that, the strong scent of humans ... when the eighth of April[1]

[1] Buddha's birthday.

P'yŏngyang fireworks go off without any particular order, the lights take over; a famous spectacle. Goblins crowd into darkness while people crowd into the light. There they try to seek life, joy and comfort.

The people who suffer from even the tiniest bit of ruthless sunlight can't help but gather beneath the lights that guide while blanketing over, the lights that shine as though they have all the time in the world, the lights that appear while wrapping around them in protection. Beneath the warm and friendly lights, they laugh, dance and jump around, forget the suffering they went through all day, and try not to think about the oncoming chaos of the following days. The April eigth fireworks best illustrate the state of mind longing for these kind of lights. Those who yearn for the light gather beneath them with all kinds of plans to enjoy themselves there. So they came up with all kinds of ideas such as outdoor dancing, theatre, illumination, restaurants and the night market. But the 'people', who are greedy and do not know the definition of 'content', were not satisfied with this. They came up with a reason to gather ten thousand people once or twice a year to entertain themselves here. For Chosŏn, that is the April eigth firework festival. When the fireworks that remained dormant for three years return, the P'yŏngyang people's hearts flutter. For eight days while there is still sunlight, five or six hundred boats prepare food and lights, and all the businesses close in preparation to go see fireworks.

So after eight and a half days, once the sun makes it past the hill and the half moon sheds its light turning the plum colored skies gradually into blue and black, the people who suffered under the beating sun and longed for the light gather below it—a flock of lonely souls who ailed in sadness and sought the joyful chatter of the crowd. A flock of minds that stressed all year long in search for a single night of carefreeness. A flock of outsiders that came to see the 'famous fireworks of P'yŏngyang'. In the middle of it all is the flock of girls eyeing their way up and down in search of a way to make money; from the pier dock that stretches a distance of five *li* all the way to Pubyŏk Pavilion are a countless number of folding screens beneath the hanging lanterns. The five to six hundred smartly decorated boats are full of the happy-go-lucky folk who were able to board. Within P'yŏngyang are only the elderly and invalids staying home while the rest have all gathered at the Taedong River. From the pier by Pan-wŏl-do the soft gold spreads across the sky. The lanterns and terrapin shells hanging from Pubyŏk Pavilion all the way to the pier, from the sand dune all the way to the torch stands in the forest, are lit up. The boats that have been waiting for this hour turn on all kinds of light at once and drift up towards the Ch'ŏngnyu Wall to the sounds of oars. Countless lights move on the water's surface. All the soft glow of lotus candle light spreads out and flows through the current like a massive applause sent off from numerous boats, the foothills of the Ch'ŏngnyu Wall and Panwŏl-do. The torch lights, standing on each sand dune across the river, dance as the occasional wind blows, teasing its own shadow reflected in the water. Fireworks go off into the sky nonstop, spreading out infinite sparks. Over the waters are all kinds of boats decorated with lights and people. Countless candle floaters, hanging on to their fragile flames like life, float on down, down from the boats.

Lights, lights, lights everywhere. Lights hang on the right and left sides of the river—lights floating on water, lights coming off the fireworks, lights reflecting from those lights in the water, lights bouncing off and emanating back into the sky, the kisaeng's song rising up from here and there, classical Korean ceremonial music. And so the Taedong River, Moran Hill, Pubyŏk Pavilion, Rŭngnado and the Panwŏl-do sand dunes turn to fire, decorated with people and covered with music.

'I want one of those boats,' are probably the words of the unspeaking people on the shore. Imagine what a wonderful time it could be to take a boat and have a ball inside all the light and fire. There are all kinds of life's transcendent issues here. And there is also as much happiness inside as there is for a person who boards a boat.

Kŭm-p'ae is one of those happy people.

3

On the boat that Kŭm-p'ae was on were two other *kisaengs* and three patrons. They filled the gaps in between boats with theirs as though filling a gap between beads on a string, and gently headed up towards Pubyŏk Pavilion. Kŭm-p'ae perched on the guardrail of the boat, gazing at the front, back and side to side of the boat as well as at the lights coming off all the other boats, listening in on the sounds of *samhyŏn yugak* instruments.[2] After having her fill of that, she went and sat next to a patron named W and spoke. They were anxious to while away the time somehow, so they exchanged a great deal of useless small talk: who was pregnant, how her father was Y or X, whose business had shut down, who was now living with whom – such were the meaningless stories exchanged and, all the while, the boat reached below the Rŭngnado bridge.

The boats that leave the shores to enjoy the fireworks (perhaps the preferred phrase is 'see') take a break here. The people who drink, drink; the people who don't drink, laugh and tease the drinkers. Some climb all the way to the top of Moran Hill to take in the sight of the Taedong River completely lit up, until the hour reaches around eleven or twelve when they each disperse and return to where they came from.

[2] *samhyŏn yugak* – the combined classical sounds of string and other instruments, typically wind instruments and drums such as the *p'iri*, *taegŭm* (flute), *hae-gŭm*, *changgu* (hourglass drum), and *puk* (drum).

Their boat was also docked there.

'Have a drink.'

'Go ahead.'

'With your delicate and lovely hands. Mm?'

The patrons who weren't satisfied demanded more booze. But before such demands even reached a complete sentence, Kŭm-p'ae's round and adorable hand had already reached for the bottle. The beer shone like gold from all the lights as it poured into a glass. Thus merriment and pleasure began to make turns about the boat. One drink, another drink, and another – they continued on. The drunken amusement spread throughout the boat as the glass was passed around and back. For reasons unknown, Kŭm-p'ae sensed the kind of joy that made her want to reveal her rear end, and she grabbed hold of the *changgu*.

'Let's – let's hear a song, sweetie!' a slurred voice groaned.

Kŭm-p'ae winked at Wŏl-sŏn. A line from the richest, most roaring song, the 'Pangat'aryŏng' came from Wŏl-sŏn's lips smoothly and beautifully.[3]

> E-he e-he-ya.
> *E-ra, pound it in. It's the rice mortar.*
> *I'm halfway over the hill so I won't be*
> *able to turn (e-ra) young any more.*

Wŏl-sŏn's smooth flow with Kŭm-p'ae's skilled *changgu* beat rose up and down, standing out distinctly among the sound of fireworks. Kŭm-p'ae picked it up.

> Et-ta, *feels good.*
> *On a night when the moon is bright,*
> *play a* kayagŭm *of twenty-five strings*
> *The wild goose can't suppress his anger.*
> *Biting down on a single stalk of grass*

[3] 'The Miller's Song.'

Pressing back a broken one behind the ear,
Flying in slowly,
A peaceful day to enjoy a song (no)
E-ra, *ain't it so?*

'Sounds good.'

'They're great.'

Such were the drunk and nasally groans erupting from time to time. Kŭm-p'ae was in a good mood. She gave and received the song back and forth while bouncing her shoulders. The pretty voices rising up through the noisy clamour of the fireworks couldn't help but grab hold of people's attention from the mass of boats. Several tour boats came and surrounded them. When Kŭm-p'ae looked at Wŏl-sŏn's face and sang the finale,

> *The yellow bee and white butterfly*
> *playing gleefully over the azleas*
> *in the spring breeze.*

A voice cried out, 'Real good!' from a boat way yonder. And so the 'Pangat'aryŏng' came to an end. Kŭm-p'ae's face was filled with love and endearment as she pushed the *changgu* aside, poured seltzer into a glass, grabbed Wŏl-sŏn and sat on the edge of the boat. She gazed out at the tens of thousands of people enjoying their lights and fireworks, reciting in a small voice, 'Let's play, let's play, let us be young and play, because once we grow old and useless, we no longer will be able to.'

At that moment, Wŏl-sŏn poked Kŭm-p'ae sharply with her finger saying, 'Hey. Look at that. Young school girls.'

'School girls? Where?' Kŭm-p'ae paused her mellow song and looked in the direction that Wŏl-sŏn pointed. At that very moment (from the boat that would eventually be dragged by Kŭm-p'ae's boat) came finger pointing and whispers:

'Look at the *kisaengs*.'

'Where? For real!'

Kŭm-p'ae threw her head back, full of hostility and charm, and gave a contemptuous glare at the boat full of students. One of the girls' fingers pointed at Kŭm-p'ae as though it proclaimed, *That one over there – she's real lovely.*

Kŭm-p'ae, as though she wanted to vent her anger or proudly gloat at the girls, let out a contemptuous laugh silently to herself then turned her head to face Wŏl-sŏn. The clock struck twelve, and for those who'd heard the clock ring for the first eight hours couldn't ignore the final four. The clock rang in the girls' ears as well as Kŭm-p'ae's.

'How indecent. If you point like that, they can see.'

'Tell them to go ahead and look.'

'What did they say? Did they curse you silently?'

'Tell them to go ahead and curse me silently.'

'But look at that silk skirt and that jade hair pin. She's sharply dressed.'

'Well, what of it!'

'What do you mean "what of it"? Are you dressed that way?'

'Well – no.'

'See? You don't dress like she does.'

'Even if I don't, I'm not jealous of her.'

'Yeah, right. What girl doesn't envy pretty clothes? They don't exist!'

'So what if they dress nicely? You just wait ten years and see what they turn into. They'll be squalid and won't even be able to get married.' After that remark they moved on to another topic. Five minutes would barely pass until they forgot that exchange. They would forget whether they even had such a conversation or not. Even if they did recall, they'd only remember having a mildly inappropriate conversation and nothing more. But for Kŭm-p'ae, that dialogue contained a point sharper than an ice pick.

Kŭm-p'ae was annoyed. But what was she annoyed about? Did those girls say something that wasn't true? No. Their words were true from the beginning till the end. Because they were true, Kŭm-p'ae was annoyed again. Had those girls spoken a bunch of lies, Kŭm-p'ae simply would have scoffed at the words and held contempt against them. Then who would be the target of such anger? Those girls ... But there was some space to be filled between her anger and those girls. Would it be the drunk patrons? No. It wouldn't be her parents, either. Nor herself. Then what? Kŭm-p'ae realized that it was her situation. Her circumstances.

(I want to take this opportunity to catalogue Kŭm-p'ae's career.)

She was of cheerful disposition. She could recall back to when she was seven years old, wandering out into the streets only in her slip and getting into fights with boys. At the age of eight, she longed to live the glamorous life of a *kisaeng* and asked to be sent to a *kisaeng* school. She succeeded. So up until age thirteen, by the time of her test, she was unsurpassable when it came to a *kisaeng*'s regular talent for performance. Kŭm-p'ae began to take an interest in men. If she caught a glimpse of a man on the street looking at her, she returned home and sat before a mirror for a long time gazing at herself and enjoying the view. The concept of 'young female students' gradually began to change. In the past, there were many 'young female students' who were in their thirties, but more youthful students started to come about. The trend of 'young female students' began to take over. Kŭm-p'ae regarded this as 'young female students emulating the *kisaeng*', and took pleasure in considering this as her victory.

'Play while you're young. When you're old, you won't be able to.' These were Kŭm-p'ae's favourite song lyrics.

When she saw young female students talking disdainfully

of *kisaengs*, rather than getting angry, she took satisfaction with it. *They (the school girls) will be jealous that they can't put on airs like the* kisaeng *can*, thought Kŭm-p'ae. And she sang, played, laughed, swaggered and entertained – wanting to enjoy her youth as much as she could till the very end. Several years went by this way. But tragedy invaded her life as well. The person who brought on such tragedy (let's call him A) was a fellow who had seen Kŭm-p'ae somewhere, and from that moment on, always asked for her. Kŭm-p'ae disliked this man. A wasn't particularly ugly, but he was lacklustre, and his ear was deformed. On top of that, he didn't have any money. But what she disliked the most about him was that A was the kind of man who completely lacked a sense of style.

One night, at some Chinese restaurant, A got stupid-drunk (he wasn't a very good drinker) and sat there dozing until he caught sight of Kŭm-p'ae and greeted her. Kŭm-p'ae ignored him. The two sat in stuffy silence. A didn't even drink any more but just stared down at the *tatami* mat. A sat still in silence for a long time until suddenly, like an elementary school kid going up to a teacher, he just barely made it beside her and pressed an envelope into her hand (turns out it contained fifty *wŏn*). Kŭm-p'ae didn't say a word. But the anxiousness inside A's eyes suddenly seemed endearing to her. A spent the night at Kŭm-p'ae's house that evening. A asked for Kŭm-p'ae numerous times after getting a taste of her warmth that one time. But the fifty *wŏn* that A had saved up over a span of months and spent all at once did not return to him again. Kŭm-p'ae kicked him aside.

There was a blizzard one night. Kŭm-p'ae wandered the restaurant till very late and returned home, where she found A covered in white snow, shivering outside her door, waiting for her return ... completely drunk. Kŭm-p'ae demanded in rage what it was that he had come for. A didn't reply. He collapsed right there and began to sob. Kŭm-p'ae stood speechlessly before the sight until she couldn't take it anymore and asked her father and a servant to come and remove A from the premises. A allowed himself to be dragged out without resistance. Kŭm-p'ae's dreams were not particularly sweet that night. She awoke from several nightmares. The following day, Kŭm-p'ae learned that A had frozen to death in a spot not too far from her home. Not only that, but inside A's pocket was a letter. It was as though he'd been anticipating his death all along.

He'd loved a woman. But this woman scorned him. His possessed mind had no way of finding release. In order to erase his tormented mind, he'd decided to end his life. But, he did not hate her or hold anything against her – this was the gist of the letter. And, of course, that woman was Kŭm-p'ae.

After this incident, Kŭm-p'ae had a tremendous change of heart. The incident taught Kŭm-p'ae two lessons. First was that before every person was the enormous shadow of death. Kŭm-p'ae knew that it definitely existed for her, too. There was no way to know when it might come. This shadow that wasn't present just ten minutes ago could suddenly appear just ten minutes later. The second was that in this life, aside from money and looks, existed two extreme kinds of longing. Kŭm-p'ae had witnessed one extreme in a man spending everything he had – fifty *wŏn* (fifty *wŏn* isn't by any means a large sum of money, but it is also one person's entire life savings) – in order to gain her love, and another extreme where he throws his life away in order to forget that intense love. This event affected Kŭm-p'ae. From that point forth, Kŭm-p'ae developed a sigh that others did not hear and shed tears that others did not see.

When she arrived at her lonely home from the restaurant in the middle of the night, she would sit before the mirror grieving in self-pity; she would play the *kŏmun'go,* with her youthful energy, deep into the moon-filled night; and when she looked around the sleeping city streets of P'yŏngyang, or listened to the oars moving through the foggy waters on a hazy autumn morning, others couldn't tell that through her laughter was a vulnerable yet intense feeling that shivered, bounced, and split. Even when she entertained and enjoyed her time with men, deep inside of her hid a particularly deep sigh – one couldn't tell when this would burst.

There's no way of knowing when it began, but a certain dilemma began to grow and permeate inside her head.

Is it true to live a bold but short life or a narrow and long life? When she thought about A, she realized her fear of living a bold but short life. However (once again pushing A aside), not knowing when this life would end for her, there was no reason for her to be so constrained either. She lamented. Fifty years was by no means a short life. Living in this world was gruelling. In spite of this, she wanted to live those fifty years young and happy. When she realized the impossibility of this, she grew lonely. And so, on the other side of her joy was her melancholy. On the flipside of her laughter were tears.

5

Kŭm-p'ae's eyes, which were filled with tears as clear as crystals, slowly turned towards the young female students' boat. But a decorative dragon had come in between the two boats making the girls who'd harshly criticized the *kisaengs* barely visible, save for their backs. However, their barely visible backs (which were bouncing as though in avid discussion) seemed to be saying: *You just wait ten years and see what they turn into.* Kŭm-p'ae didn't have a way to see what the girls' lives would be like after they got married. Therefore, she really had no clue. But she could surmise that it'd be like clusters of azaleas abloom in the spring. The ones that lit up light pink – that was the life of the girls' life hereafter. A piano, a wooden floor for reading books, a child dressed in Western clothes, travel – these would be the things awaiting those girls. What greater joy could there be. But ...

'You just wait ten years.' Would her own life from that point forth truly be in squalour like those girls had said? Kŭm-p'ae didn't want to give it any thought. But several thoughts passed through her head without any particular order. *Concubine, third class, prostitute, a fight with the real wife.* These were her thoughts. The large shadow in her way at the moment was composed of these thoughts.

Kŭm-p'ae pondered the saying, *Pleasure follows pain.* She pondered the saying, *After joy come tears.* Kŭm-p'ae couldn't tell which saying was better than the other. Neither phrase was able to take over her view, so she was able to see the darkness before her very clearly. She was afraid, and she hated what she saw.

What'll I do then ... What'll I do then ... These were the thoughts that circled inside her mind. Kŭm-p'ae lowered her heavy head. Suddenly a candle-lit lotus floated beside the boat, like a puzzle about to solve the future for her, before drifting away. She slowly raised her eyes, which had been following the candle briefly, back up. Several drops of hot tears fell onto her skirt. They were tears of despair. They were also tears of deep longing. Kŭm-p'ae was scornful of the girls' 'present'. But when looking at the future, there were two impossibly deep pits. An enormous hostility towards those girls grew inside of her. Her eyes, which shone with light, were now filled with poison as she glared at the girls' boat. But that boat had disappeared. The only boats left nearby were the ones delivering food. Kŭm-p'ae felt lonely, so she went to sit beside W. She wanted to hear some warm and encouraging words from somebody – anybody. But the patrons were all drunk and they could hardly think straight. Kŭm-p'ae returned to the boat railing and sat down.

> *Even though we live on different sides,*
> *north and south,*
> *Please don't forget this fool whose*

mind does not change.

From somewhere nearby a sound erupted. The *changgu* started a beat. It was followed by big laughter. She brushed away the tears that nearly fell onto her skirt and silently lifted her head. She could hear the classical string and wind instruments coming from where the decorative dragon had travelled to, softly drifting over towards her.

The boat turned around at about midnight. As the boat docked in front of the restaurant, Kŭm-p'ae broke past the fireworks crowd and entered the restaurant for a minute to retrieve a schedule. There were no more rickshaws in service so she decided to walk to the village. There weren't many people about. Kŭm-p'ae walked slowly with her head lowered. She became upset by a feeling completely different from when those students had insulted her.

What did it mean for a person to go on living? Eating, dressing, working, eating again, sleeping, the same thing again the next day. Fifty years would be the same, as would another hundred years, so what meaning does 'going on living' really have? People look down on the statement, 'Have an entertaining dream'. Is there a difference between experiencing moments of entertainment while living and experiencing an entertaining dream? Those who don't have, want, and those who have, want even more. People living their lives couldn't mean anything more than filling their greed. If dying young is sorrowful, does getting old contain some unexpected joy?

A *kisaeng* understands that her ranking is different from the norm, and others have the same understanding, but what is the difference? *Kisaengs* have feelings. They have sorrow. They have joy and laughter. They have love. How are they different? They, too, will walk this earth till the day they die. After that, they'll walk yet another world. After they die, the whole world will forget them completely in a matter of five years.

What does it mean to want to live long? What does it mean to not want to die? Is this yet another part of a human being's endless desire to live for ever? As though pressing against her heart and revealing herself, upsetting thoughts appeared inside her head one after the other. She nearly walked past her own house. While standing before it, she regained her composure and was about to set foot through the gate when she stopped herself. She heard a song. It was a beautiful tune. It was like a giant wave galloping in the ocean. It also sounded like a tiny bug crying out into the silent night sky, echoing. It was a strain of *kŏmun'go* from T'angmun-gun's 'Sangburyŏn.' It was being plucked by Kŭm-p'ae's younger brother, who was playing the tune while awaiting her return. Kŭm-p'ae stopped in her tracks to listen carefully. Kŭm-p'ae stood listening to the 'Sangburyŏn' playing passionately – not quite coaxing nor quite tattling – as it reverberated. Kŭm-p'ae stepped in through the main gates and made her way inside. Her brother asked who was there, and Kŭm-p'ae replied before stepping into her own room. She got changed and sat before a mirror. The upsetting thoughts returned again. They circled around and around inside her head without beginning or end. She sat there a while before running her hand over her head. The dignified light that was once in her face became a poisonous sneer.

'I was entertaining such unbecoming thoughts,' she said to her reflection. As of now, life was an easy riddle to solve as far as Kŭm-p'ae was concerned. But people did not want to see it that way, so they distorted it. They did not want to see 'life' as an easy riddle. In other words, life was ridiculous, simple, miserable and lonely. The only way to live through this miserable, simple, ridiculous, and lonely life was the occasional pleasure found in vice. What's the point in thinking about the coming days? One couldn't tell what might come next this very evening in this so-called life. *Booze of longevity, don't you lie to me. Fountain of youth – who is the witness? The*

hull of kings' graves, a king's tomb and sword – they are just
the fog of autumn's dusk over grass. Life is but a field dance
within a dream. What are you waiting for? Go on and play.
She recited the words silently to herself before getting up suddenly and walking over to her brother's room. The young boy had pushed the *kŏmun'go* aside and fallen asleep. He'd fallen asleep innocently on his back with his bare chest open, gently breathing in and out. Kŭm-p'ae sat beside his head. She fingered the long band of ribbon around his head as she peered lovingly into his face, adorable as a peony and bright as the moon's light.

'You don't know yet. What a person is. What a man is. What we kisaengs are ... You'll feel joy and gladness at everything you see. You'll want to dance and jump for whatever you greet. Now is the time. But wind and waves will find you, too. Those days aren't too far away. Your innocent eyes will shed tears of agony. There will come a time when your gentle heart tears apart. That day is close. How shocked you will be when the day comes – you, who haven't the slightest idea what filth or indecency is. How frightening that day will be. But our fate is determined for us. We can't avoid it. What's to be done?' Kŭm-p'ae clasped her brother's hand. The little boy, who'd been sleeping peacefully, opened his eyes a bit. Kŭm-p'ae couldn't hold it in any longer. She buried her face into the snow-white chest of her little brother. Hot tears fell from her eyes.

6

The days grew warmer, and the boats over the Taedong River multiplied with folks who wanted to sit across from a beautiful woman over a drink in the spring. Kŭm-p'ae grew busy. Boat rides, parties, drinks – they were always waiting for her. Kŭm-p'ae, who was constantly being called out, returned home with some joy.

'P'yŏngyang's most celebrated *kisaeng*.' This proud remark brought her happiness which bore joy, and brought her soul encouragement. But ...

You just wait ten years. The remark that stained her mind that night would not erase.

This life where we can't predict the time of our death. Could this make that stain disappear? On second thought, *This life what we don't understand even if we lived a hundred years* ... What about that? These thoughts that seemed plausible then not so plausible, visible yet not so visible remained lodged deep inside her mind and would not leave. She wanted to understand it from every angle. She tried to learn everything she could from her associations and relationships in society. But all she'd seen were patrons who were drunk and slumped over unconscious, her parents who criticized her for not taking on a husband for this long, and her now pubescent younger brother; they were the only ones she'd associated with so far. Obscene songs and words that expressed only nonsense were all she'd heard up till that point. She tried with all her brain's might to make sense of it all. But just as before, no new knowledge appeared. When she tried to think harder, her mind just played games by mixing up one thought with another. In the end, all that came of her plans was neuroticism and sleep deprivation. Everything was a mess.

During this time, she came to the unpleasant conclusion that she would never be treated as a complete person. The patrons looked down on *kisaengs* condescendingly as lovable animals. Her parents looked upon her as a gold mine that brought in income. Christians looked upon her as though she were the devil. Moralists looked upon her as a wicked being. Children teased her, calling her a doormat. They believed her to be some kind well-dressed animal. The old and the young all seemed to agree that she was just a beautiful creature who sold sex. They didn't see her as someone of character. Whether they were folks who loved her or hated her (whether it was through money or circumstances), even those who wouldn't dare associate themselves with her, they all looked upon her as an indecent being. Prior to this, Kŭm-p'ae had been leery of society folk who looked down on her or tried to befriend her. Men were indeed weak. They were clumps of hypocrisy who had good times with her but also did not regard her as a human being, and simply saw her as a pretty creature who sold her love. Such insulting thoughts tormented her mind without end. And so Kŭm-p'ae came to the realization that not a single person existed who would not cause her grief. This rang loudly inside her skull. And so, the Kŭm-p'ae who used to be so cheerful, who would smile and tell great stories, turned into the neurotic Kŭm-p'ae who laughed then cried then grew angry then fell into a deep state of thought. During this time, another terrible event caused a huge blow.

7

It was a warm day. Around noon, Kŭm-p'ae had breakfast, washed her face, then returned to her room. Perhaps it was the weather. Kŭm-p'ae was in a very good mood. (On this particular day, the southwest wind blew breezily as though to provoke youthful hearts. Pink clouds clustered together and moved about in the sky. Butterflies flitted about on the field.) She considered paying a visit to a friend's house, but that idea didn't quite satisfy her. She sat rubbing her hands together, wondering what to do, when a guest's voice was heard from the house's main gate. Kŭm-p'ae stepped out. A patron named Y, whom Kŭm-p'ae had spent time with about three or four times, had brought someone who Kŭm-p'ae had never seen before.

'It's been a while. Please come in.' Kŭm-p'ae welcomed the two men.

'Were you on your way out?' asked Y.

'That's all right. Come on in.'

'Let's go inside, then,' said Y, ushering his friend. 'You were away, you said?'

'Yeah.'

'Where?'

'Just here and there ...' Y replied vaguely.

After exchanging a few words between themselves, Y turned to his friend.

'What do you think?'

'She's quite pretty,' replied the new patron, grinning. Kŭm-p'ae sensed that it was his first time visiting a *kisaeng*'s house. But the guest eyed Kŭm-p'ae's face (quite boldly) up and down with hawk-like eyes. Kŭm-p'ae tried to avoid this look by lighting a cigarette and offering it to him. The guest accepted the cigarette. He grinned again then turned to Y, saying (in Japanese), 'How strange!'

'What is?'

'When I see a young woman, my face turns so red that I can't even function properly, but before a *kisaeng* – even though this is my first time – well, it feels no different from sitting before a hen or a bitch.'

'Enough already! This isn't a philosophy seminar.' Y laughed as he chided him.

But the guest didn't pay it any mind and continued to talk (while his eyes twinkled with a smile). 'A recluse such as yourself can't tell the difference among locations or between what should and should not be said, but to someone like me, it's another story. If I sense that someone isn't a person then I frankly claim it regardless of where I—'

'If she isn't a person then what is she?' Y cut off his friend's remark with a question. 'Do you want to know?'

The new guest nodded his head and laughed. Y sat still. There was no reply so the guest decided to answer instead.

'Actually, I won't say that she isn't human. Wait. You know what, she *isn't* human! She definitely isn't human. She's a bat.

A bat!'

'A bat? You mean she makes her living in the night?'

'Right. Just like a bat is an avian creature that doesn't quite belong in the same species as birds, a *kisaeng* is a person but doesn't quite belong in the same species as humans.'

Kŭm-p'ae felt all the blood in her body rise to her face. His words had gone too far. They, of course, assumed that Kŭm-p'ae didn't understand Japanese. Even if she didn't know Japanese, having such a conversation right in front of her was too harsh. When Kŭm-p'ae first laid eyes on the new guest, she'd already made up her mind that he wasn't up to par. But the guest didn't seem to be concerned of Kŭm-p'ae in the slightest. The conversation that began with bats changed.

He didn't even know what a *kisaeng* was, the new guest explained. The day before yesterday when he was on his way down here (P'yŏngyang), a *kisaeng* sat across from him on the train. That was the closest he'd ever gotten to one. But there was one thing he knew. That was that his hunches were usually spot on (as Y should have been aware of). When he looked upon a *kisaeng* with that hunch of his ...

The guest, who'd been giving his explanation as though he were telling a story, took a drag of his cigarette and continued, 'That's right. Easy sale. That's what that is. You so-called customers surely know of this as well, don't you? A *kisaeng*'s parents know that she is for sale. Even animals show loving care for their babies. And *kisaeng*s themselves think this way as well. Am I wrong?'

Y had no response.

The guest continued. 'A prisoner.... That's right. There are those who are people but not treated as people, and they are the prisoner and *kisaeng*. But you must be careful here – both people are treated worse than animals. You would know this better than I do. In other words, they are treated worse than those who are below you. What's worse here is that these *kisaeng*s – let's call them people – these people aren't necessarily satisfied with their lives. On top of this, they have so-called pride, do they not? You are the *kisaeng's* lord. That's how I see it. Depending on a person's environment and circumstances, they can become this handicapped, this spineless. And yet we ourselves can't even find satisfaction in our own lives ...'

Kŭm-p'ae listened without moving. Not only that, but when the guests made their way out to leave, Kŭm-p'ae said her goodbyes to them in a manner no different from the way she first greeted them. Her heart felt like it'd been torn to shreds.

8

A month into this, Kŭm-p'ae's personality grew old like a spinster's and rigid. It was one of those heart-stirring nights—a typical first summer night (not too hot and not too cool) of the new moon. The sky revealed a glimpse of Kyŏnu and Chingnyŏ.[4] At every turn of the road, there was a group of *tanso* players.[5] It was a restless night where whispers carried about and the young P'yŏngyang people could barely sit still by the Taedong River. After finishing her dinner, Kŭm-p'ae hung the 'Closed for the Holiday' sign on the door and headed for the Taedong River.

The sky had already turned black. Even the wishing star couldn't be seen any more. The Milky Way that lit up the night sky like a frosty cloud was the only light. The P'yŏng-yang folk whose blood never grows tired of the river's sight, even after sitting by the Taedong Gate or Ryongwang Pavilion watching its flow all day, had already gathered into a large crowd by the Taedong River. Kŭm-p'ae slowly walked up

[4] Kyŏnu and Chingnyŏ – a star constellation, and the names of the characters in a romantic Eastern folktale ("The Weaver Girl and the Cowherd") who are separated by the Milky Way.

[5] *tanso* – bamboo flute.

towards the Ongnyubyŏng to look down at the sight below. She watched the countless row boats floating through the pitch-black water that was lit up by the reflection of the Milky Way. A few among them were singing traditional songs. Others were singing folk songs. They drifted up and down the river in their little boats, laughing away mindlessly as if to ignore the dead who'd drowned in the deep water.

Kŭm-p'ae was looking down at this for a long time when she suddenly had the urge to go and play on the water's surface. She rented a boat and headed out. When she moved her left arm gently, the boat slipped effortlessly out onto the river. Kŭm-p'ae sat still for a brief moment, wondering where she should head. She decided to head towards Panwŏl-do and slowly rowed her way in that direction. Out in the dark, whenever she heard a noise and turned her head, she saw a row boat. In the silence, when she heard a sudden sound, she turned her head and found yet another row boat. The Taedong River was bustling as though all of P'yŏngyang had taken off on a row boat that night. Kŭm-p'ae, who'd come out on the river in search of some silence, steadily avoided the other boats as she rowed towards Panwŏl-do. She rowed her way up to the bottom end of Panwŏl-do. Although she wanted to get to the top end, her arms were tired so she anchored down in that spot. There were the occasional row boats that appeared up there, but her spot, for the most part, was pretty quiet. Kŭm-p'ae dropped the anchor into the water and stretched out on her back. The sky was endless and beautiful as though someone had created it artificially. Bright orange stars sparkled. She spotted a flying wild goose every once in a while. Kŭm-p'ae looked up at the so-called (this so-called thing being extremely vague) infinity. A star beyond a star, and a star beyond that, and something else beyond that (there's no knowing how long this can go on for), and that was no different from the symbol of infinity. A human being was quite pathetic compared to that sky. A person trying to get through life must seem like a bug trying to swim its way out from the middle of the ocean. If that bug has even the smallest opportunity to enjoy itself, then the absolutely right and smart thing to do would be to enjoy itself as much as it possibly can. Go ahead and enjoy yourself. Play. What's the point of worrying? Why fret? That too will disappear, and only the vast sky and sparking stars will remain, laughing at the people's downfall. Kŭm-p'ae lay there pondering such thoughts.

9

The sound of the water that flowed down each side of the boat made her sleepy. She tried her best to snap out of it, but as ever, the water sound brought on the drowsiness again. She didn't want to break away from her sweet dreams, but she continued to tell herself that she could not fall asleep. She sat up, splashed cold water onto her face, then returned to the far end of the boat to lie back down again. Kŭm-p'ae wasn't sure what had happened except that she found herself spitting water out of her mouth and grabbing onto the side of the boat, trying to haul herself back in. She'd fallen out of the boat somehow. She used all her might and got back on. Her entire body shook like a poplar tree. The cold and the fright agonized her, but she wasn't sure where the fright was coming from. The sound of the river's stream amplified her fear. She was so afraid that she didn't even take the time to wring the water out of her clothes. With trembling hands, she rowed her way back home. The boat was pushed along by the river's powerful stream, and like an arrow, it reached the hill close to her home. Kŭm-p'ae felt slightly reassured. She opened her eyes. She heard people's voices. At this point she'd finally regained her composure. She rowed the boat towards an isolated area where she took off her clothes item by item, wrung out the water, and put them back on again. She rowed her way back to the hill and to the rental house where she returned the boat. She didn't even go inside. Instead, she turned and went straight home (luckily for her the main gate was still open) then snuck into her room. Her room was the same as she'd left it. She didn't turn on the lights. Instead she felt her way around with her hands to remove her wet clothes, which she bunched together and tossed into a corner, before squatting down in place as though in collapse. Her heart trembled strangely. All kinds of fear swallowed her mind. But the fears were muddled together like a riddle, and it was impossible to know what was what. Within this state of anxiety, there was just one thought she could make sense of. That she'd seen the dark shadow of death just a little earlier. Mixed into this thought was her wondering why she didn't just die.

10

It was the fifth of May – the time of year that all women look forward to. There's no need to bring up complicated mythos of the past, but looking back on the beautiful customs that gradually get tainted and disappear, one painful reflection does emerge.

The fifth of May holiday is a woman's day. There's an unwritten rule to this day that excludes men and invites only women. It's the one day when those who've immersed themselves in the role of 'wife' all year long get to spend the day resting peacefully. It's disappeared now, but at the time the sight of young P'yŏngyang women dressed up in their best brought about a kind of sacred feeling. Viewed from behind, a long ginkgo-green skirt, an indigo waistcoat, a pine-green *chŏgori*, a bow that sits prettily as a butterfly and a red pigtail ribbon that flutters in the wind transcend all carnal desires in a person, and only raise feelings of sanctity. It is the penultimate harmony created by human hands. Rather than a person, that kind of beauty makes one appear closer to a doll. In addition, rather than call it nature, such an image is more like a work of art. After spending all morning getting ready, they slowly gather in groups and head towards the hill around eleven. There on the hill await swings and markets that were set up in advance. Around two in the afternoon, the hill becomes crowded with young women. At this time, if we were to head to the highest point of Moran Hill Park to take a peek at the hill below, we'd see a rich array of colours scattered, mixed, and muddled. And the pine trees with the strongest branches would have swing ropes tied over them, where ginkgo-green and indigo colours flutter while a long line of other colours await their turn like ants below them. The women who gather on the hill once a year do their best to forget all their troubles on that day. They toss aside all their reservations and manners to give their all on spending the day freely and joyfully. On any other day, they would've called powder 'tawdry', but on that day, it becomes their very desire to wear it. Standing in line with women of all classes, fighting for their turn on the swing, they bring explosive laughter to the tourists from out of town who have come to visit the May festival. Sounds of laughter, sounds of chatter, sounds of bickering, sounds of the foot stepping onto the swing, and so the day goes until the sun gradually turns bright red in the eve. The women slowly separate into smaller groups, and they each return home thinking about the following day of freedom. After spending a restful night of sweet dreams to wash away their fatigue, the women get dressed again and gather back on the hill. There, they once again spend the day in joy, letting themselves go, and another day of liberation awaits them. They spend the following day with as much joy as the day before. On the seventh day of the month (the last day of the festival), they gather at Kija's Tomb. They spend the final day of their holiday – the one that comes once a year – in the most splendid, pleasant, and joyful manner. And just as the sun is about to set, they return to their husbands and families, thinking about the chores that await them. And so, the day for all wives ends.

11

On the first day of the holiday (the fifth of May), Kŭm-p'ae cancelled all plans related to boats and parties. She decided to call upon just a few of her best clients (W, H and K) for an outing. It was the perfect weather for a picnic.[6] It was a hot day for May, but it was just right for those who needed to be in the water for work. Not only that, but the tide had come in for this party that had circled the river to picnic all the way in Chuam (the tide slowly started to come in since ten), and by the time the day reached noon, it made the Taedong River as wide as the ocean. The tide rose and rose. On top of that, the sweet breeze blowing in from the southwest gathered atop of the rising tide, giving the boats wind, making them move as fast as flying arrows, circling around Panwŏl-do and behind Rŭngnado, then up and up. The May festival didn't only take place on the eastern hill. It took over every mound and hill around. Swing ropes hung from the thick, overgrown weeping willows on top of them. The trendy ginkgo-green and indigo colours danced on those swings. As though the swings were taking flight on the gentle breeze, they went up and up and rose high above. Then the ginkgo-green skirt fluttered back down. Whenever it did, the girls made a beautiful *shwi* sound, as the swings caught more wind. Kŭm-p'ae's party gazed at this from afar on their boat, sticking to Rŭngnado, heading straight on up. Their boat gained speed from the

[6] *ŏ-juk* – the term literally means 'fish porridge', but in North Korea the expression refers to picnicking outdoors by catching and gathering ingredients directly from the site to cook. Because it's easy to catch fish, people typically gather by the water for recreation and make rice porridge out of the catch. In this case, however, '*juk*' is not limited to rice porridge but also branches out to other recipes that require boiling.

tides, aiming for the right spot.

'What a perfect spot to picnic.' It had all kinds of things – enough to make one believe that the neighbouring area of Rŭngnado and Panwŏl-do is actually not at all an easy spot to camp. At the bottom of the river was Taedong's finest sand. The water was clear. The hills were a lush green. On top of them were giant weeping willows, making a nice shade. The P'yŏngyang castle appeared in the misty distance from up ahead where Rŭngnado and Taedong River curved into the shape of a 'ㄱ'.[7] That is where the boat docked. After that, the ferryman unloaded the chicken, rice, firewood, pickled radish, and pots onto the shore. He found a spot to stack pebbles for the pot.

'Now, who's going to kill the chicken?' asked H, looking about.

'I can butcher the bird,' K replied. He tossed aside his socks and pulled up his trouser legs. He grabbed a knife and the chicken, and headed for the water. W poured water into the pot and made the fire while H rinsed the rice. And so each man took on his own task. Kŭm-p'ae felt an inexplicable joy inside, so she and Yŏn-yŏp leisurely walked around on the grass, occasionally looking up at the ginkgo-green and indigo ant-like crowd on Moran Hill, and checking in on their guests from time to time with flirtatious remarks. Whenever they did, she let out a big laugh just for the hell of it.

'Let's go see what's back there.'

'Let's go then,' Kŭm-p'ae replied lightly to Yŏn-yŏp's suggestion, and the two left behind their guests and made their way gradually towards the village, taking in the scent of grass. They'd almost reached the village, where they saw girls dressed in new clothes in celebration of the May festival. Out in the distance, they saw swing ropes spread far and wide.

'It's like silver bells hanging from pigs,' Yŏn-yŏp said to Kŭm-p'ae, pointing to the village children following after

[7] ㄱ – the first letter in hangŭl.

them.

'Wait a minute – pig or no pig, our guests might be looking for us.' Kŭm-p'ae turned around in the direction of their site. Indeed. K had killed the birds and raised two chickens high up, walking towards Kŭm-p'ae, shouting, 'Why don't you pluck one each?'

'Is the water boiling already?'

'Boiling away. We already prepped the birds in them for the plucking.'

'Let's go pick away then. Is that what the fuss is over?' Kŭmp'ae and Yŏn-yŏp dashed towards K. They took a bird each and walked towards the water. Hot water dripped from the birds. The feathers that had softened nicely in the hot water came out of the chickens effortlessly.

'They're coming out nicely.'

'Yours is easy? Mine doesn't come out in the first pull,' Yŏn-yŏp said, pointing her head towards her bird.

'Wanna trade?'

'Let's trade.'

'Eek! You think you could eat this?' Kŭm-p'ae joked, then plucked the bird completely till its red flesh appeared.

'All done!' Kŭm-p'ae shouted down to the party at the foot of the hill.

'If you're done plucking, gut it and carve it!' K shouted back. Kŭm-p'ae grabbed a knife and cut the bird up into smaller pieces. She opened up the belly and removed its insides. She threw them all into a bucket and walked over to the pot.

'Well done,' H said, taking the meat from her. He plopped it into the pot.

'No way you gents can follow my moves,' Kŭm-p'ae said proudly. As she turned, she bit into a cigarette and lit it. Yŏn-yŏp's chicken was also ready. She put it in the water. Now the only task left was for W to tend the fire. Kŭm-p'ae wandered alone towards the river, singing in a tiny voice, to pick a few mulberries and look at the leaves. The little waves – too little and lovely to even be called waves – bumped up against the river's sand, billowing over and passing it. Tiny fish teased the chicken feathers in the water, dancing playfully. Kŭm-p'ae began to daydream, imagining what domestic life must be like. Working together – husband and wife – gathering all their energies into their task, and whenever they have a moment, looking up and laughing happily, jumping with joy. Ah ... such a beautiful sliver of domestic life couldn't be any different from a blessing. If domestic life was a lot like making a picnic by the river, then it couldn't be any different from that place she heard of in stories – The Land of Happiness. Her husband's worries would become the wife's worries. The wife's anxieties would be burdened by the husband as well. If there should be any worries before them, what could they even be? They'd be snow that meets the spring. Salt that meets the water. Kŭm-p'ae sat, romanticizing these thoughts.

12

'Kŭm-p'ae, come and tear a bird with us.'

Kŭm-p'ae jumped up. Back at the picnic site, they were already removing the cooked chicken from the pot and getting started. Kŭm-p'ae ambled her way back over.

'What were you doing, sitting there by yourself?' Yŏn-yŏp asked.

'The hill, the pond, the endless sky, and the sun rising cheerfully over the horizon, high on up ...' Kŭm-p'ae replied to her question with a song instead, and began to debone the chicken. The five people sat around with buckets, deboning their chickens and collecting the meat in the pot along with rice. Afterwards, they began their long-awaited drinking party.

'You ladies can lick the bones.'

'Are you calling me a dog?' Kŭm-p'ae asked as she grabbed

a bone and gnawed the remaining meat. The sun was already setting behind Moran Hill's ridge. The red light from the sun reflected off the river's surface and made the party glow. The weeping willow leaves that nearly touched the ground shaded them; however, as the sun began to fall on the west, it turned the leaves and the billowing water bright red.

'Oh goodness. My eyes … Give me a drink, too. Are you the only one drinking here?' Kŭm-p'ae said, sitting upright.

'Do you even know how to drink, my dear?'

'My my my. How silly you are. Enough games.' K and Yŏn-yŏp's eyes became wide as they looked at Kŭm-p'ae.

'All right then. Let's give her a go.' W recognized Kŭm-p'ae's sincerity He decided to play along and pour her a drink. Kŭm-p'ae accepted and gulped it down.

'Ah – that's good,' said one of the men. But tears began to fill Kŭm-p'ae's eyes.

'*Aigu.* How bitter,' Kŭm-p'ae said, swallowing back gobs of spit.

'You see? You're a lightweight. Don't ever drink again.'

'It's totally different after tasting it.'

'Of course it's different.'

After the first drink, Kŭm-p'ae's vision blurred. She felt heat in her ears. But she took a second drink anyhow. She wasn't sure why, but her mind was set on drinking. Her neck began to grow stiff, but watching the men sipping the spirits made her want to drink more.

'My, am I thirsty.' After three, four, five – up to six drinks later, her face grew dark. She couldn't withstand the dizziness any longer, and she passed out on the ground. She could hear the men telling one another to drink. Their voices sounded faint, like they were coming from across the river. She couldn't tell if they were standing close to her or far away. It felt as though all her weight was gathered in her lungs. The weight on her chest was terrible. She raised both hands in the air and began to thrash. She couldn't take it in any longer and she cried out, 'Save me.'

'What's wrong?' someone asked.

'I'm going to die.'

'Why did you drink when you can't even hold it in? Anyhow, let's go to the boat. I'll take you back. Lie here and wait.'

'I don't want to go by boat.'

'What do you mean you don't want to? What if you vomit? Come now. Let's get up.'

'Wait. I can't budge. If I move, I'll throw up.' Kŭm-p'ae was barely able to reply as she held back vomit.

'Do I need to carry her now? Ha ha ha ha ... booze, I tell you,' he said as he placed her onto his back. Kŭm-p'ae clung to him until they reached the boat. As soon as she was let down, she put her skirt over her head and lay on her back. The man kindly rolled up a floor mat and placed it beneath Kŭm-p'ae's head to use as a pillow. Then he turned around and headed back up to join the party. The back of Kŭm-p'ae's neck was tense. The pressure pinched her all the way to the base of her skull. Tears began to fall from her eyes. They weren't tears from the drinking. The shadow of her sadness that she'd tucked away for a moment began to reveal itself again. This sadness that swept over her was different from any other. It was tremendously vast. Multitudes of sadness were muddled together. They did not come to her in a particular order. Among these was a hidden anxiety named 'domestic life'.

13

The next day, Kŭm-p'ae was called to work on one of the party boats. On her way back home, she encountered something terribly frightening. It was when the boat had been to Moran Hill and was coming back downstream, following the wall of the coast. As the boat passed a section of the wall that had the phrase 'The Way, the Truth, the Light' inscribed on it, the passengers heard something go bump. Everyone turned their heads in the direction of the sound. Someone had fallen onto a rock from the top of the wall. They saw a girl, about thirteen or fourteen years old slumped over, slightly moving her legs. All the passengers on the boat stood up. But a swarm of people had gathered around the sight, and the girl could not be seen any more. All they could make out were phrases like 'She just died a moment ago', 'Her head split open' and 'There's blood coming from her mouth'. The Japanese police came rushing over.

'How awful.'

'Is there anyone who knows this person?' the officer asked.

'Poor thing!'

'How awful. Let's go.' So went the mutterings.

The patron rushed back onto the boat. Kŭm-p'ae shivered and turned to Wŏl-sŏn, saying, '*Aigu*. How terrifying. How am I going to sleep tonight with this image in my head?'

'Too soon ... She couldn't have known a thing about this world, right?'

'How could she? She looked no more than twelve or thirteen. If her parents find out, they won't be able to bear it.' Kŭm-p'ae let out a deep sigh. Wŏl-sŏn's remark referred to sex, but Kŭm-p'ae didn't share the same meaning as Wŏl-sŏn with that phrase. For Kŭm-p'ae it meant that the girl did not experience any sorrow or fear before falling to her death. But what Kŭm-p'ae dwelled on for even longer was how the girl didn't think about dying at all before the moment of meeting her demise. That night, Kŭm-p'ae went home and couldn't sleep a wink. Starting with the young girl's death, Kŭm-p'ae began to go over all the deaths she'd encountered, including A, the young man who froze to death after getting kicked out of her home; several of her close *kisaeng* friends who passed away, especially Hwa-sŏn, who died after taking rat poison; a patron named O who treated Kŭm-p'ae like his own sister;

and another patron named N who slumped over and died very suddenly from a brain aneurysm right there at the drinking table. Kŭm-p'ae let out a deep sigh.

Death. I am not afraid of it. But thinking about it, planning ahead and executing it, was a scary act. This is how the issue of death began to manifest inside her head.

14

On the last day of the festival, Kŭm-p'ae gave in to her little sister's pleas, and they headed towards Kija's Tomb together. By the time her sister had implored her several times and they'd finally stepped out, it was two in the afternoon. The busy street was bustling with sharply dressed married women. Even up until that morning, Kŭm-p'ae had no intention of stepping out. But as soon as she joined the thick crowd on that busy street filled with other women, looking up at the white clouds with a slightly rosy shade and the fluttering dragonflies and magpies, she thought about her pretty reflection in the mirror just a moment ago, and felt her heart soar. Kŭm-p'ae and her sister navigated the newly constructed road through the dust and the crowd of women, heading out of the Ch'ilssŏng Gate and towards Kija's Tomb. The dust and bustling crowd were enough to make the thick sight of the pine trees almost disappear.

'Hey, *hyŏngae*, look at that person over there.'[8]

'She looks like a grub,' Kŭm-p'ae replied with laughter as she got off the main street. 'Kŭm-ju, where are we off to?'

'Let's go wherever you feel like, *hyŏngae*.'

'Wherever I feel like? In that case, let's stay here.' Kŭm-p'ae plopped down right in place.

'Wait a minute. There's Yŏng-wŏl. Let's go join her,' Kŭm-ju begged. Kŭm-p'ae slowly turned her head in the direction

[8] *hyŏngae* – how a younger sister casually addresses her older sister; a casual form of *hyŏngnim*.

of her sister's finger. She saw Yŏng-wŏl and about six other *kisaengs* riding swings. A couple of them were sharing a swing seat as a pair. Kŭm-p'ae stood up wordlessly and headed over to them.

'Here comes Kŭm-p'ae. Why, we didn't know a scholar such as yourself came to places like this. I tell ya. The sun rose from the west this morning.' Yŏng-wŏl, who liked to banter, began to pick on her the minute she saw her.

'Kŭm-ju wanted to come here so badly ...'

'Whatever. Now that you're here, give the swing a go. Hey, Hong-ryŏn, San-wŏl – all of you, get off. Give the scholar here a chance to ride.'

'I'm a bit tired. I'm gonna rest a bit first,' Kŭm-p'ae replied. She headed for the nearest pine tree and plopped down beneath it. At this point Kŭm-p'ae was sleep-deprived, hadn't eaten properly, and was spending her days full of worry. Her body had grown weary. She hadn't slept at all the night before, and she was now in a big, dusty crowd. She had no strength to ride the swing. She squinted her eyes and looked at the swing's rope. She noticed that Hong-ryŏn and San-wŏl had long gotten off the swing seat, and a new girl was up there swinging. Whenever she went back, a *shwi* sound could be heard. Her swing was parallel to the ground, and she fluttered like a butterfly when she came flying forward. The tremor of the pull shook the pine branch almost to the point of breaking. The branch made crackling noises. And if that branch did indeed break, that girl who was enjoying that swing would turn immediately into a corpse. Kŭm-p'ae thought of the little girl who'd died by falling from the wall. Like a flame inside a lantern. Like candlelight. Like aging. Like a moving stream. Like a dream. There'd been plenty of terrible criticisms about this thing called life, starting from long ago, but of all the hundreds of thousands of things said, could anything describe a moment as terrible as yesterday's? The little girl, just a moment before her death, must've been wandering the top of the wall looking for flowers to pick. She was probably thinking about what to wear the next day, what to eat later ... She was probably worried about not having gone to her concert practice yesterday, and anticipating her teacher's scolding. She probably felt a breeze as beautiful as a dream's – the kind that others couldn't possibly experience. The next moment, she was a corpse below the wall. *It's possible that the girl's mother hasn't heard of her daughter's death just yet. She's probably sewing her summer dress this very moment. She probably has an older brother who's anticipating his sister's return, and quickly wolfing down a snack before she arrives. But where is that girl, and what's she thinking about now ...*

'Hey, *hyŏngae*! Let's ride the swings!' Kŭm-ju had one hand wrapped around the swing rope with a seat for two, shouting in Kŭm-p'ae's direction. Kŭm-p'ae snapped herself out of it. She wandered vacantly over to the swing and hopped on. Her arms and legs shook.

Kŭm-ju pulled the swing way back then let go. Kŭm-p'ae bent her legs forward. The swing slowly rose. They pumped their legs backwards and forwards. The ginkgo-green and indigo colours moved like water below Kŭm-p'ae's feet. As Kŭm-p'ae looked down at the crowd below her, she began to appreciate them. *Shwi!* The swing rose high up into the heavens. A strong gust hit her forehead, nose, and ears before it blew past her. Past the dust and pine trees, the roof of the gazebo appeared.

'It's going up nicely,' a voice cried from below. Right at this moment, whether it was fate or fact (Kŭm-p'ae herself couldn't tell either), she felt her right hand lose its grip. The next moment, she'd fallen plop onto the ground.

15

And so, there in the midst of the large crowd, the tiny fleck of dust that had been blowing about all over the place had just barely opened its eyes to look around at its surroundings and was shocked by its vastness. It couldn't even make a sound, and collapsed right there.

'Barely Opened Its Eyes' ends here. I want to continue writing but to continue writing a short story past its season isn't any fun. Once winter comes, this writer's body won't be so fit anymore. Let's put aside a longer piece for another time, and here I'd like to complete this final paragraph. This is how this story becomes an independent piece ...

July–November 1923

SWEET POTATO

Fighting, adultery, murder, begging, imprisonment – the slums outside of the Ch'ilssŏng Gate were the point of origin for all of life's tragedies and conflicts. Pongnyŏ and her husband were farmers – the second in class ranking (scholar, farmer, artisan and tradesman).[1] Pongnyŏ was poor but raised in a household that upheld principles. The strict rules of the *sŏnbi* were left behind once the family fell into the rank of farmer, but some level of discipline, order and intelligence lingered. Pongnyŏ, who grew up in that house, still enjoyed the creek where she played naked with the other girls, and wore pants as she casually walked around her neighbourhood, but in her heart, she still held on to a vague sense of discipline and morals. The year she turned fourteen, she was married off to a man in her neighbourhood for eighty *wŏn*. Her new husband (an old man is more like it) was twenty years older than she. In his father's generation, they were pretty well

[1] Pongnyŏ (복녀) literally means 'lucky girl'.

off as farmers, owning several patches of land, but as time passed, one or two began to disappear. The eighty *wŏn* that he spent to purchase Pongnyŏ was the last of his assets. He was an incredibly lazy man. If a patch of land was given to him through an elder's connection, he would simply scatter the seeds and never tend to them. By the time autumn came, he would simply say, 'The crops were no good this year,' and bring nothing to the landowner. He'd keep the harvest all to himself. And so he could never maintain one field for more than a couple of years. After several years of this, he lost the goodwill of everyone in town.

When Pongnyŏ first got married, she was able to get by thanks to the help of her father during the first three or four years. But even he, who had a *sŏnbi* background, began to grow bitter at the sight of his son-in-law. The couple even lost credibility at Pongnyŏ's own home. They had no choice but to go to P'yŏngyang as labourers. But for the lazy husband, labouring certainly was not a good fit. He would take his A-frame to Ryŏngwang Pavilion to stare at the Taedong River all day, so how on earth could he make any wages? After three or four months of labouring, they found some luck and entered the servants' quarters of some home. But they couldn't last there, either, and eventually got kicked out. Pongnyŏ worked hard at the house, but her husband's laziness could not be helped. Pongnyŏ glared her husband down every day, but his habits could not be mended.

'Clear those rice sacks.'

'I'm a bit sleepy. Why don't you do it?'

'Why don't *I* do it?'

'You spent twenty years stuffing your face with rice. You can't manage that?'

'*Aigu*, just kill me why don't you.'

'Why, you little bitch!'

Fights like this were constant between the two and eventually got them both kicked out of the house.

Where to go now? They had no choice but to take residence outside the Ch'ilssŏng Gate – a ghetto. Generally the people there were all beggars. Aside from that there was also looting, whoring amongst themselves, and all kinds of other frightening and dirty sins. Pongnyŏ joined them. But who on earth would support the begging of an eighteen-year-old girl who is at the prime of her life?

'What's a young thing like you begging for?' Whenever she heard this, she would come up with an excuse that her husband was dying, but the P'yŏngyang people, who were tired of this kind of remark, could not show her any sympathy. The couple was one of the poorest even in the slums. But there were some who made good money. They would bring back five *ri*, one *wŏn* and eighty *chŏn* in cash. In some cases, there were even folks who went out to make money at night and returned with four hundred *wŏn* or so and start a cigarette business nearby. Pongnyŏ was eighteen years old. She had a pretty face, too. If she emulated what she'd seen other girls in the neighbourhood do and visited a well-off man's house, she could make fifty or sixty *chŏn*, but her *sŏnbi* upbringing would not allow her to do this. So the couple led a poor life, and they often went hungry.

The pine groves of Kija's Tomb became infested with moth larvae. The P'yŏngyang ministry decided to hire local women from the ghetto (as if handing out a favour) to catch the pests. All of the women from the ghetto enlisted, but only about fifty of them were chosen. Pongnyŏ was one of them. Pongnyŏ put her heart into her work. She would climb up the ladder to reach the pine trees, catch the larvae with tongs and insecticide, and repeat the process. Her bucket would fill up in no time. The day's wage of thirty-two *chŏn* made it into her hands. But after five or six days of working, she noticed some strange activity.

About ten or so young women didn't work but sat around laughing and fooling around on the ground. Not only that, but their wages were eight *chŏn* more than the actual workers. There was just one supervisor, and he not only allowed them to carry on, but would occasionally join in on the fun.

It was lunch hour one day at work. Pongnyŏ climbed down to eat her lunch before getting back up on the ladder to work when the supervisor called to her, 'Pongne! Hey, Pongne!'

'What is it?' Pongnyŏ set down her insecticide and tongs and headed over to him.

'Come here for a minute.'

She went over to him without a word.

'Hey, um. Let's go back there for a second.'

'For what?'

'Well, just go ...'

'Okay. *Hyŏngnim*.'[2] She turned and called to the women. '*Hyŏngnim*, let's go.'

'No thanks, dear. The two of you can enjoy yourselves. What fun would there be for me?'

Pongnyŏ's face turned bright red as she turned and followed the supervisor.

'Let's go.' The supervisor walked ahead and Pongnyŏ followed with her head lowered.

'Lucky you, Pongne!' She could hear the sounds of the women teasing behind her. This made her face turn even brighter. From that day forth, Pongnyŏ became one of those women who did not work but collected a higher wage. Pongnyŏ's outlook on life and morals also changed.

Up until that point she'd never considered having sex with another man. That wasn't the sort of thing a person does. It was only fit for animals. She also thought if she did

---

[2] *Hyŏngnim* (although it is more commonly used between men today) was also used among women to address another woman who is slightly older than she. In today's parlance, it is on par with *ŏnni*. This form of address is still used between sisters-in-law.

such a thing she'd drop dead on the spot. But life was indeed strange. Even as a person, she found that she was capable of such business. It wasn't out of bounds for her. On top of that, she didn't work but made more money and experienced intense pleasure; it was easier than begging ... Like the Japanese saying, it contained the joy of three beats, and there was nothing else like it. This was the life, wasn't it? Not only that, but after this incident, she found a confidence in herself as a human being for the first time. She even began to wear a bit of powder on her face.

A year passed. Her life was moving forward smoothly. The couple was no longer living in such dire straits. Her husband would stretch out on the warmest part of the floor and laugh with joy. Meanwhile, Pongnyŏ's face grew prettier by the day.

'Hey sweetie, how much did you make today?' Whenever she came across a beggar with a little bit of money, she would ask him in this way.

'I didn't make much today.'

'How much?'

'About thirteen or fourteen *nyang*.'

'You made good today. Why don't you loan me five *nyang*?'

'Listen, today I ...'

When he made excuses like this, Pongnyŏ would grab him by the arm and hang on. 'You've been caught red handed. You ought to loan me some.'

'My goodness. It's always like this with you. Okay, I'll loan you some but, uh, you understand, eh?'

'Whatever could you mean? He he he he.'

'If you don't know then forget it.'

'Come now. I get it.'

Her character had fallen to such a state.

Autumn. Around this time year, the slum women outside of the Ch'ilssŏng Gate went to the Chinese man's vegetable garden with a basket to steal sweet potatoes and cabbages. Pongnyŏ stole quite a few sweet potatoes. One night, she had taken a basketful of sweet potatoes and was turning to leave when a large shadowy figure took hold of her. When she took a closer look, she saw that it was the owner of the vegetable garden – Mister Wang. Pongnyŏ couldn't speak a word. She simply stared down at the ground.

'Let's go to my house,' he said.

'Well, let's go then. You think I can't?' Pongnyŏ swung her ass around, tossed her hair and followed Wang to his house with the basket in her hand. She came out about an hour later. When she made her way out of the furrow and onto the street, someone called out to her from behind.

'Pongne, is that you?'

When Pongnyŏ turned to look, she saw a dark figure carrying a basket on her side, stumbling out. '*Hyŏngnim*, is that you? Did you go there, too?'

'You were there, too?'

'Whose house did you go to, *hyŏngnim*?'

'Me? I went to Mister Nuk's. What about you?'

'I was at Mister Wang's. How much did you make, *hyŏngnim*?'

'That cheap bastard Nuk gave me three cabbages.'

'I made three *wŏn*.' Pongnyŏ beamed proudly. Ten minutes later, she and her husband sat before the three *wŏn* that she had made and laughed heartily over the Wang story. From that point forward, Wang would come over looking for Pongnyŏ. Whenever Wang sat around making blank stares, Pongnyŏ's husband would take the hint and step outside. After Wang left, the couple would look at the one or sometimes two *wŏn* they had made and rejoice. Pongnyŏ eventually stopped selling her love to the neighbourhood beggars. If Wang was busy tending to something and couldn't make it, Pongnyŏ would pay him a visit on her own. The Pongnyŏ household was now one of the richest in the ghetto.

Winter passed and spring came. Wang spent a hundred *wŏn* and bought himself a young girl as his wife.

'*Hŭng*!' Pongnyŏ snorted.

'Pongnyŏ, you must be jealous.' Whenever the ladies in her neighbourhood went around saying this, Pongnyŏ would respond with a snort.

Me? Jealous? She denied this fervently, but could not control the darkness that took hold inside of her.

'Wang, you bastard. You just wait.'

The day for Wang's bride to arrive drew near. Wang cut the long hair he'd always boasted. It was also rumoured that it was his new bride's suggestion.

'*Hŭng*!' All Pongnyŏ could do was snort.

It was the day of the bride's arrival. Dressed in fine clothes, she rode a palanquin carried by four men and arrived at Wang's vegetable garden just outside of the Ch'ilssŏng Gate. Wang's house filled with Chinese guests, various kinds of music, singing and noise all through the night. Pongnyŏ hid in the corner of her house with a violent glare, listening. As Pongnyŏ saw some Chinese guests leaving around two in the morning, Pongnyŏ turned to Wang's house and went inside with her face powdered white. The new bride and groom looked at her in shock. She glared them down, then went to Wang and grabbed his arm. A strange smile appeared on her lips.

'Come. Let's go to my house.'

Wang couldn't say a word. His eyes lacked focus.

Pongnyŏ gave Wang another shake. 'Come now. Let's go.'

'We have something to tend to tonight. I can't go.'

'What tending do you have in the middle of the night?'

'There's still ... tending ...'

The strange smile from Pongnyŏ's lips suddenly vanished.

'You trifling thing.' Pongnyŏ raised her foot and kicked the bride's ornamented head. 'Come on. Let's go. Let's go.'

Wang began to shake. He pushed aside Pongnyŏ's hand.

Pongnyŏ collapsed but she got right back up. When she stood, she had a sickle in her hand.

'Die, you chink! How dare you hit me, you bastard! You bastard! *Aigu!* I'm dying!' she cried out while brandishing the sickle. There outside the Ch'ilssŏng Gate, where Wang's home stood in isolation, a violent crime took place. But that scene soon quelled. The sickle that Pongnyŏ had been wielding suddenly found its way into Wang's hand. Blood spewed from Pongnyŏ's throat and she keeled over onto the ground. Pongnyŏ's body was left unburied for over three days.

Wang went to see Pongnyŏ's husband several times. Pongnyŏ's husband went to see Wang several times as well. The two had negotiated something between themselves. Three days passed. In the middle of the night, Pongnyŏ's body was transferred from Wang's house to the husband's house. Three people sat around the body. One was Pongnyŏ's husband, the other was Wang and the last was a herbal medic. Wang reached for his purse, took out three bills of ten *wŏn*, and handed them to Pongnyŏ's husband. Two of those bills went to the herbal medic.

Two days later, the medic declared that Pongnyŏ had died of a cerebral haemorrhage and sent the body to a public burial ground.

January 1925

FIRE SONATA

You, the reader, may feel free to believe that this story I am about to write took place somewhere in Europe. You may also believe that it's a story that takes place on stage in Chosŏn forty or fifty years later. But I don't know if it took place somewhere here on this earth. Perhaps it has. Perhaps it does. The only thing that exists is its possibility. That's all you need to know. And so, the protagonist of this story, Paek Sŏng-su, could be called Albert even – that's fine. Jim is fine, too. He could also be called Ho-mo or Kimuramo.[1] Just know that he's a creature called 'human' and the things that occurred took place in a human world … Let us begin the story with this premise.

'Did you know that chance can make or break a person?'

'Yes, and it's not a topic worth researching, either.'

'Now, let's pretend that there's a shop here. But there is no

---

[1] Ho-mo (胡某)

owner, no clerk – a completely empty space – and a gentleman just so happens to walk by. A young gentleman who has money and an excellent reputation. Such a man could take a peek inside this empty shop and think to himself, "It's completely empty, so a thief could enter without any hesitation. He can get inside, steal, and no one would know a thing. Why would anyone leave a shop unattended like this?" At the end of a thought like this, he might, what would you call it, *incidentally*, out of sheer perversion, grab a small (valueless) item and stick it into his pocket – could he not?'

'I'm not sure.'

'He could. He most certainly could.'

It was a summer evening. Somewhere beyond the city's outskirts in a suburb somewhere, two old men shared such a conversation. The man who was making this argument was the famous music critic, K. The man listening to him was a social culturalist called Mister Mo.

'I wonder if he could.'

'He could indeed. In any case, let's just assume that he does. Then where does the responsibility fall?'

'There's an Eastern proverb that warns us not to retie a shoelace in a melon field, and so perhaps the gentleman holds responsibility here. Does he not?'

'If so, then that's that, but that gentleman is young. If he wasn't placed in such an odd position with such absolution, he wouldn't have ever thought of such a deed or concern. Then what of that?'

'…'

'What I'm saying is, sin is contingent upon opportunity. Opportunity – this intangible item – is unable to offer punishment. And so we have no option but to call this gentleman a sinner.'

'Yes – that's right.'

'Another thing. If calling someone a "genius" depends on the right situation, without opportunity, such a genius could never appear. However, if the opportunity arrives, and a person's genius and criminal instinct intersect, then do we praise that opportunity or frown upon it?'

'I'm not sure.'

'Do you, sir, know a man named Paek Sŏng-su?'

'Paek Sŏng-su? Hm. Not to my knowledge.'

'As a songwriter he's—'

'Ah, yes. I remember. He wrote the famous 'Fire Sonata', correct?'

'Yes. Do you know where this man is now?'

'No, I don't. Well, I did hear that he lost his mind ...'

'Yes. He's currently committed at the X Mental Institution. I will now tell you his life's story, and I'd like to hear your opinion on it as a social culturalist.'

The Paek Sŏng-su I am about to speak of had a father who was also a very talented musician. This father was my peer, and even as a student, his gift was readily apparent. He majored in composition. He would write his own pieces late at night alone, and the sound of him banging the piano would wake us up. The sound of that savage melody in the middle of the night used to frighten us. He was a wild man. If someone – even teachers – got caught on the wrong side of his wild and outrageous spirit, he would beat them. Even bar owners near the school – there wasn't a single person who hadn't been subject to his thrashing. Even in his wild state, he was constantly locked inside his music. It's possible that this savagery fuelled his talents even further. But upon graduating, that wildness gravitated elsewhere. Booze! Booze! It was that terrifying booze. From morning to night, from night till dawn – the glass never left his lips. After getting drunk, he would harass women. The police would detain him and, once he got out, he repeated the cycle all over. His work? Whatever do you mean, 'work'? After drinking, he'd be hyped up on his drunkenness and sit before the piano, improving some tunes, but looking back, that frightening sound had the power to paralyse his listeners. (No different from a modern-day Beethoven.) Even if it was a gem of a tune, we were each so absorbed in our own day-to-day lives that we wouldn't think of copying that kind of drunken music – not even in our wildest dreams. We all thought of his impending funeral, and we occasionally tried to get him to control his drinking, but what use is a friend's intervention for a wild drunk such as he?

'Booze? Booze is music!' he'd cry out, laughing loudly, 'Ha ha ha ha!' before grabbing a bottle and running off again. After seven or eight years of this, he turned into a complete wreck. When he didn't drink, his hands shook. His eyes were always crusted over. And whenever booze entered him ... whenever booze entered him, he displayed madness. He would grab any random person and just pour liquor into their mouth. He stopped caring about his surroundings and passed out anywhere to sleep. It's a shame how his genius went to waste. We would often sigh amongst ourselves at the thought of this wasted talent, but the world was oblivious to the frightening prospect of the death of this genius. During this time, he met a bar girl and got her pregnant. But he didn't even see the birth of his child. He died of a heart attack. That son who was born into a world without a father is Paek Sŏng-su. But we only heard of the birth of Paek Sŏng-su through the grape-vine. After his father's death, we didn't hear any news of the boy, nor of his mother. Well, rather than not knowing, that household's issues were simply erased from our memory.

———————————————

Thirty years passed. When ten years pass, even the mountains and skies change. How is one to speak of the change that takes place after thirty years? Anyway, during that time, his name was completely erased from my mind. As you may know, when we mention the name 'K' today, I am regarded as one of the top five music critics in the country. When it comes to K – a reliable ear – his authority and judgment in the music world create cultural value. Many musicians trained beneath me. And many musicians became recognizable names today because of my guidance.

It was spring the year before last. At the time, I had a habit of going to XX Cathedral to spend a few quiet hours of meditation at night. It was the only building that sat at the very top of a hill. I would sit there all by myself, listening only to the sound of startled pigeons flapping their wings while fluttering from the crossbeams. If it wasn't for someone with a peculiar temperament such as myself, one couldn't pay a person to step inside such a dreary place. But for someone like me, who enjoys meditation, it was the kind of building that had all kinds of perks that couldn't be found anywhere else.

It was isolated, quiet, and gloomy, and made mysterious sounds from time to time. In the distance, the startled whistling of a train could be heard occasionally. This sound alone was quite considerable, but on top of this, this cathedral had a piano. Cathedrals typically have organs, so finding a piano inside one wasn't typical. If I felt compelled, I would go and play a tune on it. This felt pretty good.

That night (it was probably past two a.m.) while I sat there alone, enjoying the sweet silence of the place, I suddenly heard the sound of chatter from somewhere below. When I opened my eyes, I saw a flame rising high up. When I peered outside the window, the house at the foot of the hill was on fire. People scrambled about. It was chaos. I don't know what you might think of me saying this, but seeing a fire display from up close was quite nice. The rising flames, the billowing smoke, the flying embers, the spotted pillars appearing through them, the darkened corpse of the house, the noisy crowd – these things could be regarded as a poem, or a musical composition. Back when Nero saw the Great Fire of Rome, it is said that he took up a lute and began to sing. From a musician's standpoint, this is not something to criticize. I, too, looked at that fire and felt excitement.

Why don't I pay tribute to Nero and improvise a tune? I thought to myself numbly while gazing at the fire in a foggy contemplation. It was at that moment. Something went bumpety-bump and the cathedral doors opened. A young man, who appeared to be in distress, came rushing in. He looked around nervously. I guess he didn't see me. He rushed to the window and crouched below it. He then peered out of it to watch the flames below. I couldn't move. He definitely wasn't some ordinary man. He was either an arsonist or a thief in my eyes. What else could I think? So I stood there without moving a muscle, and the man finally let out a deep sigh. He stretched out his arms languidly then turned to walk back down when he suddenly spotted the piano beside him. He pulled the stool over and sat before it. I was elated by the sight of another who shared my profession. So I waited to see what he would do next. He opened the lid and struck a key to give it a test. A moment later, he hit a couple more keys still testing out the sound. His breathing grew heavy. He began to pant like a madman. His body shook and both hands finally fell like a lightning bolt onto the piano keys. An allegro began in C sharp. I'd only begun watching him out of curiosity, but as the allegro burst into the air, my heart did not stop pounding with excitement and anticipation until the end of the song. That sound was purely wild. It was too powerful to be called music. It wasn't even art. But it contained such suffering, weight and intense emotion that it was difficult to not call it music. It was enough to make a person's heart grow dark and heavy like the sound of the bell toll at midnight. It also contained both a savage and human cry that was enough to make one's skin rise from the realization of frightening emotions. Ah – that wild energy! That savage clamour! That hidden suffering, hunger and pain! That pure and undisciplined expression!

I plopped onto the floor. I ignored my instincts as a trained musician and reached into my pocket to grab a piece of paper and pencil. I followed the tune coming from the piano and scribbled it onto the paper. The poverty that began at such rapid pace, the hunger, the life that slowly faded like flames, the slow melody that continued in spite of all these things, compressed into emotion. The fury came bursting out without warning. There was also a hint of pleasure and laughter – and so the tune found peace and the performance ended.

The compressed emotion, the violent fury, the ghastly outrage that entered the heart – due to my submersion in the spoils of what we call civilization, I thought about how I'd overlooked this feral being. Even after the tune was over, I sat there blankly, unable to pull myself together. Anyone with the slightest bit of musical knowledge would recognize that this person's sonata did not have any traditional discipline but was ingeniously improvised. He paid no attention to the seventh and sixth chords, and confused them. He endured up to the fifth and eighth chords. He'd completely forgotten the scales. It was the kind of sonata that was immune to labels such as 'bold' or 'ignorant'. It was a completely liberated sonata. At this moment I suddenly recalled Paek XX, who'd died thirty years ago due to a heart attack. If I drew out traditional training from this young man's music and added more wildness to it, then I would have Paek before my very eyes.

Like a person seized by a spirit. That energy, that uninhibited expression and wild spirit – this was a rare gem in modern music. I'd been locked in a long trance by his sonata. I slowly crept up behind him and placed my hand gently on his shoulder. He had been resting there for a moment after completing his tune, and he jumped up in alarm and stared at my face.

'How old are you?' This was the first question I asked him.

I felt such urgency inside that I couldn't think of anything else to say. The moonlight that beamed in through the large window hit my face. He stared at this for a long time before he finally turned away from me.

'Are you hungry?' This was my second question to him.

He turned around again as if my questions irritated him. After staring at my moonlit face for another moment, he finally said, 'Oh. Aren't you Professor K?'

I said that I was and he replied, 'I saw you only in photos.' He languidly turned his head away from me again. As he turned, I got a glimpse of his face for the first time in the moonlight. I was caught off guard when I saw my dead friend Paek XX from thirty years ago.

'What's your name?'

'Paek Sŏng-su.'

'Paek Sŏng-su? You're that Paek's boy ... the fellow who left this world thirty years ago, just before you were born ...'

His head bounced up and looked at me. 'Excuse me? How do you know that?'

'Are you Paek XX's boy? You look just like him. I'm a classmate of your father's. Ah – indeed. The apple doesn't fall far from the tree.'

He let out a long deep sigh and lowered his head.

I brought Paek Sŏng-su over to my house that night. The whole house was a mess, with original compositions strewn all over the place, but it would have been a pity to lose a sonata that was so full of ardour and wildness. I asked him to sit at the piano once more. The notes that I'd taken down on paper were towards the end of the allegro. What I wanted to document was what came before that. He sat at the piano and craned his neck forward. He hit the keys a few times with his fingers, and he tilted his head thoughtfully. He tried five or six times but it was useless. The sounds that came from the piano could not surpass the level of unprincipled noise. Wildness? Power? Haunting? None of that prevailed. They were only ashes of emotion.

'It's not working, professor.' He lowered his head as if in embarrassment as he spoke to me.

'Not even two hours went by, but you already forgot?' I pushed him aside on the stool and opened up the notes that I'd written down on scrap paper. I began from the point where I'd written. Flame! Flame! Poverty. Hunger. Wild power. A strange emotion that had been repressed! I got carried away playing what I saw on the notes. Indeed, in that moment my eyes were flashing like a madman's. My face turned red with passion. At that moment, he pushed me aside and took over. He played instead. I'd fallen from the chair but couldn't stand back up because of the excitement. I looked at his profile from there on the floor. He began to read what I'd written after pushing me aside. Ah, that face! His breathing grew heavy, his eyes flashed like a crazy person's. Then he tossed the notes aside, and both hands took over the keys. The 'C Sharp on the Minor Scale' – that eerie sonata began again. The power was like a tornado. It was like a frightening wave. It was enough to make a person suffocate. It was greater than Beethoven's. It was a violent wildness that didn't exist among us modern musicians. A frightening and miserable hunger, poverty, compressed emotion. A spark of fire that jumped out. Horror. A mad laughter – ah, my chest ached for a breath of air. My arms flailed.

He worked himself up that night and told me everything about his past. His story went more or less like this:

After his mother became pregnant with him, she was kicked out of her home. That's when their poverty began. But his refined and benevolent mother worked hard as a labourer, and raised him the best she could. She found a humble organ and played Schubert's lullaby for him to aid his sleep. When he woke up, she played 'The Second Waltz' to start his day off cheerfully. When he was three, he sat in his mother's lap and played the organ. After his mother saw him play, she saved her money over the years and bought him a piano by the time he turned six. In the morning, the sound of birds, the sound of fluttering poplar leaves in the wind, his mother's love, the sound of soup boiling in the kitchen – all of these sounds contained a mysterious charm and sentiment. He sat at the piano and played notes that came to him. He completed his elementary and middle school education at this time. All the while, the adoration for music that collected inside of him was enough to make him burst. After completing middle school, he couldn't continue his studies for the sake of his mother. He was employed at a factory somewhere. But due to his compassionate upbringing by his mother, he grew up to be a kindhearted person in spite of being a factory worker. And his obsession with music had not diminished in the slightest. Although he didn't have the means to receive any official musical training, he would sit before the gramophone or attend the cathedral on Sunday nights to satiate his young heart's desire for music. When he was home, he never left the piano. On a number of occasions, a strange poetic inspiration took over, and he would grab a sheet to jot down whatever came to him. But strangely, even with all that intense passion and bursting emotion, as soon as he wrote them down, it turned lifeless. Why? You might ask why someone with that much talent and that much passion could only write down music that turned to ash. I'll explain that a bit later. Passion, an insatiable passion, exceptional thrill; the inverse of that was a pathetic result. Ten years passed with this dissatisfaction still intact.

––––––––––––

His mother came down with a sudden illness. The cost of her

dietary supplements and medicine gradually ate up the savings he'd gathered over the years. He put the money away so that when things got easier, he could get some official musical training, but that money wound up going entirely into aiding his mother. But she showed no signs of improvement. His mother, unable to hang on any longer, fell into a critical condition one summer day of the year before he and I met at the cathedral. But by that point, he'd already spent all of his money. He left his mother behind that morning and went to work at the factory. But he felt anxious throughout the day, so he left in the middle of work and headed home. His mother had fallen into a coma. He felt his heart drop. He ran out of there in a state of panic. But where to run? To do what? After fleeing the house, he ran around aimlessly for a long time until he finally came to his senses and decided to look for a doctor.

It was at that moment. The 'opportunity' that I mentioned earlier appeared before him right at that moment. It was a tiny cigarette shop. The door that separated the owner's house from the shop was closed shut, and there was a chance that a person was indeed back there, but no one was in sight. And on top of the cigarette box was a fifty-cent silver dollar and several pennies. He himself wasn't sure what he was doing. He'd made the dim rationalization that a doctor's visit would cost him merely several dimes. He looked around once more; then, like a lightning bolt, he grabbed the money and ran like hell. But he didn't make even twenty steps before the owner rushed out and grabbed him. He pleaded with the owner several times. He even tried reasoning: because his mother was nearing death, if he could please be let go for just an hour, he would bring a doctor to her then return. But all of that was dismissed as bullshit, and he was dragged to the police station. From the police station, he was taken to court. From court, he was taken to prison. He spent the next six months grinding his teeth in anger. He wondered whatever happened to his mother. He wrung his hands and stomped his feet in frustration. If she did pass away, she must've searched for him in her final moments. There wasn't a single person near her deathbed to even offer her a glass of water. That image of agony. The image of his mother dying of thirst. Such images haunted him to the point where he himself felt as though he'd die of thirst. After spending half a year away, he returned to the bright and shiny world. He went to the shack that used to be his home, but someone else was already occupying the space. He heard that, six months ago, his mother came crawling out onto the street looking for her son and died there. He went to the cemetery but couldn't find her gravestone anywhere. And so, unable to find a place to spend the night, he ran into the cathedral where he met me.

K abruptly stopped his story at this point. He removed a Madoros pipe, lit his tobacco and turned to Mister Mo.

'Have you found any inconsistencies in my story yet?'

'I'm not sure.'

'Then I'll ask instead. Paek Sŏng-su was a very gifted musician, but why is it that after he turned his music – the "Fire Sonata" (we began to call the piece "Fire Sonata" after that night) into a written composition, it became completely lifeless? The music that was once full of excitement, anticipation and tension?'

'It's most likely that he just couldn't duplicate the same amount of energy that he had when he was creating the "Fire Sonata".'

'Is that your understanding? After hearing you say it, I suppose that makes sense. But I didn't see it that way.'

'Then what is your understanding, Mister K?'

'Well, rather than give you my interpretation of it, I'll just show you a letter that Paek Sŏng-su sent me. You're not busy today, are you?'

'I don't have any plans, no.'

'Then would you like to come over my place for a bit?'

'Sure.'

The two old men stood up. K's home was situated between the city and the suburbs. By the time they reached his house, it was around four or five in the afternoon. The two old men sat in K's study, facing each other.

'This is the letter that came to me from Paek Sŏng-su a couple of days ago. Please take a look.' K removed a long letter-sized envelope and handed it to Mister Mo, who took the letter and opened it.

'Wait. Try reading from here. Everything before that is just a useless greeting.'

> *[...] and so, I was out looking for a place to stay the night yet again, and while wandering around I just so happened to find myself before the shop where I stole fifty cents. It was very late at night, and the whole neighbourhood was quiet, but while I was looking for a place to get some rest, standing before that house I suddenly felt a terrible urge for vendetta. If it wasn't for this shop ... if this shop owner had the slightest bit of decency, my poor mother wouldn't have crawled out of the house and died in the street like that. This shop had turned me into the bastard who couldn't even find his mother's gravestone to place flowers over. I couldn't stop thinking about this, so I found some hay in front of the house and lit it on fire. I stood there and watched the flames slowly take over the house. I suddenly felt very afraid, so I ran away. During my getaway, I saw a few people already gathering to intervene. My mind was preoccupied with thoughts of delightful satisfaction and the urgency to flee. I saw the cathedral before me so I ran inside*

in order to hide. I was going to leave after watch-
ing the flames die down, but I saw the piano [...]

'Excuse me, sir,' K called to Mister Mo, who was reading the letter. 'The reason why he couldn't duplicate the music in spite of his unusual passion and motivation is precisely because of this. Sŏng-su's mother was an incredibly virtuous woman, and so ever since Sŏng-su was a boy, she raised him to become a good person. It's because of that virtuous child-rearing that he was unable to reveal his wildness – his innate brute. When that wildness, passion and power got written into a musical composition, it turned into beer that lost its fizz. The calm and virtuous lessons of morals – they got in the way of his ability to exhibit his gift.'

'Hm.'

'Sŏng-su was able to free himself of that somewhat during his incarceration, but a person isn't able to undo his cultivation completely. And after a while, he found himself standing before his enemy's shop, and suddenly, out of nowhere, the wild brute within him came out and started a fire out of plea-sure. It was after this that the "Fire Sonata" came bursting out of him. The rising flames, the people's screams, the power of the fire spreading without regard for anything – these elements are the foundation of what brought on that wild pleasure.'

'...'

'Do you understand? Okay then. Please continue to read the letter from here then.'

> *[...] That night's incident continues to plague me.*
> *When I think back on the time when you (you*
> *who'd introduced numerous musicians to this*
> *world) sat before the piano in your elderly state and*
> *played my 'Fire Sonata', my eyes well up with tears.*
> *That time when a patron and his wife both passed*

*out, I can't deny that it was your great influence
on the 'Fire Sonata' which caused it. You put me
before a large audience and said, 'This person is
the composer of the "Fire Sonata" and the son of
a remarkable talent who left us behind in this
world. His name was Paek XX.' When will such
kind and moving words ever be spoken of me ever
again in this lifetime? After that, the room you
prepared for me was by far the best room I ever had.
A large space that faced the north. In the southeast
corner, a strong and sturdy bedframe made of oak.
In the northwest corner, an oak desk and chair. A
piano. And the only décor in that room was a large
mirror. This enormous space was enough to bring
me goosebumps, especially at night when I sat
beneath a lamp. The room's interior was painted
completely black. Outside my window was a dead
locust tree. It was a ghastly sight. All this time, you
put your efforts into helping me to create new music
organically. Just think of how hard I must've tried
to create great music in that environment. When I
requested a more technical musical training from
you, you replied, 'You don't need that kind of training. Just do as your heart tells you. If someone like
you receives any technical training, your music will
turn mechanical. Work freely, and ignore discipline and rules. Just work as your heart desires ...'*

*I didn't quite understand the meaning of your
words. But I did understand the overall gist of
what you were saying. And so I tried to cultivate
my music as freely as I could. Strangely, though,
the work I created did not surpass the level that
I'd accomplished in my past (back when my
mother was still alive), and just like back then,*

my music had no power. It was mere child's play.
Imagine how anxious I must've been. At times,
you would say things that would exacerbate my
anxiety. And the more I grew anxious, the softer
my music became. There were times when I tried
to imagine the sight of that fire. I tried to duplicate that satisfied feeling I had at the sight. But I
always failed. On occasion, a rare feeling would
come over me and I'd jot down some music, but
when I returned to it after a few hours, all I
saw was a helpless concept. My heart gradually
grew heavier. And I couldn't help but feel sorry
for you who had such high expectations of me.

'Music is different from a handicraft. It doesn't work
whenever you want it to. So give yourself some
peace of mind and whenever you feel inspired, just
...' Whenever you said such words of encouragement,
my skin felt as though it was being peeled off. I felt
like I could never create such powerful music ever
again. Several months went by in idleness. One
evening, my heart felt so heavy and my chest so
cramped that I decided to take a walk. I wandered
aimlessly, carrying a heavy mind, a heavy heart,
dragging my heavy legs until I came across a large
haystack. I'm not sure how to describe my state of
mind at this moment. I felt tense and aroused as
though I'd come face to face with a terrible enemy. I
looked around me then ran over to it and lit it on
fire. I suddenly felt afraid, so I turned to run, but
when I got some distance and looked back, the fire
had risen to the point of nearly piercing the sky.

'Whoa! Whoa! Hey! Hey!' I heard people shouting. I returned to the spot to take in the terrifying

sight of the haystack engulfed in flames, taking over the house next to it, making it collapse. I became excited by the sight and hurried back home. The music that came to me that night was 'Raging Wave'. Since then, all the fires that went off in the city were all started by me. And each night that I started a fire, I gained new music. Whenever my heart felt heavy, and my chest felt cramped and stifled like indigestion, I hit the road without a point of destination. And on these nights, there was always an arson incident and the birth of a new musical composition.

But as the number of incidents kept growing, the proportion of excitement for those fires began to decline. That ruthless and unforgiving fire could no longer make my heart stir. It was right around then when you looked at my music and said, 'The power is gradually shrinking.'

But I had no other means to continue. For a while there, I pretended like I'd forgotten music completely and put it aside.

This is the point where Mister Mo had read Sŏng-su's letter to when K called out to him again.

'Spanning from last spring and through the autumn, there were a number of mysterious fires, were there not? They were all acts of crime committed by Sŏng-su.'

'And you didn't know anything about this?'

'Me? Of course I didn't know. I was thinking one night to myself about how I'd brought Sŏng-su to my home, bewitched by my expectations of him, and how he hadn't created anything powerful since his arrival. I was wondering what it was that I could do for him. That's when I saw from way over there ...' K lifted his finger and pointed towards a window facing the south. 'W-a-a-y down yonder I saw flames. I thought to myself, if Sŏng-su saw this, perhaps he'd be able to revive the feelings he had from back then (I couldn't imagine, not in a million years, that the fire that occurred at the cigarette shop was started by Sŏng-su). While I was thinking this, I suddenly heard the sound of the piano ringing from his room. I stopped in my tracks towards his room. Once again, C sharp on the minor scale. There was no opening. The adagio began. It was a quiet, gentle sea. It was the sun that was slowly fading over the horizon. This temperate mood slowly evolved into a scherzo and turned into a spring shower. Wind and water, lightning, the frightening sound of wind, thunder, a boat overturned at sea, an exhausted seagull plummeting, the cries of people swept away by the tsunami – excitement within excitement, outrage within outrage, wildness within wildness, all kinds of horror and violent scenes played before my eyes. My old body couldn't handle such excitement. You can bet that I shouted, "Please stop," without meaning to. I went up to check in. He had finished playing and was leaning against the piano in exhaustion. He'd already written down this piece entitled "Raging Wave" on a music sheet.'

'So you're saying that Sŏng-su created two fires and two musical compositions, correct?'

'That's right. After that, for about ten days or so he wrote one piece at a time. They each occurred whenever there was an arson incident. But as his letter indicates, after some time passed, the power and wildness gradually faded from his music. And so ...'

'Wait a minute. Didn't he also write "Blood Melody" and many other famous tunes after that?'

'Well, that's the thing. For an explanation on that, please continue to read the letter. Go ahead and read from here.'

I was coming down X Bridge when something got in my way. I lit a match to take a closer look. It was an elderly person's corpse. I was frightened, so I turned to run off. Then I stopped and turned back around. Now, this is where I need you to understand me.

This was such a mysterious incident that I myself can't quite understand it. I sat upon that corpse. I ripped apart all the clothes from its body and threw them in all directions. I raised the nude corpse high up into the air and threw it far into the distance with all my might. Then, I ran over to the corpse and threw it back like a cat playing with an egg. It went on like this many times. Its head was smashed. Its belly split open. The corpse had become a terrible sight. When the corpse no longer had any part left over to destroy, I sat on the ground in exhaustion. My heart was suddenly taken over by fear. I ran back to the house. That night, I wrote 'Blood Melody'.

'Do you, sir, understand this kind of psychological state?'
'I'm not sure.'
'You probably don't. An artist's mind isn't that readily discernible. And read here ...'

[...] The fact that this woman died was not my concern. I went to that woman's grave by myself that night. I dug up that grave which was freshly plotted just seven or eight hours ago and pulled her corpse back out from the ground. Her body which lay beneath the blue moonlight was as beautiful as an angel's. Her pale complexion with her eyes slightly shut. The high bridge of her nose.

The loosened black hair – her face which lacked
expression. A plain and silent face. It added to
her overall plaintiveness. I became aroused – I
was taken over by something very suddenly and
... oh, Professor, I do not have the courage to write
out what took place from here on out. You'll know
what took place if you read the court's documen-
tation. That night, 'Spirit of the Dead' was born.

'What do you think?'
'...'
'What?'
'...'
'Is it the poor wording? It may appear as such in your eyes,
sir. Continue to read from here on out.'

I was suddenly committing murder. When-
ever I did commit murder, new music appeared.
From that point forth, whenever I wrote new
music, it was at the cost of a person's life.

'There was nothing left to read here. But you must understand Sŏng-su's actions by now. Do you have an assessment of
this situation?'
'...'
'Well?'
'What kind of assessment do you mean?'
'This opportunity that you speak of – if a genius had it,
a genius with a criminal's potential, would we curse that
opportunity or would we bless it? If we speak of Sŏng-su here,
we're speaking of arson, assaulting a corpse, raping a corpse,
murder, all kinds of criminal activity ... We at the artist's society went through various hurdles to petition to the government that Sŏng-su was a mental patient, and we just barely
got him into an institution. But even so, doesn't this warrant

execution? But as you might've discerned from his letters, in our day-to-day, he was an incredibly level-headed and gentle young man. But every now and again, how should I put it, because of that excitement, he would lose sight of right from wrong and become a terrible criminal. After committing such heinous crimes, he would birth a wonderful new piece. In a situation such as this, do we look upon his crimes with disdain or do we forgive him for his crimes due to the art that he creates?'

'Well, if he hadn't committed those crimes and created these works, wouldn't it be all the better?'

'Well, of course. But how would this Sŏng-su fellow find a solution to this predicament?'

'He ought to pay for his crimes. How could anyone just watch his sins continue to thrive?'

K nodded his head. 'Yes, indeed. As fellow artists, we can also see from this angle. Ever since Beethoven, music gradually lost its strength. All we did was praise women, flowers, and affairs, not realizing how bold we grew. On top of this, we had very strict rules when writing music, quite similar to mathematics, and so there were severe restrictions to writing new music. It became a new trade – not new art. This is what makes the artist so lonely. Art that has power. Art with clear boundaries. Art that contains extreme wildness. I'd been in wait for this for a long time. That's when Paek Sŏng-su appeared before me. In all actuality, each of Paek Sŏng-su's work is a bright and shimmering gem that will shine for all eternity. They are to be commemorated as part of our culture. Arson? Murder? An unworthy house, an unworthy person – if it means the creation of one of his great works, they are ultimately not that difficult to sacrifice. A gift that comes once in a thousand – no, once in ten thousand years ... To say that a few useless crimes are worth smothering his talent – wouldn't that be the ultimate crime? That's what we artists believe, at least.'

K took back the letter that the old man sitting before him

handed over and put it back inside his drawer. There, in the bright red light coming from the sunset, the old man's eyes were full of tears.

January–December 1929

LIKE FATHER LIKE SON

That old bachelor M finally got engaged. When we heard the news, we looked at one another blankly. M was thirty-two years old. As social conditions changed – or perhaps due to economic reasons or defiance against traditional early marriage – there was an increase in bachelors waiting it out, but a bachelor at thirty-two? No matter which way one looks at it, that's a bit extreme. Whenever his friends had the chance, they'd press him to settle down. But when he heard this advice (we know that deep inside he was quite interested in the prospect) he'd turn them down with a wry smile. This was M who'd gotten engaged on the sly.

M was poor. He was a salaryman at a highly unstable company. It's possible that his precarious fiscal state kept him a bachelor till his old age. This is why M's friends regarded his bachelorhood with pity and wished for him to tie the knot already. But only I have a different interpretation as to why he refused marriage. As a doctor, I am aware of M's physical defects. This is why M postponed his marriage till he reached his thirties. This is my belief. Ever since M was a student, he led a life of debauchery. He, who lacked the means to lead such a wild life, often debauched in the lowest form possible. When fifty *chŏn*, or even a single *chŏn*, turned up, he would go straight to a udon house or the red light district. He had a high libido. In order to satisfy his lust, he never let an opportunity pass. Even when he met his friends, he wasn't interested in treating himself to a meal. He was interested in treating himself with a visit to the brothel.

'I don't know about quality, but I can beat anyone in terms of quantity.' He never failed to speak of his female encounters in such a way. Furthermore, he wasn't interested in a *select choice*. He was more about checking off boxes. By the time he reached twenty-three or twenty-four years old, he announced that he'd been with over two hundred women. By the time he reached thirty, he was probably already looking down at the Buddhist monk Sin Don. This is probably why he contracted nearly every venereal disease there is. Not only that, but he was a supreme drunk. Because of his high libido, he did not abstain from sex even while he was infected. Out of the three hundred and sixty-five days in a year, there was not a single day when he was in good clean health. He was always dripping pus. He'd visit me to get a shot every other month or so, barely able to walk due to orchitis. Even so, whenever fifty *chŏn* or even a single *chŏn* turned up, he'd use it to find another partner.

Of course, this lifestyle did not support his ability to reproduce. I, who was fully aware of this, connected his long postponement of marriage to this reason. Out of general morality, I even felt compassion towards him. He had led a penniless life. Even in his old age he'd be lonely and childless, with no one to look after him. He'd be swimming through the bitter world all on his own to the end of his days. It was such a pitiful existence. Then, out of nowhere, M had gotten engaged. But several days beforehand, there was an incident.

I had just finished eating dinner that day. I was reading a treatment report alone when M paid me a visit. His face was relatively gloomy that day, and he answered my questions as though they were a chore to him until he finally threw me a question.

'If a man contracts syphilis, is he unable to reproduce?'

'He's probably fine.'

'What about gonorrhea?'

'Well, if it doesn't invade the testicles, it should be fine.'

'Testicles. A friend of mine has testicular inflammation and he says he's infertile now. You can't imagine the negativity of this fella. If his testicles are infected, does that make it impossible? They both seem infected.'

'Well, if the infection isn't too bad then it should be fine.'

'Now, if it's not too bad, then would I fall under that category? Or is it serious?'

I looked at his face point blank without meaning to. His condition was beyond serious. The fact that he was even asking me this sounded like a joke, but M's face was dark and heavy. He looked like someone awaiting an important sentence with his eyes wide open.

'It's not too bad, is it?'

'Of course,' is how I replied. This is how we ended our conversation and said our goodbyes. Now that I think of it, that response is probably what led to this engagement.

It was our friend T who relayed the information regarding M's engagement. About four or five of us (all friends of M) had gathered.

'Today we lose an ancient, national treasure,' someone quipped.

'So, does it appear to be an engagement of love?'

'Love? Some love. A guy like him who knows nothing but prostitutes – where would he find such a thing as love?'

'Was there at least a dowry?'

'Are dowries that easy to come by?' It was at this point that I sensed the most distasteful aspect of this engagement. If this strange object called love was able to bring that thirty-some-thing-year-old bachelor to his knees, it was a reason to cele-brate, not criticize. Even if the engagement was for a dowry, considering the world we lived in (especially since we knew full well what his circumstances were like), we couldn't pass judgement. But this was neither love nor dowry related. We couldn't come to any other conclusion but the most unpleas-ant factor.

'Then ...' I started, making my way into the unpleasantness, 'it seems he's gotten a wife in order to save the money that he would typically spend at the whorehouse.' T threw me a look as though to chastise my remark.

'We shouldn't speak of it as such. M's already thirty-two or thirty-three years old. In any case, it's about that age when a man wants to hold a child of his own on his lap. And that's not to say that finding the right woman is easy ...'

'A child? A fellow with orchitis as severe as that hold a child? A child is—' I abruptly stopped mid-sentence, as I'd broken the doctor-patient confidentiality in my haste. But there was no way for me to swallow back the words I'd thrown up.

'What? What do you mean?' Several questions came at me regarding M's reproductive condition. I had no choice but to take responsibility for my words so I tried my best to refash-ion them, although with little success. I hadn't confirmed it but there was a good chance that M was unable to reproduce. But given that I had not tested him yet, there was a possibility that he still could. I said that I'd overreacted to the news of this bland engagement with a critical comment and tried to take it back.

Then a twenty-something year old man asked, 'Isn't it more comfortable to live a life without children anyhow?' I steered the conversation in a different direction and told the young man that he had no inkling of affection for blood-related kinship and that this ignorance seemed to be the common trend.

M even wedded in secret. Not a single one of M's friends knew of his wedding date ahead of time. Not only that, but he didn't go with everyone's preferred mode of the Western style wedding. Instead, he held it at his home in the old-fashioned way. Word was that the bride, who was a graduate of X High School, didn't want a traditional wedding, but M insisted on it. This is how the red-light district lost one of their most loyal patrons.

'There is something very pleasant about a monopoly.' M supposedly said this to some friend after his wedding. Ultimately this wasn't a wedding that came from love. With that said, it wasn't a failure, either. This old bachelor who went around spending fifty *chŏn* – even his last *chŏn* – on satisfying his lust had now hit an unimaginable jackpot. He must've been extremely proud. The marriage hadn't blossomed out of a romantic relationship, but romance appeared to have budded between the two since the wedding. His face had always been gloomy. Perhaps that's the reason why it seemed relatively brighter.

'Many blessings.' I and the rest of us congratulated their matrimony. At first, I wished them a happy marriage for the sake of his young bride who'd become a tool – a martyr – for satisfying M's sex drive. Regardless, may their marriage be fruitful. *May your wife not become a victim of sacrifice. Your poor wife who will never experience the joys of motherhood – make sure your wife experiences multiple joys that others couldn't dare taste.* Whenever I thought of M, I sent prayers like these his way. A few days after their marriage, I heard a rumour here and there that M was abusing his wife. I even heard that he was using physical abuse. But I didn't think too much of it.

Whenever such rumours entered my ears, I repeated the *Arabian Night* story of the genie inside my head: some fisherman was out casting his net. When he pulled up his net, he didn't find any fish. Instead, there was a bottle. The bottle had a stopper, which was sealed with lead. After a moment's hesitation, he removed the stopper. Then, a black smoke rose up into the sky. The dark smoke began to clump together until a genie appeared. 'The prophet who trapped me inside this bottle is Solomon. I swore to myself while I was trapped here that I would reward whoever rescues me within a hundred years with great wealth. But a hundred years went by and no one rescued me. So I swore to myself once more that I would give the person who rescues me within the next one hundred years every treasure there is in this world. Then, after another hundred years went wasted, I waited another hundred years with the promise to reward my rescuer all the power and glory this world can offer. But a hundred years went by and no one came to save me. And so I finally swore to myself once and for all that I would kill the bastard who rescues me right there on that spot and relinquish all the bottled-up disdain that I'd been brewing.'

This was the genie's story. When I heard the rumour about M abusing his wife, it was impossible not to think of the genie's story. All that pain and solitude that had bottled up inside of him over the years of his bachelorhood was now directed onto his wife. So I prayed, 'Go ahead. Beat her all you want. Beat her with all your might,' and sent it their way.

One night, a year into their marriage, M and I were having dinner somewhere. His face was especially gloomy that day. He barely touched his food and kept drinking. He was usually a bit closed-mouthed as it was, but on that day he was especially quiet. By the time he got incredibly drunk and couldn't drink any further, he finally spoke. His bloodshot eyes flashed towards me in a frightening manner.

'Hey. Hey listen. Don't try to fool me. Be truthful. Do I have the ability to reproduce?'

'I'm not sure. We need to take some tests.' And this is how I wanted to leave it.

'Then examine me, will you?'

'Why all of the sudden?'

He was about to respond immediately to this but stopped in his tracks and swallowed his words right back. He took another drink, then spoke with his eyes downcast. 'It's just that, if I'm sterile, I'd feel really bad for that woman.' (By which he meant his wife.) 'If this fact is confirmed then I should at least give her the opportunity to change her fate while she's still young, shouldn't I? That's the reason I ask.'

'We should examine you.'

'Let's do it then.'

A few days later I heard a rumour that M's wife had gotten pregnant. The news shocked me. There was no need to examine him, because M was most likely sterile. But M's wife was pregnant. It was then I finally realized what M must've been going through several days ago. Ultimately the exam wasn't for the sake of his wife's 'future'. It was because he harboured suspicion against her. It wasn't like he was completely in the dark about it. The chance of his infertility was nine out of ten, but his wife had gotten pregnant. If I think about it, it's an entertaining scenario. M, who is unable to reproduce, doesn't reveal this and gets married. The woman who marries him becomes pregnant. The wife, who is unaware of her husband's infertility, flaunts the seed of her sin before M without any remorse. M, who didn't reveal the fact that he might be impotent, has no right to reproach his wife at this point no matter how deep his suspicion runs. He's willing to go through some tests but if the test results show that he is, in fact, impotent, then there's no telling what he's going to. In order to chastise his wife's obscenity, he would have to reveal his own deceitfulness. In order to hide that deceit, he would need to endure all the more pain.

He showed up one day claiming that he wanted an exam. I was already swamped with patients at that time, so I asked him to wait in the office and said that I would meet him once I finished seeing my patients. When I told him this, he didn't wait for me but simply turned around and went home. He returned a couple of days later, but again, he just went right back home. I myself wasn't sure how to make sense of this situation. What if the results confirmed his impotence? My medical oath denied me the ability to lie to him and say that there is life when there isn't. But the thought of breaking news of his impotence and ruining his life was just as difficult for me to face. M's wife, who had left M and indulged herself in a momentary pleasure with another, was most certainly the one to reproach. On the other hand, when considering this scenario, if I just turned a blind eye to the whole thing, then M would find comfort in raising a loving child and everything would resolve itself amicably. Standing between the two choices that diverged before me, I hesitated over which road to take. But the problem resolved itself four or five days later.

M came to me that day with another gloomy expression. I asked him as a matter of duty, 'Should we examine you today?'

To this, he responded, 'I've already done it.'

'Huh? From where?'

'At P Hospital.'

'What was the result?'

'I'm fertile.'

'?' I stared at him without meaning to. I was surprised to hear a response that differed from my expectation but, more so than that, his distressed tone confused me. While feeling relieved of the grave task that I had nearly taken on myself,

I couldn't help but reveal shock with my eyes at the result he heard from P Hospital. Then M's eyes, which met mine, began to wander this way and that as though they were lost. I realized then that what he'd just told me was a lie. So why did he lie? In order to preserve his wife's honour? So that he could fool himself and the rest of the world while raising this child? I had no way of knowing how he felt. He finally opened his mouth. A heavy and sorrowful sound emitted.

'Listen. Do you understand this feeling?'

'What feeling?'

He took a moment's rest before he began. 'A salaryman receives his paycheck. Whatever he makes, he spends it immediately. He spends his money however he pleases. He is on his way home. He's certain that there are a few bucks left inside his wallet. But he can't open it. Perhaps it's because he hopes there is a lot more left than he thinks. If he opens it, though, wouldn't the fact that there isn't much left simply reveal itself? He's afraid of this, and so he continues to fool himself. He plans to buy rice. He plans to buy a plant. If he opens it, the reality will make itself known, and he won't be able to buy any of those things. And so he keeps his wallet far from his hand's reach and goes straight home. Do you understand this feeling?'

I nodded my head.

'All right.' He grew quiet again. But I knew it then. M didn't even get examined. He was too afraid. He was avoiding the exam. His wife was pregnant. Logically, that child was most likely her husband's. No one would doubt this. There was no reason to doubt this. Why? Because, when a woman comes together with a man, shouldn't a pregnancy occur simply based on principle? When a person doubts something that doesn't deserve any doubt, there can only be self-destruction and contempt. Poking a hornet's nest is a stupid thing to do. M avoided the exam in order to evade the unsavoury result, which may be a nine out of ten chance. In order to avoid his own anguish, in his state of pain, still clinging on to a ray of hope, he decided to desperately avoid that dangerous hornet's nest called 'exam'. He decided to force himself to love that child inside his wife's belly. Should he go through with the exam and find that there is a sperm count, it'd be convenient for everyone, but if there was none, then all the tragedy, rage and contempt would be secondary to knowing that he couldn't continue his lineage in this lifetime. He wouldn't be able to avoid the despair of knowing that there is no one to turn to in his old age. This is a frightening thing. There was no need to deny the logical decision and go down this dangerous path. And so he gave up the idea of the exam, but he couldn't seem to get rid of his suspicion.

Then one day, while talking about this and that, he mentioned the following. 'I hope the child takes after the father....'

I began to mention all the ways a child could liken a father.

He sighed. 'When a woman conceives, it must be worrisome for her. If the kid takes after the father or grandfather, it's fine, but if he takes after the mother's side of the family, or no one in the family, it must be worrisome. If the kid takes after the father, it's the best. Ha ha ha.'

I replied, 'Indeed. This isn't my field so I can't recall the exact title, but among German tales there's one called "Father" or something along the lines of that. A child is born, but the father can't tell if it's his or not so he falls into despair. Had the kid simply taken after the father, there wouldn't have been any issue.'

'Ah – ah. It's all so irritating.'

M's wife gave birth to a son. The child grew to be about six months old. One day, M brought his sick child to me. He had a case of mild bronchial deterioration. M accepted some medication and sat down. Then he spoke up, unprovoked. 'This kid looks just like his great grandparents.'

'Is that so?' I was quite intrigued by his comment and so I looked around. To my eyes, there was no relation between M and this child. The remark that the child looked like his grandfather was strange. Seeing as the child looked nothing like the father's side or the mother's side, it appeared that he had no choice but to claim that his son took after his dead ancestors. And out of his enormous suspicion and his even greater hope (the hope that his suspicion might be a mistake) placed onto the child, he must've come up with this explanation.

M, who saw that I took an interest in his remark, hesitated for a moment before delivering the next thing he had prepared, 'On top of that, there's a part of him that takes after me, too.'

'Where?'

'Look here.' M moved the baby to his left arm. With his right hand, he removed his own sock. 'Look at my toes. My toes look different from others', and the middle one is the longest. It's hard to come by. But look …' M lifted the swaddle and revealed the baby's foot. 'Look at this kid's toes. Don't they look just like mine?'

M searched my face desperately as though to find an agreement. He so wanted to find a likening image that he found it in the baby's toes. I was moved to tears by M's heart and effort. The effort that M made to quell his enormous suspicion was most tragic.

Without looking at the baby's foot that M had produced for me to see, I gazed at M's face for a long time and finally said, 'It's not just the toes. I think his face takes after yours, too.' With that, I turned around and sat back down, avoiding his gaze which darted around my face, mixed with both suspicion and hope.

January 1932

RED MOUNTAIN

A Doctor's Memoir

It happened when Yŏ was travelling through Manchuria. He wanted to sightsee the Manchurian autumn and research diseases among those who were not yet graced with civilization. He spent a year researching every last detail of Manchuria. He happened across a village named XX, which will be the details of this story.

XX was a small village where only about twenty Chosŏn farmers lived. Not a single mountain could be found within sight. It was an expansive Manchurian field without a name. While riding a mule with a Mongolian servant in tow, he came across XX village while travelling the countryside. By then, autumn had passed and the fierce northern Manchurian winter had begun.

There weren't any Chosŏn people to be found in Manchuria, so when he came across a rural town with only Chosŏn people, he was very glad. Furthermore, all the Chosŏn people in that town were relatively honest and warm. In spite of their naivety, they were at least familiar with the thousand-character classic text. After having led a dreary life in dreary Manchuria, coming across a relatively peaceful town with Manchurian-Chosŏnites after a year of travelling was heartwarming. It would have been gladdening even if it had been a foreign town because they were Easterners just like him. Yŏ spent at least ten days there paying a visit to each house and spending the days swapping stories with the locals. He was finally able to take pleasure in such leisure. He met a person named Chŏng Ik-ho here, who had the nickname Wildcat.

No one in XX village knew where Ik-ho's hometown was. Based on his dialect, he appeared to be of Kyŏnggi origin, but when he chattered on in a fast pace, he sounded like he was of Yŏngnam origin. When he fought, he sounded like he was from the northwest. In any case, pinpointing his hometown from his dialect alone was impossible. He knew simple words in Japanese. He knew some Sino-Korean characters. He definitely knew Chinese. He knew some basic Russian as well. There were definitely some things he had picked up along the way, and his knowledge in these areas was quite rich, but no one knew exactly what his experiences were.

About a year before Yŏ arrived at XX village, Wildcat had come to town empty-handed in a flustered manner. His face was like that of a mouse. His sharp teeth and cunning eyes gave off an intense energy. His tiny nostrils had long, jutting nose hairs. His body frame was small but he appeared nimble. He seemed to be somewhere between twenty-five and forty years old. His body and face must've suffered a great deal of hatred, as he gave off an energy that repelled people. His talent was in card games. He was also a good fighter, an excellent nitpicker, and a sword-wielder who was great at chasing after the town's virgins. His looks attracted hatred. On top of that, his behavior wasn't any better. No one in XX village associated with him. Everyone avoided him.

He was homeless, but when he went to someone's place to

sleep, the owner wouldn't say a word and would provide the bedding while going into another room. Ik-ho would spend two whole days sleeping well and getting up as if it was his own house. He would request breakfast then leave without a word of gratitude. If anyone declined his request, he would start a fight. When he started a fight, he always brandished a sword. The village maidens and young girls could never walk through town in peace ever since Ik-ho arrived. Several people even experienced public mishaps this way.

'Wildcat.' No one knows who came up with this nickname, but pretty soon everyone in XX village called Ik-ho by this and not by his real name.

'Whose place did Wildcat stay at?'

'Mister Kim's house.'

'Any trouble?'

'Thankfully no.'

Every morning, when the townspeople awoke, rather than greet one another they all asked the whereabouts of Wildcat. Wildcat was a major cancer to this town. Because of him, no matter how scarce the hands were on the farmlands, several young and sturdy men needed to stay behind to protect the maidens. Because of Wildcat, women and children stayed indoors no matter how hot it got in the summer nights. They couldn't even walk outdoors to take in the breeze. Because of Wildcat, the townspeople stayed up all night to protect their chickens and pigs. All of the town's young and old congregated several times to discuss a way to throw out Wildcat. Of course, everyone agreed to do this, but there was no one who could do the actual deed.

'Uncle can initiate and I'll take care of the rest.'

'Don't concern yourself with the backend. You talk to him first.'

Each man was eliminated as they avoided taking on Wildcat first.

And so the villagers had come to an agreement, but Wildcat coolly insisted on staying.

'Have the bitches made any breakfast yet? Have your grandsons prepared a place for me to sleep?' Wildcat treated the entire town as though it were his own home and went from this house to that house as he pleased. Whenever anyone at XX village died, they always wondered why it couldn't have been Wildcat instead of their own relative. They cursed him at every turn. When someone fell ill they said, '*Aik*! May this illness befall Wildcat!' Cancer. No one pitied or loved Wildcat. Wildcat had also long ago foregone the love from others. No matter how anyone treated him, he never faulted them for it. If someone ever mistreated him out in the open, he was sure to wield his sword in retaliation, but if someone said anything behind his back, he never reacted, even if the rumours reached his ears.

'*Hŭng* ...' This was all he said, and it was his way of life.

He frequently went to the local card dens to gamble. Every now and then he would get beaten to a pulp and return with bloodstains. But he never complained. Even if he did, there was no one around to listen. No matter how badly he got beaten, after a day of washing his wounds in fresh water and limping around for a couple days, he healed right up.

It was the day before Yŏ was about to leave XX village. An elderly man named Song loaded up some harvest onto a mule and headed over to the countryside where the Manchurian landowner was. But when he returned, he was a corpse. Song, who had taken a beating for not producing enough harvest, just barely made it back to the village. When his shocked relatives took his body from the mule, he passed away.

XX village clamoured, 'Let's get revenge!'

All of the village's young men became excitable due to the untimely passing of Song. Each man seemed like he was about to rise up to the task. But that was it. No one wanted to take the lead. Had someone stood up to take the lead, they would've already reached the landowner's place by now. But no one stepped up to the plate. Each person looked at the other. They stomped their feet. They shouted. Mourning the harassment of one man, they cried. But that was it. They had all gotten up for the sake of someone else's issue, but no one could bravely take the lead. As a doctor, Yŏ did as a doctor should and examined Song's body. On his way back, Yŏ bumped into Wildcat, and looked down at the short man. Wildcat looked back up at Yŏ.

'Pitiful life. Human leech. Valueless life. Mealworm. Parasite!' Yŏ cried out to Wildcat. 'Do you know that Mister Song is dead?'

Wildcat, who'd been staring at Yŏ the entire time, dropped his head at these words. As Yŏ was about to leave, he noticed a deeply upset expression in Wildcat's face which he couldn't get over. Thinking about this being who'd suffered all kinds of abuse after leaving his hometown, Yŏ could not sleep that night. Mulling over our pitiful and enraging state, Yŏ could not stop his flow of tears.

The next morning. Yŏ woke up to the sound of people's voices calling for him. Wildcat had been found outside of the village entrance, beaten to a pulp and left for dead. As soon as Yŏ heard the name Wildcat, his eyebrows crinkled. But he was a doctor, so he grabbed his bag and ran over to the site. Several people who'd gathered for Song's funeral followed after Yŏ.

Yŏ looked. Wildcat's back was broken into a '⌐' shape and tossed into a furrow. There was still a slight sign of life.

'Ik-ho! Ik-ho!'

But he did not respond. Yŏ took emergency measures. Wildcat's four limbs were in complete spasm. He finally opened his eyes.

'Ik-ho! Can you hear me?'

Wildcat peered into Yŏ's face. He stared at him for a long time.

His eyes glistened. He finally seemed to come to his senses.

'Doctor, I went there.'

'Where?'

'That bastard ... that landlord bastard's house.'

What? Yŏ's eyes filled with tears, but he shut them with all his might. Yŏ grabbed Wildcat's hand, which was already turning cold. They both fell silent. His limbs continued to spasm. It was the sign of death. A small sound came from his lips. It was barely audible.

'Doctor.'

'What?'

'I want to see it. I want to ...'

'What?'

He moved his lips, but no words came. He seemed to lack the strength. After a moment, he moved his lips again. A sound emitted.

'What is it?'

'I want to see it. The red mountain and white clothes!'

Ah, because of death, he must've thought of his homeland and fellow countrymen. Yŏ gently opened his eyes again. At that moment, Wildcat's eyes opened as well. He tried to raise his hand. But his hand was already broken and it could not be raised. He tried to turn his head, but he lacked the strength. He gathered his final words onto the tip of his tongue and opened his mouth.

'Doctor!'

'What?'

'What ... what ...'

'What?'

'There's a red mountain ... there are the white clothes ... doctor, what are those?!'

Yŏ turned and looked but all he could see was the vast open space of the Manchurian fields.

'Doctor, please sing to me. It's my final wish. Please sing to me. *Until the East Sea and Paektu Mountain dry up and wear down ...*'[1]

Yŏ nodded his head and closed his eyes. He parted his lips and the anthem flowed out of him. Yŏ gently sang to him.

'*Until the East Sea and Paektu Mountain ...*' As Yŏ sang the anthem, the people who'd gathered to the sounds sang along with him in chorus.

> *Roses of Sharon, three thousand* li
> *Magnificent rivers and mountains ...*

In some corner of the endless Manchurian winter lay a mealworm named Ik-ho, dying, and a funeral song that rose and spread. In midst of that, Ik-ho's body slowly but surely grew cold.

April 1932

---

[1] *aegukga* – the Korean national anthem

A LETTER AND A PHOTOGRAPH

I saw her again today. She sat there in that same spot looking like she was waiting for someone ...

A beach resort somewhere. She was there yesterday as well, like she was waiting, sitting vacantly. Age, about twenty-four or twenty-five. No matter which way he sliced it, she didn't appear single. At a beach, the most obvious thing to do was go for a swim, but she didn't even do that. She just sat there in the same spot and stared out into the sea. This woman grabbed L's attention, and he found himself pacing back and forth before her.

'Such lovely weather we're having,' he finally initiated.

'Yes, indeed. It's a very lovely day.' The words fluttered out of this woman's red lips. Her teeth were more than just white. They were translucent.

'Are you here to swim?'

'Yes. I'm here on vacation.'

This is how the gate to their relationship opened.

'Would you like to go for a walk?'

'Sure.'

'Shall we lunch together?'

'If you'd like.'

The two people became a bit closer. Then one day, L saw a portrait photograph of a man hanging in her room (her name was Hye-gyŏng).

'Who is he?' L pointed at the portrait and asked. His question contained a hint of hostility.

'He's my husband.'

'Is that so? He must be a great man,' he replied.

That night, L couldn't fall asleep. The portrait he saw hanging in Hye-gyŏng's room lingered before his eyes. A handsome man, a rugged man, a man of good looks – there were many ways to describe the men of this world, but L had never seen a man who had the looks of the one in that portrait. His face wasn't pretty like a girl's. It was manly and noble. The owner of such looks could've been a Greek sculpture in his past, but it's hard to believe such a person could exist in the flesh. He was of a rare refinement. L was also known to be a handsome man. He was confident enough not to feel inferior to anyone when it came to his looks. This is something he was convinced of. But when he compared himself to the subject of that photograph he'd seen earlier, he found himself beating his chest. In other words, he was of an ordinary tailor's swatch or hat advertisement status, whereas the status of that man in that photo could not be surpassed. L lacked refinement. When he compared himself to the subject of that photo, it was like comparing the sun to a terrapin – a useless comparison.

Then why leave a great husband like that and show any affection to a fellow like me? he wondered. But just because such doubts occurred, it didn't mean he would give up on her. Hye-gyŏng definitely showed an interest in him, and as long as they left such doubts by the door, the affair would continue. On the following day, L brushed his hair for half an hour in preparation to pay Hye-gyŏng a visit. He fixed his tie over ten times and put every effort into dressing himself up. He sent a message to his home and had his entire wardrobe sent to the beach resort. He changed his clothes every morning and afternoon in attempt to improve his looks somehow. From that point forth, he and the subject of that photograph were locked in a fierce competition. He went through every means to improve his looks, no matter what it took. Due to this, L's looks (in spite of his already decent reputation) improved day by day. To top it off, his relationship with Hye-gyŏng deepened.

The beach season passed. The urbanites who'd come to enjoy the summer by the shore returned to the city. Hye-gyŏng headed back as well. So did L. But even upon their return, L and Hye-gyŏng continued their affair.

'Hye-gyŏng!'

'Yes?'

'Where is he?'

'Travelling in Italy.'

'When he gets back, please introduce him to me.'

'Goodness, L. Why do you say such things? As soon as he returns I should go back to him, don't you think? Pardon me for saying this, but L, you're a temporary companion just while he's away.'

What? Such violent rebelliousness. *I'll make myself even better than him, so that even if he does return, she'll never leave my side* – and so L continued to spend all his efforts on his looks. An inexplicable anxiety came over him. At this moment, he was definitely trying to take over all of Hye-gyŏng's affections. But there was no way to predict when she would return to her husband. Whenever he and Hye-gyŏng walked side by side down Chongno, he would occasionally catch a reflection of himself with her in a shop window and renew his sense of confidence – that he was indeed worthy of accompanying Hye-gyŏng. But then the memory of that photograph he saw in her room at the resort would make his heart grow weary once more. On a typical scale, his own looks were quite fair, but compared against the subject of that photograph, he barely reached the subject's heels. The thought of Hye-gyŏng walking with that man, linking arms, made L burn with jealousy. It even made him throw air punches.

I can't lose against him. No matter what it takes, I have to win. With determination, L devoted himself even more to grooming.

Autumn passed. So did winter. The following spring, Hye-gyŏng's husband, who'd been travelling in Italy, did not return. L and Hye-gyŏng's affair continued. One spring day, Hye-gyŏng paid L a visit. She stayed around till sundown. After Hye-gyŏng left, L found a piece of paper lying in the spot where she sat. When he picked it up, he saw that it was a letter. Hye-gyŏng had mistakenly left it behind. L opened the letter. Hye-gyŏng's friend had written to her with the following:

> *We heard that your husband has returned from*
> *his trip to Europe. How happy you must be! Let's*
> *meet at X Theatre the day after tomorrow. After*
> *the play, we should have supper together. It's*
> *been too long. Please come. Hope to see you.*

So he's back! L's heart sank. Now that the subject of that portrait had returned, Hye-gyŏng would return to her husband's arms (just as she'd always planned). Looking back, it made sense why Hye-gyŏng seemed so cold. Had he known of his return, he would've tossed her like an old pair of shoes. The thought of the subject of that portrait – an elegant man of high pedigree – sitting side by side at the theatre with Hye-gyŏng made L's teeth chatter. The evening after next, L also went to X Theatre. He himself did not know why it was necessary for him to go and see for himself, but he just had to.

He spotted Hye-gyŏng immediately. But her husband? The elegant man of high stature that he'd seen in that motel room – Hye-gyŏng's husband? L searched for him all over the theatre. L traced every inch of the place, but the man he'd seen in that photograph was nowhere to be found. Instead, there beside Hye-gyŏng was a man that appeared to be her father – an elderly man who sat next to her and watched the play. He appeared to be around fifty years old. His face was covered in a beard like an animal. His eyes were so small that they were barely visible. His nose was flat. The world's ugliest man sat beside Hye-gyŏng and watched the play leisurely.

'?' L was dumbfounded. That man was too hideous to father a beauty such as Hye-gyŏng.

But later, when he found out through a friend that that hideous man wasn't Hye-gyŏng's father but in fact her husband, how great his shock must've been. At first, L did not accept this. He couldn't accept it. But after the play ended, on his way back, L happened to walk by the two and overheard the hideous man say to Hye-gyŏng, 'Watching such an unsatisfying play only made my back ache. Let's hurry up and get that supper with your friend and head home.'

After hearing these words, L had to accept it as the truth. His love for her also completely cooled. The thought of Hye-gyŏng folded inside that ugly thing's arms did him in. Because L had believed that man in the photograph to be her husband, he worked very hard on improving himself, but after seeing that hairy thing as Hye-gyŏng's husband, L realized he could've stopped bathing for ten years, stopped grooming for three years and gone without shaving for a month and still best that creature.

And so L stopped his self-improvement. L, who used to complain of itches if he didn't shave three times a day, began to walk the streets *au naturel* with a dark moustache below his nose.

The final afternoon. Hye-gyŏng and L decided to call off their long affair and say their goodbyes at a quiet place.

'L!'

'Yes?'

'Here are the love letters you sent me. Please take them all back.'

L accepted the bundle of papers that she handed him.

'Well then, goodbye. Why don't you head down left and I'll walk right?'

'Hye-gyŏng!'

When she turned to look at him, L suddenly came back to his senses.

'Yes?'

'I have one final question.'

'What do you mean?'

'Remember the photograph you showed me at the beach? You said that he was your husband?'

She began to smile. 'Yes. I did say that.'

'Whose photograph is that?'

'Ha ha ha ha. Why do you ask? I don't know whose photo that is. I bought it at a photography studio in Shanghai for a couple of *nyang*. He's probably some Chinese actor or a nobleman of some kind.'

'Shanghai? A couple of *nyang*? Then why – why ...'

'Why did I fool you and say that he was my husband, right?'

'Right.'

'You still don't know? You should know yourself just how much you adored me after I told you that the man in the photo was my husband. If I am to have an affair, I'd like to do it with a much more decent-looking man, which is why I pulled that trick. It wasn't to be spiteful. Forgive me, but to tell you the truth, after I showed you that photo, your looks improved by three or four times.'

L was speechless. He sat there for a long time just moving

his lips without sound. When he finally was able to speak up again, he said, 'So what you're saying is I'm like some dog that high class ladies drag around, wash with soap and spray perfume on. Is that it?'

'Is it necessary to take it that far? Ha ha ha ...'

'Okay, fine. I must commend your tactic. But why is the ending so bland? Why couldn't you take your cleverness all the way to the end?'

'What do you mean? Please elaborate.'

'Okay, I'll tell you. One day you came over to my place, spent some time and then left. But as you left, you dropped a letter. It was that letter that led me to see your husband. I learned of that hairy man – forgive me – that hairy monster. That monster—'

'Please watch what you say.'

'Then are you saying that that monster isn't your husband?'

'Of course he is my husband.'

'Well, there you go. Because I saw that monster, we grew apart, did we not? Before that, when I saw that two *nyang* photo, I became a much more handsome man and pulled all kinds of tricks to improve myself, but after seeing that hairy monster – forgive me – I forgot all about that kind of maintenance. If I compare myself to that monster, I could go without shaving for a year and still look a million times better than he does. So why did you let a letter bring you to failure like that?'

Hye-gyŏng looked at L for a long time. She smiled as she did.

'L.'

'Yes?'

'Listen to me. Hearing you now, I realize how primitive you really are.'

'Why?'

'It's mighty silly of a woman having an affair to go around dropping letters here and there, isn't it?'

'Then you're saying you didn't drop any letter?'

'No, that's not what I'm saying.'

'Then what do you mean?'

'I definitely dropped a letter, but it wasn't a mistake. I did it on purpose. I wanted you to see it, so I left it behind on purpose.'

'What do you mean? Because you dropped that letter, I went to the theatre, and when I went to the theatre, I came across that monst— excuse me – that monster. But you meant to show me that letter?'

'Yes, exactly.'

'Then, because I came across that monster, I stopped grooming myself and because of that our relationship came to an end. You're saying you did it all on purpose?'

'L, don't get worked up, and listen. That was my plan all along.'

'For what reason?'

'Goodness. Men are so slow. If I put it simply, the photo I showed you at the beach is the same photo I will show some other man. So what I'm saying is that even if you stop grooming yourself, it won't affect me any longer. Understood?'

'…'

'L, listen to me and listen to me good. Men can be manipulated any which way with a single photo and letter. Don't ever take a photo or letter you come across for what it is. It's all a trick. *Aigu* – why do you glare at me with such scary eyes? This is our final farewell, so let's end it with a smile and remain friends. Now then, as I mentioned earlier, you go left and I'll go right. I have plans to meet a man I showed that Shanghai photo to, so I'm a bit busy. Take care then.'

A dusky street. She headed right on the street towards the light while humming to herself. She'd told L to take the left, but he could not move. He stood there like a man without a thought and watched her as she left.

A half-lit street.

A barren street.

April 1934

NOTES ON DARKNESS AND LOSS

'*Mother is in critical condition.*' *Your sister.*

'*Mother is anxious. Head straight over.*' *Your sister.*

Telegrams. Two. A sudden chill clutched my chest. I'd gone to visit a friend out in the countryside a couple of days earlier, then took the earliest train back home. These two telegrams were awaiting me that morning. Over the past forty-odd hours I hadn't slept a wink in order to catch up with the friend I had not seen in quite a while. I'd run into the house to find a spot to finally get some rest, but I found these two telegrams waiting for me. They came out of the blue. I looked at the dates that each telegram was sent. The first had arrived two nights before. The second arrived the next morning. The second telegram contained an urgency. Because the first telegram had not received a reply, a second attempt was made. This was certain. After sending the second telegram from P'yŏngyang, the lack of response from me must've been interpreted as a lack of filial piety, and another telegram was not sent. I hadn't slept in two days and my senses were completely dulled. It was difficult for me to get my head straight.

'What am I to do, dear?'

'You should take the morning train.'

Of course I needed to go. What I was asking was if the entire family should go, or if I should go alone. Living in this modern century, all kinds of issues are contingent upon finances. We were already in the middle of the month. There was no way that we had any money to pay for train tickets to take the whole family, nor pay for whatever costs there might be once we got there. There was nowhere to go to so early in the morning and find the kind of money to cover these costs.

Eight ten a.m.

There was barely an hour left before the morning train was about to leave. My chest felt chilly, and I still couldn't get my head straight. When I'd gone down to the country two days previously, I went without telling my wife. After receiving such alarming news, she'd waited for my return all night. Since early morning the day after, she went to every possible spot where she might find me. When she grew tired and went home, there was another telegram awaiting her. She waited up for me until last night. She decided that if I didn't get back the next morning, she would take the train down to pay a visit herself and got ready to make the trip.

The hour for the train's departure drew near, and we couldn't think of any real solution, so I decided to head down first. We decided that I would go and survey the situation before sending for the rest of the family. Caught in a whirlwind of chaos, I didn't even have a minute for breakfast. I didn't even get a chance to change the underwear I'd been wearing for two whole days. After settling on the decision with my wife, I rushed to the station. I've been telling this story for a while now, but by the time I'd gone down there, then made my way back up, my one and only mother had already passed on.

I was thirty-four. I wasn't at that age where one should be missing his mother. She died at sixty-six, and one can indeed argue that she could've lived a few more years. The anger in my chest when I think of why she couldn't have lived just a little while longer never goes away.

My mother was quite a healthy person. It had been three years since my mother collapsed from her first cerebral haemorrhage. Recovering from a cerebral haemorrhage is difficult enough, and even if she could pull through such a recovery, the chance of paralysis in half if not her entire body was extremely high. In spite of all this, she was able to overcome this terrible hurdle thanks to her physical health. She was able to pick up the cane again, and she felt well enough to walk the streets. She was making a gradual recovery when, early that spring, she suffered her second cerebral haemorrhage. Even the doctor refused to provide any physical examination. He said there wasn't any point. But my mother's incredible physical endurance helped her brave yet another hurdle. By the summer of that year, her health had improved vastly. She was able to use the cane to go to the toilet alone, and if she ran into anyone in need of help, she had no problem coming to their aid. And so my mother was able to make a long-awaited trip to Seoul to visit me. Nevertheless, my mother, who'd suffered two cerebral haemorrhages, was in a pitiful state. During her half-month stay here in Seoul, she only smiled once. She smiled while watching my young daughter play. Aside from this, she retained a gloomy expression throughout her visit. The tiniest thing brought her to tears. *This is your son's home. This is your son's wife and your grandchildren.* Even so, she always believed she was inconveniencing us. She never asked us to bring her anything or buy her anything. If she needed something, she went to get it herself despite her physical discomfort. If she wanted something, she put her hand into your pocket, pulled out some money and asked the children to fetch it for her. Seeing how my mother's disposition had weakened so, I felt incredibly forlorn.

'Tongin-*ah*.' Not once did I hear her address me in this familiar way. Whenever she spoke to me, she seemed to struggle terribly.

Doesn't even know how to greet people any more ... Even if she was glad to see somebody, she didn't know how to express it. This upset me. She was constantly scowling, and so my immature son avoided his own grandmother. In the past, he used to call out to her, '*Halmŏni, halmŏni*,' and never leave her side. But all he did now was avoid her.

'Go sit with your grandmother for a bit,' I would say. Then he would obey and sit with her for a minute, but as soon as an opportunity to leave her side appeared, he was off again. *Watching your immature grandchild leave your side like this, a loneliness would creep over and you'd be sniffling again.* She was like a child. She spent half a month like this here in the city. A few days before she was set to return to P'yŏngyang, a small boil appeared behind her neck. At first it was insignificant in size.

I got her a medicinal patch. But my mother said, 'I'm going to need surgery. A bump on the neck is a sure sign of death,' she added ominously. Because the patch was itchy, she peeled it and put it back on several times an hour.

That boil became a pain. We thought it might get better, but by the time she got ready to return to P'yŏngyang, it had turned into the size of a fist and hardened. We received word that she did undergo surgery for it in P'yŏngyang. The word was followed by the message that the post-surgical results were not good, but I remained relatively calm. I simply assumed that if the boil was excised, then it would heal just fine. Then after just a few days, I received those telegrams.

I took a sleeping pill on the train. I wondered if things had gone further south since those two telegrams arrived. If things had taken a turn for the worse, then I had to prepare myself for several nights of staying up. But I simply could not sleep. After passing Kaesŏng, I dozed off for a moment, but by the time we reached Sinmak I woke up again. I couldn't fall back asleep after that. In the midst of all this, my mind wandered to a vast expanse. Seventeen years ago, when I was studying in Tokyo, I received a telegram that my father was about to pass. I recalled the day that I'd scrambled back home immediately. By the time I completed my four long days of travelling back home, my father had already passed away. I wasn't able to be at my father's side on his deathbed. Was I not going to make it to my mother's either? If the telegrams had come just two days before and again the next day, but none since then, couldn't it be a sign that she'd already succumbed? I was seventeen when I lost my father. I was still full of bravery and hope in the face of life back then. But as soon as my father died, they did not reverberate inside my chest as loudly any more. I was thirty-four now – the age to feel the loneliness of middle-age the most sharply. On top of this, I was constantly filled with concerns about my mother.

My mother, who'd lived her youth and middle-aged years without any leisure whatsoever, experienced a great deal of precarity during her later years because of my bankruptcy. This always made me anxious. My plan was to bring my mother to live with us as soon as I reached a point of stability in my own life. Once I gained footing, the plan was to ideally get her own house with a sitting room and meals brought to her. This is what I imagined. Even after her son's bankruptcy, not once did she ever complain or indicate displeasure. In fact, when I think about the mother who took on her son's guilt and apologized, believing she was the cause of her child's inconvenience, it broke my heart. This is how I felt, but considering my family's shy tendencies, I couldn't express any of it despite knowing that it would bring her joy.

Perhaps this is why, when I rushed to the house in P'yŏng-yang to see my mother upon hearing news of her hospitalization, I felt an unstoppable rush of joy fill my chest even while my mother was in critical condition. She was lying in bed at the Christian Wives' Hospital while my sister and older brother's wife were at her side. My mother opened her eyes and looked at me. She looked at me with eyes that contained no emotion. She appeared to not even recognize me. Then she turned her back towards me to face the other direction. Not a minute had passed before she suddenly flipped her body over to face my direction again. Then she flipped over once more. She couldn't pass a single minute in a still position. She was completely restless. From what I heard, the boil on her neck had worsened and she'd gone to P'yŏngyang to have surgery, but she didn't take care of the wound well and so it resulted in an infection, which led to this state. Because of her age, the hospital refused to conduct any major surgery on her without a relative's signature. That was the night of the telegram. The following morning, the entire back region of her head had swollen red. Without a moment's hesitation, the infection spread. The surgery had to be done. That's when the second telegram was sent. The spreading infection could not be left alone any longer. Any further delays would result in tragedy. The only person who was around to see this was my sister. She called our older brother, but he said he would come by after finishing breakfast. She sent word to my younger brother, but no news from him so far. A telegram was sent to me the other night, but even I was unresponsive, and so, unable to postpone this grave matter any longer, my sister went ahead and signed the contract on her own so that our mother could undergo the operation. My mother did regain consciousness after a few hours in the recovery room; however, it took nearly thirty hours for her to come to her senses completely. Even now, she was still in the recovery stage. My sister shed tears, wondering aloud if funeral arrangements shouldn't be made.

My mother would ask for a fan when she felt stuffy, or some water, but aside from these requests, she didn't say a word. The only person she seemed to recognize while surrounded by all these people was my sister. I spent the night at the hospital alone. My older brother sent a maid over, but I sent her to the nurse's station and decided to look after my mother alone. It was a little embarrassing, but I wanted to be a good son to her even if it took just being at her deathbed. She was restless even in her sleep. She flipped her body this way and that. One bed was not able to sustain this activity so another bed was placed beside the one she lay on. She rolled this way and that all throughout the night. I tried restraining her arm at one point, but she yanked it back with a surprising force and continued her restless movements. My mother recognized me in the middle of the night. I tested the waters and asked if she knew who I was.

She looked at me blankly for a long time then replied shortly, 'Seoul boy.' But she did not express any joy, or ask me when I got there. She simply turned her body over again. Water, fan – she wanted nothing else aside from these two things. I was told that even up until the night before her surgery, she made a request for a telegram to be sent to me. The following morning, right before her surgery, she had asked for me once more.

Around ten a.m., when the doctor was making his rounds, I was finally able to see her surgical wound. My older brother and sister were both there, but neither had the strength to bear it. They all stayed outside the patient's room, and I was the one to hold my mother up by her underarms. I watched her sit upright with her arms, and straighten her back with the support of her legs. The sight of the surgical wound was separated by only a piece of cloth. A width of about five inches and a length of about six inches were cut out of her scalp. The skull's two hemispheres were plainly visible, and the pieces of skin dangling in places were all rotten. Yellow pus oozed from where the scalp remained.

'It hurts. It hurts.' My mother, who couldn't enunciate her words clearly, expressed her suffering in a tiny voice. I'm a person of relatively cold and brutish disposition who can look at this objectively, but even I shivered at the sight of this horrible wound. My arms shook while holding up the entirety of my mother's weight, which was well over seventy-five kilograms. A chill came over my chest. I tried not to look at the wound, but hearing her weak voice cry out, it was impossible for me to take my eyes from it. I admired my mother's ability to withstand this pain so courageously even while bearing such a frightening wound. Just by looking at the wound I felt my entire body soak in cold sweat, but my mother withstood this pain with a surprising amount of tolerance. As they dressed the wound and placed some material between her scalp and skull, her body flinched slightly, but she pulled through it beautifully. I wondered if it was possible that the pain was so great, perhaps she couldn't even sense it anymore.

'It's healing very well,' the doctor said reassuringly. But I was sceptical of such confidence. I didn't know what the capacity of a person's physical condition was. My mother's weakness, which originally began with her illness, now had this wound added to it. I wondered if she would be able to pull through it so easily. Upon my younger brother and sister's insistence, I left the hospital around two p.m. to catch up on some sleep, as I had not slept in several days by then. I went to my sister's house, which was close to the hospital, for some shuteye. I took a sleeping pill to get some rest, but I spent barely two hours in a state of neither sleep nor wakefulness before rushing back to the hospital again. My mother, who requested constant fanning and cold water due to her fever, continued to thrash about. I spent the night by her bedside alone again. My sister asked her husband to try and force me into getting some rest that night, but I didn't trust anyone else with the task other than the nurse from the other night. A person like myself who suffered from insomnia and couldn't sleep a wink was just the right candidate to be the night nurse of an ailing patient. I needed to be present just in case she was thirsty in the middle of the night, or needed to take a trip to the toilet, or in case there was a sudden change in her condition. I couldn't leave my mother's side while she was in such a critical state. But this night was fairly unpleasant for me as well, as I hadn't slept in many nights at this point. The drowsiness pressed down against my every nerve. The suffering from sleepiness which I hadn't experienced recently had arrived for the first time in almost ten years. My mother would appear to be asleep then wake up suddenly. She'd appear awake then pass out just as suddenly. When she was awake, she would vacantly stare straight ahead into a limitless vast. And through all of this, another night passed. She must've had someone she wanted to see. She must've had something she wanted to request. But she'd lost her appetite for the world's trivial matters. Perhaps she'd completely lost interest. If it wasn't that, then it was because her body was so swollen and in discomfort that even acknowledging the doctor was an annoying task for her. She would sometimes lie down facing me while her eyes gazed in a direction right above my head, but she would then turn her body in another direction, completely expressionless. I was sceptical as to how conscious she even was. Just as the day was about to break, my mother woke up again. While taking her temperature and checking her pulse, I asked her if she knew who I was because the situation was such a sorry one.

'Excuse me?'

'Do you know who I am?'

'The doctor.' She continued to assume that this son of hers was the doctor. Tears began to pour from my eyes.

'What do you mean I'm the doctor? I'm Tongin from Seoul, aren't I? It's me, Tongin, who arrived the day before yesterday.' When I quietly explained myself this way close to her ear, I hoped to see at least an expression that indicated familiarity. But even after I said all this, my mother would say, 'Tongin?' in a completely stoic tone. This would be her only response. She wouldn't make any attempt at recognition. Her once chubby face had grown lean over the summer. Her cheekbones jutted out prominently, and her limbs lost all their weight, revealing fine wrinkles throughout. As I massaged her limbs while she lay, tears fell ceaselessly from my eyes. Although she was breathing and had a pulse, seeing my mother, who didn't understand human emotion, brought tears to my eyes. During the day, the doctor came by again to make his rounds, reassuring me once more that she was recovering very well. When I asked him what he meant by 'well', he said that seeing that the area where the abscess was removed did not continue to rot, it was a good sign. But while they redressed the area before my eyes, the smell of rotting flesh still pinched my nose. When they pressed the rim of the wound, the pus no longer oozed as there wasn't any left.

'How is she internally?' I followed the doctor outside and asked. He seemed suspicious of the fact that I'd asked him about her internal state when his professional concerns were of the patient's external condition.

'She's great. She's really great,' he responded before walking away from me. But shortly thereafter, the doctor returned with a stethoscope. He'd initially only brought tools for examining her external condition. This was the first time I'd seen something for an internal medical examination since my mother's hospitalization. The doctor scowled slightly.

'She's showing symptoms of pneumonia but as long as we are careful, there shouldn't be any problems. She's doing well. Very well.'

There was an inflammation in her left lung. Three to four days passed, but my mother's condition did not seem to improve. Whenever the doctor made his rounds he said, 'She's doing well.' But we couldn't see how she was doing well. The only thing that had changed since I arrived in P'yŏng-yang was that she'd finally stopped her restless flip-flopping. To our eyes, this was just another sign of her frailty. She simply didn't have the strength to move her body any more. I brought a fan from my brother's house and left it beside her. My mother quietly lay with her eyes closed beneath the whirring of the fan. The way she lay there was so quiet and still that I would shut off the fan just to see if she knew that it was even on. Then she'd open her eyes and say, 'Turn on the fan.' As per usual, she would ask for some cold water and fruit, but aside from this, she didn't show the slightest desire for other things.

My mother's illness persisted without change. There weren't any signs of a sudden turn of events for the worse, so I began to worry about the house back in Seoul. The family barely scraped by on the income I brought in after turning in a manuscript. I'd rushed over to P'yŏngyang, leaving everything behind. I was concerned with the day-to-day back at the house. My older brother was the wealthy one here. He and my sister lived without any worry, and could pay a visit to the hospital for days on end without concern, but my family back in Seoul ate from the stroke of my pen. My wife had already sent a letter indicating the financial difficulty back in Seoul. With the end of the month approaching fast, this concern could not go ignored. Should I pay a quick visit to Seoul? Should I return to Seoul and make sure things were taken care of so that I could return to P'yŏngyang and continue nursing with some peace of mind? While entertaining these thoughts I also considered my mother in her critical state, who wasn't thinking lucidly. I did not want to leave her side. Because my mother's illness was of utmost priority, I didn't have the leisure to consider the state of things back at the house in Seoul, but it bothered me relentlessly.

One night as my mother slept silently, I stood beside her bed and checked her temperature with my right hand. I thought to myself, considering how well she was sleeping, the chances of her illness taking a turn for the worse seemed very dim. But given her advanced age and her serious illness, how could I just leave her side? It was past midnight. Between one and three a.m., I placed my hand over her forehead absent-mindedly. Then I thought of my dilemma and began to cry. The nurse who stopped in during her nightshift must've seen me crying and assumed that I was mourning my mother's dangerous condition. She probably felt rooted to the ground – not knowing whether to come near or keep her distance. There wasn't anyone around to share my pain. At the crack of dawn, I sat in a chair with the lamp turned towards me and read a magazine. My mother looked up and asked, 'Who is that there?'

I quickly set the magazine down. When a person experiences joy, his face typically glows. When the feeling surpasses joy, he cries. If the feeling surpasses that, he laughs uncontrollably. I finally understood these feelings. She'd regained consciousness. My mother, who would only ask for water, for the fan or express physical pain, had come to her senses and was now even asking how her son-in-law was doing. She'd come to her senses – enough to recognize who this person in a suit was, sitting beside her. I tossed the magazine aside and went before my mother, unable to suppress my laughter. I placed my hand over her forehead and told her, 'It's me, Tongin. It's Tongin.'

My mother looked at me. But just as she'd lost her expression since the summer, she peered back at me as vacantly as ever. She looked at me for a while until she finally closed her eyes again. From this day forth, my mother slowly began to come back to her senses. However, despite regaining her consciousness, she didn't ask for anything or make complaints. She was just able to recognize the faces of those who came to visit her, and when they did, she'd catch up on whatever was going on in their lives. This was just enough to help her exercise her mind again. *Just as before, you didn't show any signs of your wants or desires.* That afternoon when my older brother stopped by at the hospital, I made an awful request.

'The end of the month is near. I'd appreciate it if you could send some money to my family back in Seoul. My mind is a wreck. I can't think of anything else to do at the moment.' My wife had just sent another letter to me that morning. She said there wasn't a cent left back at the house, and if she could just find out any outstanding payments for my manuscripts, she would go and gladly pick them up herself. They were in desperate straits.

My brother, who listened to my request, replied, 'I don't have any. If I come into some, I'll send it,' turning me down. This was unfortunate. I couldn't just leave my family that way in Seoul. Then again, what was I to do with my mother in her current state?

That night, I wanted to get some long-needed rest, so I asked my brother-in-law to look after my mother. I went to the house my mother stayed at, took a sleeping pill and laid my tired body down to rest, which soon fell asleep (if my doctor heard of this, he'd be shocked). But my mind was anxious due to my current dilemma, so I could not sleep restfully until morning. Whenever I did fall asleep, I had nightmares. While my anxiety kept me in a cycle of sleep and sudden wakefulness, I made a very cold-hearted determination. *Let's return to the city. I'll return to the city for two days and, during that time, bring some order back to the house then come right back. Even if I'm not here, she has two sons, a daughter-in-law, a daughter and a son-in-law, so there's no reason to worry, but back in Seoul my own family will start wandering the streets without me.* My wife hadn't experienced living a life of debt just yet, and so whenever she ran out of cash, she didn't know what to do with herself. *Let's go back up and at least temporarily tidy things up and return.*

Upon daybreak, I spent the entire day in a depressed state. Perhaps it was because I'd made up my mind to make a trip back into the city for a bit the day after. I was very concerned with my mother's condition. Her health seemed to have improved since the other day, but when it comes to the elderly there really is no way to know when things might turn. This is what concerned me. I asked the night nurse, physician and the doctor in charge – I asked all of them, going around one by one. If they all answered that she was in a critical state, then I would not make my trip back home. If they all reassured me that she was fine, then I would make my trip back into the city. But the doctor in charge said that she was fine, and the night nurse said she was in a critical state, while the physician said that there was no way to tell. There was no opinion for me to rely on. That night after my mother fell soundly asleep, I sat by her bedside, looked around the environment and heaved a heavy sigh. I bemoaned my circumstances. I had no choice but to leave behind a mother who couldn't speak of her condition herself, and pay a visit to the city. *I'll be gone for just two days. Until then, please be all right,* I prayed silently to myself.

'Hey.'

My mother, who'd looked asleep, opened her eyes. She was looking at me. I immediately stood up and grabbed the kettle full of water to bring to her lips. This was because my mother never looked for anyone unless she was thirsty. But my mother took just one sip, as though she wasn't looking for water after all. She then just stared at me.

'Where are my clothes?' she finally asked. She wasn't quite articulate due to the stroke. She spoke in a scolding tone. I couldn't possibly understand this speech. I had no choice but to ask.

'Excuse me?'

'My clothes.'

'Your clothes?'

'Yeah.'

I did not know where my mother's clothes were.

When I told her that I didn't know she remained silent for a long time. Then she asked irritably, 'In my murse. In my murs – my p-pur-se.'

'Your purse?'

'Yeah.'

I still had no way of understanding her.

'I got m-money in the purr-se.' What she was trying to say was that the clothes she'd taken off also included a purse containing cash. But this kind of talk, which had nothing to do with her current state, sounded like random nonsense to me. I just figured that she was in so much pain that she couldn't help but speak nonsense. I grabbed her wrist to check her pulse. My mother shut her eyes again as if to fall asleep. But about ten minutes later, she spoke up again with her eyes still shut.

'Put. Money. Use. Need.' Her speech wasn't crystal clear but she was definitely trying to tell me to put it to use as I saw it fit. I couldn't stop the flow of tears pouring from my eyes. If she came to her senses entirely, there were probably a million other things for her to consider, but she was most concerned about where I needed spending.

'No. No need. I have plenty to spend.' When I replied this way in the midst of shedding tears, my mother sealed her lips shut. But a moment later, she opened them again.

'You need send Seoul. The murse also has rin.' I couldn't hold it in any longer. I buried my face into her arm and cried. My mother heard what I'd asked my brother yesterday. *And you offered me the one valuable item you own – a ring made of pure gold handed down from a noble family. You were telling me to sell it and use the money.*

While I cried into her left arm, I felt her place her right hand over my head. It had been twenty or so years since I'd cried while my mother stroked my head this way, and I cried like no tomorrow.

'Don't say things like that. You need to get well again and wear your ring.'

'What do you mean wear ... Do you think I'm going to

survive this?!'

Whatever happens, let's just take a trip into the city tomorrow and then return. Let's go to Seoul and take care of the urgent situation there, find peace of mind and then return. Then let's nurse Mother with all the care and attention I can offer. Even if it's with all my devotion, let's try and get her out of this hospital bed.

'Even the doctor in charge spoke highly of your improvement. You'll be better in just a few days now, don't you think? Don't you worry about my problems. There's always a solution.'

My mother sealed her lips completely this time. Whether she was asleep or awake, she shut her eyes silently. Like a well-mannered person, she only broke the still silence with her breathing. And so another night was endured safely and the day broke. During the rounds the next morning, the doctor in charge introduced a woman named B to us and said that she was the new physician taking over. Afterwards, my mother went to sleep. When my sister and I were the only ones in the hospital room, I explained to her that I would be taking a trip back into the city that evening. I said that I would head into Seoul then take the late-night train back in on the day after next.

'Is that doable?' My sister was surprised but tried not to show it.

'Well, what can I do ... I don't want to leave, but it doesn't seem like mother's condition will change in the next couple of days ...'

'But she'll look for you.' Indeed. She would look for me. If I was gone, the only two people who could keep vigil were my younger brother and brother-in-law. The two were notorious sleepers, and they wouldn't be able to stay up through the night. Just the other day, I'd asked my brother-in-law to take the night shift due to my fatigue, but the next morning, my mother complained. She'd asked for water during the night, but he slept right through her request. She'd wanted to use the restroom, but he kept on sleeping. She'd wanted to shift her position at night, so she used all of her strength to do so. She was in a great amount of pain as a result. She could hardly bear it. I did not want to leave my mother's sight even for a second. For the sake of her caretaking, I didn't leave the hospital room for more than five minutes (aside from completely necessary tasks such as eating and sleeping) at a time. Other than myself, there wasn't anyone who could devote their all to my mother's care. To make sure that my mother was completely accounted for without complaints would be difficult. Considering the circumstances, taking this trip (even if it was just for a day) was completely shameful of me. I wound up not making the trip. I changed my plans.

That day, my mother woke up and suddenly started speaking strangely. She called on my sister and asked, 'Where are my clothes?'

I'd already heard this request the night before. The request pricked my conscience.

'Where are my clothes?'

'Your clothes? I took them back to the house. Why?'

'What about my purse?'

'It should be with your clothes. Why do you ask all of a sudden?'

'Go get it for me, please.'

'Why?'

'I want to see it.'

So went the conversation. A chill crept over my chest. Tears were about to fall from my eyes. I couldn't help but interrupt their conversation.

'Hey. It's a purse she really cherishes. That's probably why she's thinking about it.' And so I got my sister to wrap up the conversation and change the subject. Up until then my sister had been taking care of Mother. It seems that Mother's real estate fortune would be handed over to her. Such was the case. Things could grow awkward between she and I if the discussion moved in that direction, so I was hesitant to bring up anything of the sort. It was hard to determine whether it was necessary of me to say that Mother's words were nonsense. But at the time, I had no choice but to nip that conversation in the bud. *You must've known that your daughter was planning on inheriting your assets.* She found it difficult to continue the conversation, so she stopped without getting any further into details. But from that day forth till the day she passed, she asked for her clothes and purse every day, several times a day. Her words were almost meaningless at this point. My heart ached whenever I heard those words.

Starting that night, she complained of extreme pain in her surgical wound. We asked the nurse for some painkillers. Looking back, I'm always grateful to these nurses, but I'm especially grateful for one particular reason. Most hospitals typically are rumoured to have unkind nurses, but in our room, the nurses were very co-operative. The following day, my brother-in-law came by. I took the opportunity to go to the bathroom. During that time my mother had awoken and asked my brother-in-law, 'Did Tongin go to Seoul?' She'd overheard my conversation from the day before.

'What do you mean go? He's staying here.'

My mother, who paid no heed to any of the world's problems these days, to the point where she'd even lost interest in her grandson, who she once greatly adored, was showing concern about my suggestion of taking a trip into the city. The fact that I'd caused her such alarm made me feel terribly sorry. From that day forth, her condition became strange. It wasn't like her fever or pain grew worse, but she seemed to hallucinate some kind of incessant threat. My mother said that two children died at the hospital the other day, and that she couldn't sleep because of the sounds of the dead children's crying. It was a foreboding statement.

When I asked the nurse if any children had died at the hospital recently she said that aside from my mother there weren't any patients in critical condition. I relayed this message to my mother. I tried to eliminate these delusions and hallucinations, but she eventually grew angry with me. She said that they were definitely dead, and that I was trying to fool her. That was not all. When she was briefly awake, she always hallucinated an image. Usually, she never opened her mouth aside from asking for cold water or to turn on the fan, but she would now and then say needless things, like how the whole place was going to get torn down, so we needed to take cover. She said that Il-hwan (my son) had come down here, taken off his hat and tossed it there on the side and walked off. She asked of his whereabouts. She would then ask when she was going to be discharged. It was as though she were a child, begging us to leave. Whenever she saw us, she would ask to be discharged. This tendency was difficult for us to witness. The elderly are old, and the invalid are ill. We knew very well that she wouldn't be able to stand up again, but a child's hope awaits a moment of gladness even in the most impossible circumstances. Whenever we tried to consider these awful circumstances, we did so coldly and rationally. But even so, when we imagined her body growing for ever still and the silence at the funeral, it was impossible for us to wrap our minds around such thoughts. She ultimately implored us for discharge. We disobeyed her request all the way till the end.

'I have to leave the hospital. There's something I must do.' Whenever she said this, we lied to her and said that we would let her leave the hospital as soon as she showed a small sign of improvement. That night I heard Mother say what it was that she needed to do upon leaving the hospital. It was a completely trivial task. Another time, she declared that she needed to leave in order to make final preparations before her death.

'Please don't concern yourself with that. Such thoughts

can have an impact on your health.' She didn't listen to us, of course. Till the very moment when she was drifting in and out of consciousness, she worried about this son of hers who was about to turn forty any day now. I couldn't help myself from tearing up at the thought. The folks who came to visit us at the hospital all returned feeling sorry, but we didn't give up hope. When we considered things coldly and logically, we knew that it would all end in death, but we didn't believe that the end was imminent. Furthermore, a person like myself who had never seen a person die before had no idea what death was like. After the Western woman, B, took over the head physician's tasks, the food during meal times was always mysterious. Grilled meat, bracken fern and kimchi. Before the change, the meals rotated items such as rice porridge, thin rice gruel, milk, an egg and others along those lines, but after B took over, the menu changed. The patient despised the new menu. We raised the softened foods to her lips, and only then did she take to them. Even so, there was no way she could like these kinds of foods.

'She has diabetes,' was B's remark.

'No. I want an apple slice.' Whenever I brought meat to her lips, she shook her head and refused it. However, this was another form of treatment, and we had to refuse her wish and offer her only meat and bracken fern to eat. My sister once offered her a piece of crab apple and got caught by B, which resulted in a long scolding. We were told that tomatoes were okay for diabetic patients, so we gave her some, but pretty soon thereafter even tomatoes were forbidden. What an unlucky patient. Whenever I looked at Mother carefully, I sensed her grief thoroughly. I knew that for a patient in a critical condition, even if something wasn't allowed by the hospital, we should still give them to her. I knew this. But in her critical state, we couldn't make a single one of her wishes come true.

'Let's leave. Bring me my clothes. Bring me my purse.' We

took all of these remarks as an invalid's drivel and ignored them. I understood the meaning behind them, but I was in a tricky situation myself and so I could not speak up for her.

'Give me a crab apple. Let's have some peaches. Bring me some quince.' We couldn't satisfy these requests because of B. Someone making a hospital visit brought some peaches and quince. We thought Mother didn't see them, but as soon as the visitor left, she asked us to bring her some peach slices. I felt my heart break whenever we refused these things. One night, while I thought my mother was asleep, I ate a crab apple. My mother then woke up very suddenly and stared at my crab apple point blank. I felt terribly sorry for her at this moment. I disobeyed the doctor's orders and gave her a slice. My mother seemed to savour it. When she said she was thirsty, I offered her only water. The meat and bracken fern were too dry, and they didn't quite go down easily. Even when she complained of this, we couldn't do anything about the doctor's orders.

'Can't I have some cold noodles?' She woke up very suddenly one day with this request. She must've craved something cool and refreshing for a long time to ask us of this. If we wanted something cool and refreshing, we had the option of eating fruit. If we wanted something like that, then we could always step out of the patient's room and eat on the porch. But after we ate and returned to the room, we always felt like we'd committed some heinous crime and felt guilty.

The doctor said that the inflammation in her left lung had worsened, but that we should not concern ourselves over it too much.

Seventeenth of August. She asked to be released from the hospital again that day and for her clothes. Her condition remained the same, however. She seemed neither better nor worse. Around five p.m., a nurse came by and gave her a shot before leaving. When I asked about it, I was told that it was an insulin shot to treat diabetes. There were only two people in the patient's room – my mother and myself.

Mother seemed to have fallen sound asleep, so I picked up a lifestyle magazine to read. A while later, her breathing suddenly grew sharp. I tossed the magazine aside and rushed over. When her forehead felt as hot as a coal fire under my hand, I grabbed her wrist and felt a terribly fast pulse. My heart froze. In a state of panic, I wasn't sure what to do. I can't remember for the life of me how I handled things from that point forth, but I did take her temperature. I called the nurse. I asked the nurse for an adrenaline shot for my mother but was told that a doctor's prescription was required. I coerced the nurse for the shot regardless, and I recall seeing a shot be administered twice in a row. I didn't know what the hell kind of hospital this was where the hospital director, night duty doctor, and physician with the authority all remained unreachable. I remember sending all the nurses in search for a doctor at one point. Her sons had to be called upon urgently, but no one knew where the house was so it took for ever. My older brother's house did have a phone, but there wasn't anyone around who could make the call. Every single nurse was out searching for a doctor. Meanwhile, I couldn't leave the patient's side – not even for a second. During this time her temperature rose to thirty-nine degrees Celsius. Then to thirty-nine point three. Then to thirty-nine point five. Then to thirty-nine point eight. It kept rising. Her torso retained heat, while her feet grew cold as ice. I shook her, but she didn't regain consciousness. Despite my screaming and shouting, the only response was her quickened phlegmy breathing. She didn't show any other signs of awareness. Someone arrived right at that moment. My sister came rushing over in tears at the sight. I tried to calm her down and asked her to go to Kirimri (where my younger brother lived) and bring him over. No one else except my sister knew where my brother's house was as he'd moved very recently. I instructed my brother-in-law to first call my older brother and then to find every doctor associated with this hospital and bring them here. Meanwhile the temperature in her knees had dropped. My younger brother and sister rushed over first. By the time my sister-in-law and older brother arrived, the patient's thighs had gotten cold. The nurses who'd gone out in search for a doctor returned unsuccessfully.

A camphor injection. Then another. And another. No signs of improvement showed despite multiple attempts. The patient's breathing remained sharp, and her consciousness did not return. The hospital director arrived first. He gave her a checkup, then lowered his head as though he felt sorry. He prescribed two shots of something, then turned around and left. B, the physician in charge, arrived next. She basically said the same thing as always. The night doctor also arrived. The internist also took a look. They could all only offer words of regret. My younger brother's wife, who'd taken their son to P Hospital due to scarlet fever and were both quarantined, managed to escape and rushed over here upon hearing the news. The patient, who was unaware of her children surrounding her, was fast asleep, while phlegm could be heard through her breathing. The temperature in her legs was finally returning to normal. The fever had gradually spread down towards her feet. Around eleven p.m. in the evening, her whole body was warm from head to toe. Her temperature was thirty-eight point eight degrees, which was typical for her. I asked how long the effects of adrenaline typically lasted. I was told it took about five to six, if not seven to eight, hours. Could this state be solely due to the adrenaline shots' effects? Her body, which had gotten cold, was suddenly getting warm. Her breathing had also returned to normal. Could this all be the effects of just one medicine? Once the effects of the medicine wore off, would her body just cool right down again?

Eleven p.m. Twelve a.m. One a.m. While her children

surrounded her without a word, not making a sound, even suppressing their breathing, the patient continued to breathe sharply in her sleep as though abiding by an unwritten rule. I tried calling for her close to her ear. I even tried giving her a little shake. But her face didn't change in the slightest. She just continued to sleep. I even quietly gave her arm a small pinch. It brought a chill to my spine. For a brief moment, Mother winced a little bit in pain. It wasn't anything to write home about, but seeing my unconscious mother's face move slightly felt to me like witnessing some frightening amount of movement. It was enough to make my skin rise. In continuation of this experiment, I even tried touching her feet. Based on our last experience, we knew that her feet would grow cold first, so someone was holding on to her feet at all times.

Weeping. Guttural wailing. No one present could directly admit that her condition had finally taken a turn for the worse. None of us had prepared ourselves emotionally or mentally for her death. We all wished for Mother to open her eyes again and to look at us once more. What if there was something she'd like to say before she passed, but her body just turned cold? Could there be anything more cruel than this? Time passed while our hearts remained heavy and in pain. Three a.m. Four a.m. Five a.m. Within that terrible silence, the only thing that remained consistent was her breathing. The time was around seven or eight hours since her last shot. The effects of the medicine should have worn off at this point. The horror of waiting for that final hour felt like a large stone was pressing against our chests. The nurse entered. She followed standard protocol and took the patient's blood pressure, temperature, and checked her respiration. Then she put her hand beneath the patient's shoulder and proceeded to lift her up and down. How am I to express the horror I felt at the sight of this ... *This must be the end* was the only thing on my mind. Open? The patient's eyes had opened. They were eyes containing horror. Those eyes rolled and wandered the room. We couldn't tell where she was looking. She seemed to be focusing on a void. She rolled her eyes around aimlessly several times, but she didn't seem to be able to see our faces or the lamp.

'Ah-ma.' She let out a strange noise that sounded like it came from a machine. After that she closed her eyes again. The sound of phlegmy breathing. It was the same deafening, terrible breathing, but at the very least it shattered the eerie silence. In midst of this we all stood and shook like poplar trees.

Morning. As the day grew bright, our mother regained consciousness, going against our anticipation of horror. Her eyes opened and she said, 'Give me some water.'

When she said this, our hearts nearly burst with joy. The doctor, who arrived at our urgent request, cancelled last night's prognosis after examining her. They say that when a patient nears death, it is common for her to return to her senses while her lips remain ashen. But this patient's lips were flush with colour, and so last night's prognosis was to be postponed. Breakfast arrived around eight a.m. I couldn't contain my rage against this hospital's strange manner of handling things. The breakfast was grilled meat, seasoned bracken fern and kimchi. I called the chef and asked who had prescribed this meal, and the reply was that it was Doctor B. When I asked when this was prescribed, I was told that it was that morning. I called for B. B entered the patient's room wearing a stethoscope around her neck.

'Do you mean to give this food to the patient?' I was struggling to breathe due to my anger.

'Yes. Why do you ask?'

'Right. So for this patient, it's meat, bracken fern and kimchi.'

'Yes. There are lots of nutrients in them. The calories are—'

If my brother-in-law hadn't held me back, I probably would have inflicted some brutal injury onto this woman of a civilized country. A little later, when a nurse entered to administer an insulin shot, I stopped her. It was my first time hearing of such a medical treatment – this insulin. The other night, within thirty minutes of the insulin shot, Mother's condition had taken a bad turn. I felt uneasy about it, so I stopped them from administering another. After breakfast, I gave a call to a doctor friend, and asked about this insulin. Upon hearing his answer, I nearly fainted from shock. Insulin was used to treat diabetes; however, even if the patient was relatively healthy, after the insulin shot a dextrose shot has to be administered immediately thereafter in order to balance out the levels. Otherwise the patient could suffer a heart attack. If the patient was weak, it could be particularly hazardous.

'Why was she taken to this sort of hospital?' When I reproached my sister this way, she explained that it was simply because this hospital was the closest one to home.

It wasn't too late. I wanted to transfer her to a different hospital immediately. As soon as the sun went down. all the doctors at this hospital went their separate ways to pursue their leisurely activities without leaving behind a night doctor. I realized that in a state of emergency, we wound up running all over the place. The fact that this hospital treated its patients in such an ignorant manner was frightening. But how to transfer a patient in so critical a condition ... It was a child's greed to see the day of their mother's fast recovery. Even so, I just couldn't find a way to get back some peace of mind. I began to make preparations for the funeral. But we couldn't have imagined that she would pass away that evening. Our wish was not unreasonable. We, who could not predict the next hour, spent the day in a relatively indifferent state. There was just one change in Mother's overall appearance. The other day, she would not leave the blanket over her body alone. She continuously tried to remove it, but that day she remained completely still when we placed the blanket over her body. She briefly awoke then fell back asleep. After falling asleep she woke up again. Whenever she awoke, she would just raise her bandaged right arm. Other than this she didn't move at all. That afternoon, during her brief state of wakefulness, she suggested once more that she be discharged from the hospital.

'Hey. Let's leave the hospital.'

All we could do was glance at one another. Were we to leave the hospital or not? This was in fact a big deal. If there was absolutely no chance of her ever recovering again then we had no reason not to take her up on this request. But we were all waiting for the last grace from above, so none of us could take our critically ill mother out of the hospital. Of course, you could say that there was zero chance of Mother making any sort of recovery, but to our minds, that simply could not be.

'Either this evening or tomorrow, we'll be sure to get you discharged.' All we could do was lie to her this way, just as we had been all along. Of course, Mother's face expressed disappointment. She could barely roll her eyes around freely. She just about brought her focus towards my sister.

'Give the skin now.'

'Excuse me?'

'The skin! Now! Give it to me!'

'Leave the skin? What skin?'

'Give the skin! Skin!'

There was no way I couldn't interrupt this impossible conversation.

'Yes, we understand. Please don't worry.'

Then I told my sister that she was probably hallucinating about eating some kind of fruit and laughed it off. But my mind scattered in all directions. Whatever she felt must've been extremely urgent if it took her all her strength to speak up about it in her critical state. What made it worse for me was not being able to understand Mother's words, despite her painstaking manner of delivering them to us. She must've heard what I said and withdrew from speaking even more. She simply shut her eyes. Those were her final words during her long-lived sixty-six years. That night, we had dinner together at the hospital. It would've been perfectly acceptable to have eaten at a spot nearby, but for whatever reason, we just didn't feel comfortable at the thought, so we decided to bring our food to the hospital and dine there. We ate our dinner on the hospital porch, and while sipping our scorched rice drink without quite tasting anything, we returned to the patient's room and found our mother snoozing, snoozing, snoozing away. There was a nurse pouring some medicine into our mother's lips. Upon a closer look, I saw that it was dextrose.

'Is that dextrose?'

'Yes.'

'Did you give her an insulin shot?'

'Yes.'

My heart dropped. I didn't even have the strength to shout at the nurse as to why she would do such a thing. Although the nurse had poured the medicine onto a spoon to feed the patient, she wasn't able to open her lips. It seemed she couldn't swallow the medicine at all. My vision began to blur. In order to pour the dextrose down her throat we held her mouth open, but she couldn't swallow it. We needed to check her pulse and temperature as well. The sight was too pitiful for words. My brother-in-law entered. My sister came in after him. At that moment, the final drop of dextrose was fed. Afterwards, the nurse turned around to leave, and I removed my hand from Mother's lips in order to check her pulse. Right at that moment, her breathing stopped.

'Hey – this ...'

It was such a sudden moment that came down like lightning. In the middle of my shouting, I heard her breathing return again for a few seconds. But those breaths were Mother's final moments. By the time my sister ran out to fetch my sister-in-law and our younger brother returned, our mother had stopped her sixty-six years of breathing.

Shot – shot – shot. Five or six shots had no effect any more. Mother's healthy condition was able to take on the first insulin shot, however, after putting all her strength into overcoming the first, she was unable to take on the second round. Our mother, who might've lived at least a few more days, had lost them to an idiotic doctor's misdiagnosis and treatment.

From the hospital to the funeral home. Three days later, from the funeral home to the funeral. My heart was in constant turmoil. The slightest thing brought tears to my eyes. It was mostly from whenever I thought back to the times I'd mistreated my mother. Although she'd never experienced starvation, near the end of her life she did suffer moments of financial instability. This is the sin that I'd committed against my mother, whose hair had grown white due to this anguish. On top of that, she never expressed disappointment or hatred towards this son of hers. When I think about the mother, who in her final stages of life worried over this son of hers who was nearly forty years old, there was no end to my heartache. My mind and heart's devotion to her was incomparable, but I could never express this to her out loud as a son, because I was simply too shy. I had a mind to show all of that devotion to her as soon as my own life started getting sorted out, but before the possibility of that was even realized, our mother left us forever.

After saying goodbye to my siblings in front of P'yŏngyang Station, I hopped the train back to Seoul, and sobbed without giving any concern to who was looking.

My mother, who passed at nearly seventy years old, had certainly lived long enough, and me at nearly forty years old, who wasn't at the age where one should miss his mother, had a heart filled with a void, so I sobbed and sobbed. It's been three or four months since Mother has passed. I still imagine myself finding a point of stability somewhere ahead in the

THE MAD PAINTER

Inwang.[1]

A young pine tree stands on top of a rock. Below the tree, moss glistens in the sunlight. Crouched down, several orchids spreading open their blossoms can be seen. An orchid leaf bumps against the stone bed as a chilly wind makes it tremble. Yŏ leans over and swishes his stick back and forth down there. The orchids are still about four to five feet away. When he shifts his eyes, there is a mountain stream. It is completely blanketed over by pine trees. Although glimpses of iron-blue stones are visible through the gaps, the ground is completely out of sight. If Yŏ trips and falls, he'd tumble way down into the pine forest, then into the valley and disappear. Behind Yŏ is a stone about twenty-three *chang* in length.[2] When he stands on top of the rock, a large valley appears over Muhak Hill. There is another massive rock

[1] A mountain in Seoul.

[2] One *chang* equals approximately three metres.

below Yŏ. It has several orchids. Below that are some young pine trees. A waterfall appears at the precipice. Right as the mountain stream ends, just above the pine trees, the edge of Kyŏngsŏng finally appears.[3] The darkly paved streets for cars are visible. The usual hustle and bustle is probably going on in that world. But this here is a mountain valley. It has all the conditions that a mountain valley should possess. It has wind, a cavern, wild herbs and flowers, a stream, living creatures, a cliff, a thick and wildly grown pine forest – in other words, it has the serene depth and quality of a deep mountain valley. The city was once a deep mountain valley. Over five hundred years of carving and polishing replaced it with present-day Kyŏngsŏng. One cannot know what Yi T'aejo's intent was by founding the nation's capital on a ravine. But from a hiker's perspective here today, Seoul is a city of beauty like no other. What city in the world can compare to Seoul? A city where loosely clad residents can take an after-meal walk through the deep, dark woods?

Yŏ bends over to see the five-hundred-year-old city lying silently beneath a charcoal-grey roof.

Alpine plants grow all around him. The sound of the mountain stream and the exotic landscape below touch him with ecstasy. Yŏ fits his hiking stick between a crack in the rock, and he positions himself against the young pine tree to keep from falling. He wanted a smoke and he'd stepped out thinking it would only be a short walk, but his feet carried him all the way over here without even packing any cigarettes. A rock of two or three *chang* is on one side of him. The blue sky on the other. A few strands of pine needles also appear in his view. The fragrant scent of resin rushing in. The wind among the pine trees. Nothing compares to this. How many people have walked along the very spot that Yŏ is sitting on? Could it be that Yŏ is the first to have stepped on this rock ever since its formation? Just how many others could've done

[3] Kyŏngsŏng – colonial Seoul.

such a risky thing and crawled all the way over to this very spot here on the edge of this boulder?

It's unlikely that there'd be that many brave souls taking this risky Inwang hike so deep in the woods just to get a taste of thrill.

There's a cave inside the rock behind him. For fear of snakes, he didn't enter it but after waving his stick inside, he figured about three people could easily sit inside it comfortably. Couldn't the cave be put to use for something? Hanyang – a city of machinations – had all kinds of treacherous acts occur over the last five hundred years. From the edge of the city, it would only take a half an hour to get to this cave here. If someone knew this, wouldn't it have been used for acts of conspiracy?

Daydream! Yŏ is wrapped up in a profound sensation. Thanks to the cave, he is about to fall into a nasty daydream. All kinds of conspiring. Its associated slander, slaughter and banishment. The Chosŏn era's five hundred years of unsightliness is about to make Yŏ fall into a terrible daydream. Yŏ frantically digs through his pockets in search of a cigarette in order to snap out of this awful trap. But, just as before, a cigarette can't be found.

When he opens his eyes again and bends over – a branch! Right there before him! Flash! A stream of water appears. The water that's visible through the pine tree is most likely the stream falling between the boulders. That rumbling is probably the sound of the wind. There's no way the sound of that stream could be heard all the way up here.

A spring! Couldn't he come up with a story with that spring over there? The sound and shape of its flow are both beautiful.

Its taste must be just as beautiful. Couldn't Yŏ come up with an entertaining story with that spring? The conspiracy that was about to erupt with that cave ... Couldn't he come up with a more beautiful story other than the awful daydream about slaughter? Yŏ reached down and pulled the stick out of the wedge. While lightly tapping the boulder beneath his feet, he came up with a story.

A painter. The painter's name? It's annoying to come up with one so let's use an artist's name from the Silla period and call him Solgŏ. The era? As for the era, let's make it a time when this city in view was the most energetic and beautiful – during Sejong's reign. How about that?

A place that came to be from the flow of tunes. It was where Kyŏngbuk Palace was found – a place containing all of Hanyang's spiritual vitality. Just outside of the palace's North Gate, there in the thick of the mulberry trees, was a young lad squinting, his face in agony. He was an artist. The mulberry leaves shaded him from the ripe summer's heat. But the warmth penetrated through the leaves, and the humidity rose from the earth below. The artist hid in the mulberry thicket. From the looks of the tiny bundle containing his lunch, he'd be at this spot till the evening. But what was he up to? He just sat there with an agonized expression, sweating bullets. This mulberry patch where the Queen herself handled the silk farming was restricted to outsiders. Not a single soul could be found in the area. Every now and again the wind blew through the mulberry leaves, but not a single gust of wind reached the spot where the artist sat. The artist jumped in the dampness whenever there was a breeze. All the while, he kept his eyes fixed up ahead as if he were waiting for something. Finally, the sun set, and twilight took over the city. He'd been waiting for darkness to fall. The artist slowly crept out of the thicket.

'Today was a waste. Maybe I'll return tomorrow.' He let out a deep sigh and headed back over to the hut. The day had passed into darkness, but from the touch of remaining light, the artist's one-of-a-kind yet hideous face could be seen. His nose looked like a clay bottle. Eyes like brass bells. Ears like rice scoops. Face like a toad. He was the owner of a face that would contain all the descriptions of ugliness. Not only that but his face was so huge that it could be recognized from afar. Walking around in broad daylight with such a face was embarrassing. Ever since he learned this, he had no reason to walk among daytime folk.

At age sixteen, through a teacher's arrangement, he was able to marry a daughter of a decent household, but she fainted after taking a look at his face then ran away as soon as she came to. He got remarried and spent the first night with the new bride, who'd been unconscious, but she too pleaded with her parents, saying she couldn't stand to live with him because she was afraid. And so he was dealt two tragedies. After these incidents, he began to avoid women altogether. As this strange habit progressed, he didn't want to show his face to people at all. On the one hand, he wanted to devote himself to his drawings, but for the most part he wanted to avoid people. It's been thirty years since he left his home and hid himself inside a small shack in the woods.

If he needs supplies and is forced to step out into the street, he always does so at night. If he can't avoid a day trip, he always wears a wide-brimmed bamboo hat and covers his face with hemp cloth.

Forty years of painting. Living in forced seclusion for thirty years. All that sexual energy he couldn't use on women welled up inside his head, and that stamina reached the tips of his fingers and spilled out onto the page. He produced several thousand paintings effortlessly. At first, he had no complaints. His talent was a gift from the heavens and his teacher's training. Whenever his virility turned into a new painting, he gazed at it and felt a sense of pride all to himself. Then, suddenly, a dissatisfaction that gradually began to sprout over the last twenty years. In some ways, this dissatisfaction is perhaps very orthodox. Couldn't he come up with something new? Mountain, ocean, tree, creek, an old man with a cane, a sail boat, flowers, the moon (an absolute necessity), a cow, a herdsman. What else but these has he drawn? Something with a distinct flavour. He wants to come up with something beyond the most unique traditional painting. What he learned from his teacher was how to paint an old man with white hair and a white beard, or a herdsman playing the *p'iri*. Now he wanted to draw a person's face with more movement. He wanted to draw a face with expression. And so Solgŏ spent his days putting all kinds of traditional methods to use in order to illustrate a person's facial expression. But the artist, who'd lived his life apart from the world, could not recall a person's face anymore. The tradesman's sly expression. A pedestrian's plain, flat face. A woodcutter's insipid look. These were the only kinds of faces that he encountered in the meantime.

Wasn't there a new look out there? A look with a new colour! A look with a new colour! As the desire began to ripen and grow inside the artist's mind, one particular drunken memory sprouted inside his head. Although she was nearly gone from his memory at this point, every now and again his mother's face burst up to the surface. The image of her holding him inside her arms and looking down at him with her eyes glistening with tears. His mother was a rare beauty. Her beauty was enough to steal the 'b' in beauty from all the beauties in her family, generation after generation. The artist was still inside this beauty's belly when his father passed away.

Holding this fatherless baby against her chest, she peered down at him with a tearful look. Ever since he matured, people reacted with nothing but shock and horror at his face, but whenever he missed his mother's face, full of love and beauty, it was enough to make his whole body shudder. This is what he wanted to paint. Giant eyes filled to the brim with tears. Eyes that still contained a longing. Eyes that seemed to caress. A smile rising from the corners of her lips. This phantom vision that came and went like lightning is what the artist wanted to draw. In this artist's strange heart, which had slowly turned over the years of hiding from the world, also contained an intense passion. Just as his heart was also filled with pent-up resentment and anger. The gloomy artist thought of all the young men and women clutching on to each other with pleasure as he frantically moved his brunch. The artist, who was becoming stranger by the day, made a firm decision to draw a portrait of a woman.

At first, he simply set out to draw a pretty woman's face. But given how he hadn't seen a pretty woman's face up close, he would grow angry at his brush – but he eventually changed his concept of a 'pretty face'. He wanted to draw his wife's portrait. The world had not given him a wife. If one looks, an insect – even a feathered beast – is capable of finding a mate to enjoy. Of all the living things, the most supreme creature – he, a human being – could not find a mate. This was his biggest grievance. The worldly bastards that hadn't given him a partner, and the women who wouldn't come to him, forcing him to be single his entire life. The thought of him dying up there in the woods alone made him feel sorry for his poor self, but he mostly hated the cold cruel world. He would create a wife with his own brush – the wife that this world refused him – and he'd laugh in its face. He'd make a woman more beautiful than any other woman in this world with his brush. The ugly things that pretend to be beautiful would be laughed off. It would squash all the men who believed they had the most beautiful wives in the world flat. It would bring those dancing chaps who enjoyed four to five mistresses at once down to their knees.

Beautiful woman! Beautiful woman! He thought of her with his eyes open and shut. He clasped on to his skull and thought with all his might but couldn't conjure a beautiful woman's face. Of course, a face with no blemishes and pro-portionate features is what the world typically calls a beauty. If he added some rouge to this type of face, it would become more beautiful – for sure. Such a face was easy to see with his own eyes, and it wasn't worthy of painting with his brush. For in this artist's mind was the faint shadow of his mother's face; it was impossible for this artist to be satisfied with a simplistic beauty. In all his anguish and distress, a year then another year went by without progress.

––––––––––

The lower half of the woman's portrait had been complete for several years now. How to place a face on top of that body was impossible to fathom. This painting that hung at the far end of his hut rebuked him constantly, as though begging him to hurry and paint a face and neck already. Looking at this painting made him uncomfortable. This painter, who didn't walk around during the daytime, began to frequent the town with his face wrapped up. It was in the hopes of running into a beautiful face out on the street. If he ran into a beautiful woman on the street, he would catch the image vividly inside his mind and paint her. This was the chance he banked on. But given the city's tough regulations that forbade men and women's face-to-face interactions, there was no woman walk-ing the streets with her face held high. The only girls that were around were servant girls or ones of lower class. Sure

– there were beauties among servants and lower-class girls. But no matter how pretty they were, their facial expressions were dirty and base. None of them were worth catching. He would cover his face and wander towards a place where women might gather to. He'd go to the well and creep towards pretty girls to catch a glimpse and research their faces, but he could not find one that satisfied him. Perhaps he'd find a girl he'd like at a *sim-gyu*.[4] *Sim-gyu! Sim-gyu!* If he could collect all the girls and make them stand before him to inspect their faces …

After a long and restless day of hunting for a pretty face, he finally entered the Queen's mulberry field to catch a glimpse of a palace maid's face. But unfortunately for the artist, no one had come to pick mulberries that day. But given how it was the height of the summer, and the season for silkworm farming, he figured if he put up with it and waited it out, one of the maids would come by. His intent to draw his wife's face made him flush with fever. The next day, he returned to the mulberry field and hid.

He couldn't resist. He packed his lunch and went to the queen's residence every day for a month. But every night, as he made his return to the hut, he let out a long sigh. It wasn't that he couldn't see a palace maid. As if they intended to tease the artist, the palace maids came and went in a rotation. They'd come in a large group and flap their skirts while gathering mulberries. He saw a total of about forty or fifty palace maids. They were all equally beautiful. They were a great deal more refined than the girls he could easily see gathered by the well. But it was the eyes. What the artist remembered were those eyes. Those eyes that could caress. Those eyes filled with yearning. Eyes overflowing with love. The palace maids didn't have eyes like those. In other words, these were just ordinary girls. He wanted to take vengeance on this stubborn world that wouldn't give him a woman by drawing the most

[4] *shimgyu* – a woman's quarters.

insurmountable beauty there ever was through a portrait, but these types couldn't possibly do it justice. Whenever he trudged home, he let out a long sigh. After a month of this long sighing, he decided not to return to the queen's residence.

A crisp, clear autumn day. His heart filled with discontent and anguish, he trudged down to the creek with a basket pressed against his hip to rinse some rice. Then he stopped dead in his tracks. Through the pine thicket he caught sight of a young woman sitting atop a boulder by the creek. She was sitting beneath the shade of the pine needles and staring vacantly into the moving water. Who was this young woman? A spot quite removed from the residential area. An area quite elevated from the village. This place that didn't even have a pathway. During his thirty years here, he'd encountered the occasional woodcutter or shepherd boy, but no one else besides. What was a young woman who couldn't possibly be living apart from her family be doing in a place such as this? The artist stood and stared blankly. As he stood, a heavy anxiety began to grope his chest. One step, two steps – the artist quietly walked forward. As the space between them shrank, the young woman's face became clearer. Blood filled the artist's face. She was a rare beauty. Aged about seventeen or eighteen. It was her expression that was more beautiful than her overall looks. Her eyes and ears were completely focused on that stream. Her gigantic eyes seemed to have forgotten how to blink. They were enraptured by the creek's movement. Was the underwater palace visible through that crystal water? What was the young woman staring at, leaning over that pine tree there as the wind lightly blew over her hair? All her youthful passion and reverie was captured in an exquisite smile beaming through her eyes and lips. What was it that she was gazing at with all her attention?

Ah.

The artist had finally found it. He had spent ten years wandering residential paths, the well, and even the Queen's chambers in search for this discovery, until at long last he met this beautiful face in a place where he least expected to. The artist sped up his walk. He completely forgot about how his face might be too dirty, or how his face might cause this young woman fright, and hurried towards her. At the sound of his feet, the young woman quickly raised her head and looked at the artist. Her eyes, which seemed to stare off into space, were peculiar.

'Ah ...' His chest felt cramped and the artist stammered between words and noises until the young woman spoke first.

'Where is this place?'

Where is this place?

'This is the foot of an unknown mountain called Inwang, but what's a girl like you doing here?'

'I see ...' Suddenly a very lonely expression. 'I followed the creek over here.'

The artist cocked his head. He moved his body a bit. Her eyes, filled with that long-lost stare, barely moved. They remained open and large but didn't have any focus. The artist finally spoke up.

'Can you see?'

'I'm blind.'

She was blind. Upon hearing her sorrowful answer, the artist crept closer towards her.

'If you can't even see, what did you come all the way over here for?'

The young woman lowered her head. She seemed to be saying something in response, but the artist could not hear her. What caused him to lose some interest in her was that her face had lost the charming expression it had earlier. Even so, there was no mistake about it: this was a rare beauty. What had caught the artist by such surprise earlier wasn't just her pretty looks. It was that distinct quality that drew him towards her.

'You poor thing. It's almost suppertime. Get yourself home before it grows dark.'

The artist decided to give up on the young woman with these few words, but to this she responded, 'I don't have any issues with the dark, but dusk must be very beautiful, right?'

'Indeed. Very beautiful.'

'In what way is it beautiful?'

'Streams of golden light shine from the west of the mountain. Then the whole world appears to be dyed with bright red. Even the green pine trees, the blue boulders, the dark tree trunks – they all get submerged under golden light ...'

'What is "golden light" and what is "bright red"? What are these colors supposed to be? They say that the day is bright, but how is a day's brightness different from a red light? I heard that the view of this mountain is marvellous, so I came here, but I can't tell from just the sounds of the wind, the water over the rocks ... It's hard to know its beauty just from these sounds.' Again, that strange expression gradually appeared on her face. Waves of yearning reflected in her giant eyes. For now, the beautiful expression that had disappeared looked like it might reappear. The artist finally sat before the young woman.

'If you follow this creek there is an ocean. Inside the ocean is an underwater kingdom. There are pillars wrapped in seven colours. There are terrace stones engraved with jade, wind chimes made of gold, and gates made of pearls ...' As the artist sat before her weaving this yarn, the young woman's eyes seemed more and more enraptured as time passed. The artist finally began to plan on taking this young woman back to his hut.

'I'll tell you my underwater kingdom story, as long as your folks back home won't be too worried about you ...' As the artist began to say this, the young woman turned her giant eyes up towards the sky with a profound and distant aura and said that no parent of hers would miss a disabled daughter such as herself and enthusiastically followed the artist's footsteps.

The story that had come so quickly to Yŏ halts. How to improve this story? Distracting thoughts emerge. The sound of a pop song flows into his ear at the same time. Yŏ raises his head. Some people must've arrived. The distracting song entered Yŏ's ears when he least expected it, messing up his mind. Such annoying lyrics. Damn those lyrics. Because of those damn lyrics the story won't fall back into place. But what's a story without a conclusion? He must come up with a conclusion, no matter what. So should he say that the artist takes the young woman to his hut, tells her the underwater kingdom story while he draws her face, and finally satisfies his long-awaited heart's desire, and wrap it up? But what a boring ending. It was indeed an ending, but it would make the beginning so meaningless.

What then? How about ending it differently? The artist brings the young woman back to his hut. Then he tells her his underwater kingdom story. But because the story isn't as fascinating as it was earlier, she doesn't feel any emotions and that facial expression doesn't return. The artist's efforts go to waste. But the artist cannot leave the portrait unfinished. Another unsatisfactory ending. Well, let's try again then ... The artist brings the young woman back. Back at his home, the more he looks at the young woman, the more desirable she appears, so he decides to wed her. The blind woman has no complaints about his ugly looks, so they live happily ever after. The artist who wanted to create a wife through a painting has found a wife whose beauty is unsurpassable.

Lousy. How annoying. Damn that pop song and its lyrics!

Yŏ stands up. He doesn't want to continue sitting in that spot where he lost his inspiration. That song ... He decides to move to a spot where he can't hear it. When he bends over, he can see a glistening stream through the pine trees. That's the mountain spring from earlier. That spring. The origin of this story. Let's go down there. Getting down from the cliff is a lot harder than climbing it. If he makes a mistake while climbing up and falls, he'd fall right in place, but if he misses his step while climbing down, there is no telling how far he'd fall. He might fall all the way down to Ch'ŏngundong. And whereas the stick is helpful while he climbs up, on his way down it is a nuisance. It takes nearly a half an hour, but he finally arrives at the spring. A boulder by the stream. It is perfect for a person to sit upon.

Is this where the artist sat to rinse his rice? Is this where the young woman sat and daydreamed? He thinks the water below is a deep dark pool, but it's a shallow stream moving over a dark rock. This valley couldn't be more silent. Even the wind flows from a distance. The ravine is surrounded by pine trees and boulders, and it is probably the kind of secluded location that the artist enjoyed. Now then, shall we complete the tail end of the story here at the ravine?

The artist brought the young woman back to his hut. His heart was so full of anticipation and excitement that he didn't even want to make dinner. When he entered and looked at the picture on the scroll, the torso that had awaited a head for so long seemed to match the one on this young woman.

'Here. Have a seat.' The artist spread out the painting that had been rebuking him for years. The paint was ready. His heart fluttered and it felt like it would burst. He sat the young woman on the south side where the light was. He dipped his brush in the paint and began to tell the story. Twilight already. He had to race against the sun to complete this long-awaited piece. The ten years of energy that had collected inside of him moved towards his fingertips.

'And so ... got it?' His eyes looked at the young woman's face, his lips moved to tell the underwater kingdom story and his hand holding the brush moved like lightning. 'There in the kingdom is a pearl called 'cintamani'. The cintamani is a wish-fulfilling jewel. If it were to be rolled over your eyes, you'd be able to see the bright sun and moon.'

'Really? There's a pearl?'

'Of course there is. As long as you do as I say and stay here, I'll take you to the underwater kingdom and say a prayer to the cintamani to heal your eyes.'

'Then I'll be able to see the bright sun and moon, too?'

'Of course. The bright sun and moon. You'll be able to see the brilliantly strange seven-coloured thing called a rainbow, the beautiful forest, the eminent valley – you'll be able to see it all.'

'Aigu – hurry up and find that cintamani and...' Ah – it was a shockingly marvelous expression. The artist didn't lose a single ounce of that expression overflowing from her face and transfered it completely onto the painting. Dusk turned to night. At this point, the only part that wasn't complete was the woman's eyes. Other than that, the painting was near completion. He wanted to paint her pupils as well. But it was too dark to paint the pupils – the very last thing that would give this portrait life. So what if he put the pupils off until daybreak? After all, he'd waited ten years. He felt an insurmountable joy.

'Ah – ah!' This exclamation was a cry of joy he had long awaited. His mind finally felt a sense of calm security, but another passion began to spark inside the artist's heart. There in the darkness, the artist had gotten quite close to the young woman in order to see her face. He sat close enough to the point where his knees touched hers. The reassurance he felt with the painting so far, the young woman's scent that entered the artist's nose, and her body that felt so completely accessible were enough to paralyse him. As time went on, he began to shudder. There in the darkness, those eyes that radiated light and those passionate lips were enough to knock him unconscious. By daybreak, the artist and the blind woman were no longer strangers.

'I'll paint the pupils today.' The bachelor of thirty years had finally shed his old skin and shared breakfast with the blind woman, which he'd eaten alone up until now. Afterwards, he sat before the painting again.

'What about the underwater kingdom?' Those eyes shining with joy! But the beauty that he'd seen the night before was nowhere to be found in the morning. No other eyes could compare to such beauty. However, those eyes now contained the look of a woman who sought a man's love. The virgin who wanted to free herself from the humiliation of being a cripple had finally awakened to her sexuality last night, but this morning her eyes were that of a wife's. Her eyes contained lust.

'What about the underwater kingdom? Hurry over to the kingdom and get that cintamani to open my eyes. I want to see the bright earth and sky. I want to hurry up and see your face!' She appeared to still believe what the artist had said to her last night – that he was a handsome twenty-three-year-old.

'Sure. I'll get it for you. That place of seven wondrous colours!'

'I want to see those seven colours, too.'

'Right, right. Anyway, try thinking of those things with your mind for now.'

'Yes. I want to see it soon.'

There upon his knees, the painting waited for him to draw those pupils. Though the blind woman's eyes were beautiful, he could not see past the lustful expression any more. He hadn't waited ten years to draw such eyes.

'Now. Imagine the kingdom!'

'What good is it to imagine it? I need to see it with my eyes.'

'At least try to imagine it.'

'I'll need a sense of it in order to imagine it.'

'Imagine it the way you did yesterday!'

'All right ...'

The artist finally lost his patience.

'Now then! The kingdom! The underwater kingdom!'

'Right ...'

'Keep imagining the kingdom! Now then. What's it like?'

'The seven colors are bright ...'

'Right. What else ...'

'And the golden pillar – no, the silk-wrapped pillar, and green pearls ...'

'It's not a green pearl! It's green jade.'

'Was the jade a roof or a door—?'

'*Eik!* You idiot!' The artist took his giant hands and grabbed the blind woman by the shoulders and shook her.

'Again. Think hard. The underwater kingdom.'

'The kingdom is in the ocean ...'

The artist couldn't help himself and slapped the blind woman, who stammered from fear.

'Idiot!' What an idiot. The cripple didn't even know how to blink her eyes. They stared off into nothingness. Looking at those foolish eyes, the artist felt more enraged. The artist grabbed the blind woman's throat with both hands.

'*Ei* – you idiot! You moron! You cripple!' The artist cursed the blind woman in all the ways he could while shaking her by the throat. And he detected contempt in the cripple's watery eyes. This enraged him even more and he shook her harder. He shook her until he finally let go. Her body had grown too heavy. As soon as he let go, the blind woman's body collapsed onto the floor with her eyes rolled back inside her head. The body's fall overturned the ink stone on the floor. The knocked-over ink covered the blind woman's face. In shock, the artist shook the blind woman, but she was already gone. The artist didn't know what to do. The artist thrashed and panicked. He then looked up at his painting and screamed before collapsing. There on the painting, somehow, the pupils had appeared. When the painter came back to his senses and looked at the painting once more, he saw that indeed a pupil had been drawn over each eye. The shape of those pupils made the artist fall back onto his rear end once more. The eyes that appeared on the painting had the same look of contempt that had appeared on the blind woman's face when her throat was locked inside the artist's hands.

The fact that she fell directly onto the ink slab is strange as it is. So is the fact that the ink spilled in such a way that caused it to splatter. But how could the splatters have landed on the painting like so? On one side, a corpse. On the other side, a portrait of the corpse. The painter sat there in a daze, shaking uncontrollably.

After a few days, within the gates of Hanyang, a madman with a hideous face carrying a strange portrait appeared. No one knew where he came from or what his story was. He cherished that portrait of his so dearly that whenever someone asked him to see it, he overreacted and fled. After spending several years this way, on one snowy day, he rested his head over a rock and ended his life. Even in his death, he clutched on to that scroll tightly in his arms.

You, old painter! Yŏ will commemorate your lonely life's story.

Yŏ splashed the water a couple of times with his stick then slowly propped himself back up. When he looked up at the sky, the sunset was already dancing on the horizon, crossing over this time-old valley.

December 1935

THE OLD TAET'ANGJI LADY

The sun rises and falls then rises again, repeating the same task over and over. We came to this earth after all its spinning and rolling for hundreds of millions of years, but there's no way to predict how much longer it can go on for. Its endurance is surprising. It's a marvel. The people born into this world, as well as their society, are meaningless. These humans who repeat the same bland task over and over again are complete fools. The sages of the past invented the saying that past mistakes must be avoided, and so people remain alert, but seeing as it is the world that operates people's lives, how could they count on such a saying? The fact that I indifferently write these words as if they have nothing to do with me makes me a criminal. The so-called 'fiction' I've been writing for ten years or twenty years all share more or less the same voice and same noise except that the characters have different names, and to this, I laugh with satisfaction. I suppose this is our fate, and nothing can be done about it. In any case, I've already picked up the brush. Whether it's another story much like the ones

I've written before or not, let's go ahead and write. I turn on the record that only knows how to repeat the same few songs. I'm a novelist that this world continues to chase. There's no rule telling me to come up with a completely new story each time.

The café waitresses and *nakai* always add 'ko' to the end of all their names. The place had names like Hanako, Yukiko, Sadako – even Mariko and Bobiko. Following that logic, the protagonist I am going to write about now has the name Tabuk'o. There's no romantic association or particular reason for the name Tabuk'o. As a toddler (while still breastfeeding), whenever anything good or bad happened, she said '*tabu tabu*' while bouncing around in dance. The story carried into her career as a *nakai*, so she took this joyful word and added 'ko' to the end and made it her name. After she became a *nakai*, she suddenly put on weight. She was dull when it came to registering anxiety or concerns due to her fatty nature. Plus, whenever guests didn't finish their food, she ate up their greasy leftovers (although she'd never eaten such foods before), and put on a disgusting amount of weight which turned her unsightly. She put on so much disgusting weight and sauntered in a *dabu dabu* manner that a patron began to refer to her as 'Tabuk'o'.[1] Some patrons said her name backwards and called her 'Butako'. Tabuk'o, who knew of no other language aside from Korean, would respond to 'Butako' with a long and dragged out '*Ha-a-i-i*', thinking it was the foreigner's way of calling her name. She'd grab a liquor bottle and hop (I'd like to believe it was hopping, but it was more like thumping) into a patron's room. After some time she finally came to realize that *buta* meant 'pig', but she wasn't the type to pay any mind to that sort of thing.

[1] *dabu dabu* – a Japanese expression that describes an overweight person's walk.

One might think that since she went there as a *nakai*, she at least had a decent looking face to serve the elite, and because of her rotund body, it was easy to assume that she was the wife of some wealthy household, but these are majorly misguided assumptions. She had a hideously chubby face – even her forehead was clumped with fat. She looked remarkably like a *buta*. There were a great deal of wrinkles between her eyes which made her look even worse. Her eyelids and lips were enough to make people say, 'How could they be this thick?' and tilt their heads sideways in wonder and disgust. To top it off, her torso was wider than its height, making her body appear like a round barrel. Her back was hunched. No matter which way we looked, she appeared more like an animal than a person. She was more of a *buta* than an animal.

Her name is Tabuk'o. Her nickname is 'Butako'.[2] If a blowfish and a pig could wed and give birth to a child, it'd be our Tabuk'o. Tabuk'o was born into a poor farmland somewhere in Sunch'ŏn, P'yŏngannam-do. She is the tenth in a family of thirteen siblings – five boys and eight girls. Below her are three younger brothers, and above her are two older ones. Seven girls (one a grown woman) also crowded her. There were times when she endured humiliation and hatred but she suffered through it all in order to grow. Of course, she's never had her own bowl of rice. She's never had her fill of the leftovers either. She had siblings ahead of her, so one might assume that there'd be plenty of hand-me-downs for her to wear. But if the first child wore something and handed it down to the second, that would later be handed down to the third and so on. After going through a number of siblings this way, the clothes would be a composite of patches. The left sleeve would be red and the right would be blue. The torso would be yellow and the back would be black. This is how she spent her childhood years. After growing up this way, she found herself working as a *nakai*.

[2] *k'o* – 'nose' in Korean.

Becoming a *nakai* wasn't her own idea, nor was it her parents'. She didn't get lured or manipulated into becoming one either. One of her friends was a *nakai* worker in town. When Tabuk'o stayed home, she'd only be scolded. There was no one there to look after her either. So she headed over to town on foot and found her friend. Her friend would offer her tasty leftovers which she'd enjoy, and upon the urging of her friend, she found herself sitting at the drinking table on occasion as well. Through this and that, she got acquainted with men, and without any particular course of action or direction, she became a *nakai*.

Her parents paid no heed. There's no way to know if they are even aware of having such a daughter. They were so immersed in getting by that it's quite likely they don't even know how many kids they birthed. This is how the aforementioned Tabuk'o came to be.

Sunch'ŏn is northeast of P'yŏngyang. When the train departs from P'yŏngyang and reaches Sunch'ŏn, Kanggye appears just north from there. If the train goes east then it reaches Yangdŏk, where the line divides. Kanggye is currently hectic with the Manp'o rail construction taking place. There's nothing but dirt, lumber and labour. Yangdŏk, however, is a hot spring district. Within the Yangdŏk county alone are the *taet'angji, sot'angji* and *tolt'angji*.[3] Of the three, Yangdŏk hot springs boasts the *taet'angji*. It is, without a doubt, an authentic P'yŏngyang locale. Some even come all the way from Honam.

Finding an inn with its own tub at the hot springs in Chosŏn is a rare luxury. The inn typically provides meals, and it's normal for guests to share a public tub. Furthermore, during the

[3] *taet'angji* – large tub; *sot'angji* – small tub; *tolt'angji* – stone tub.

winter months, the inn's public tub becomes inconvenient for wandering (due to the cold). Therefore the spring and autumn are customarily hot spring seasons. But Yangdŏk is not like this. It's at such a high altitude that the climate is always cool. It's the perfect summer resort. A summer resort with a hot spring. What more could one want?

The summer is a lustful season. For one, clothes are sleeveless and there are less restrictions, making it easy for one to spill out of them. For another, there is plenty of shade to hide away from people's eyes. Finally, people can enjoy themselves however they please without concern over catching a cold. Yangdŏk has a hot spring for members of the summer resort. The springs are where people push aside their manners and graces. It is where they only hide one part of their body and mingle among men and women.

The summer weather, holiday resort, hot springs … If one asks which location has all three luxuries at once, Yangdŏk would hands down be the answer. Adulterers from P'yŏng-yang. Adulterers of Wŏnsan. Long-distance adulterers. Local adulterers. Adulterers of the whole nation can't wait to gather at Yangdŏk. Not a moment too soon. When the male adulterers gather it's impossible for female adulterers to not show. Male adulterers are set on girls. Female adulterers are after money. The women spin webs in this and that motel and wait, hoping for a catch in their net. If they do well in the summer – making about one *wŏn* and fifty *chŏn* per day – they'll be able to cover their hotel fees plus petty expenses with about a hundred *wŏn* leftover by autumn. During the off season, they get a free stay at the resort, and they get to enjoy some fun as well. The gig isn't half bad for women.

It's been three years since she became a *nakai*. Tabuk'o, who was better known as Butako, rumoured to be of fat proportions, known for frowning even when she is laughing, recognized for her ugly looks and her dim-witted brain, her inability to sing, and for pouring drinks with both hands (when she pours with just her left hand, she drops it), the same one that takes about five or six attempts to stand up from a seated position before she finally succeeds – this Tabuk'o also headed over to Yangdŏk one lousy summer to enjoy the resort, make some money and play.

She'd saved eight *wŏn* and sixty-odd *chŏn* on her own. A fellow *nakai* friend had given her six *wŏn*, and the *nakai* madam gave her another five *wŏn*. She took her twenty *wŏn* and some big hopes for her trip as she left for Yangdŏk. She had a mirror (albeit spotted) in her room, so why she didn't at least consult her own reflection before heading out like that is impossible to know. If she'd consulted a trustworthy mirror, it would've advised against her taking this trip.

Tabuk'o, who was simple in character, was also simple in her way of thinking. When she was in Sunch'ŏn as a *nakai*, she was a heavy drinker. She figured the men she'd encounter in Yangdŏk would be the same as the ones she dealt with back home. However, when she finally arrived at the inn (among Chosŏn inns, she entered the largest one), it was different from what she expected. She was a *nakai* who was used to greeting men, but she suddenly encountered hotel guests. Here at the inn, the men were guests but so was she. At the bar, the guests called for a *nakai*. Even if the guest didn't necessarily call for one, it was standard procedure for a *nakai* to appear before the guest. But here at the inn, she couldn't do this. The guest over there couldn't call her over to his side, seeing that she too was a guest. And she also couldn't possibly just wander into someone's room without giving it any thought. On top of that, the guests here at the establishment were quite different from the ones Tabuk'o had encountered. They were of a different breed. There were quite a few invalids. A man who was concerned with his own health couldn't possibly have the luxury to throw glances her way. Those who weren't invalids had already brought their own partners along. Numerous couples milled about. To top it off, this particular hot spring had more women than men. Everything was different from what Tabuk'o had imagined. Sharply dressed young men who would wander over when a woman passed, slowly eyeing their target before chasing after them, trying to get her to speak – this was the sort of thing Tabuk'o had imagined. She was surprised not to find it at the inn.

From what Tabuk'o had heard, as long as she knew how to fish in an area full of men, it'd be easy to reel them in. Alas, this was completely untrue. Tabuk'o was slowly losing patience. One *wŏn* and fifty *chŏn* per day. This is how much it cost to stay. Even if she remained completely still, one *wŏn* and fifty *chŏn* vanished just like that. During her three years of working as a *nakai*, she'd barely saved eight *wŏn*. Here, she spent one *wŏn* and fifty *chŏn* per day (she skipped lunch) without even trying. Three years' worth of savings disappeared within days. The money she had been able to scramble together was twenty *wŏn*, but the trip over cost two *wŏn*, and the return would cost another two, so that cut her budget down to sixteen *wŏn*. Skipping lunch, skipping cigarettes and avoiding the hot tub would give her enough to make just ten days' worth of meals. She consoled herself the first night after going without a catch by telling herself, *Well, whoever said the first try is easy* ... and she waited another night, and another night after that. But six nights went by very quickly. Her meal budget was down to nine *wŏn*, which was more than what amounted to her three years of savings. If she didn't catch anything good within the next four days, that twenty *wŏn* would be wasted. Seeing as twenty *wŏn* were mere peanuts out in a place like this, and thinking of the three years she'd saved plus the twelve *wŏn* she'd borrowed from her friend and the madam that she'd have to repay, gave her a headache. With only four days left she had no choice but to come up with something. A hundred *wŏn* in one season? It was unfathomable.

Seeing as her meal and travel stipend had already been spent, couldn't someone at least offer to pay the thirteen *wŏn*? Just so she'd have twelve *wŏn* in her pocket when she headed back down to Sunch'ŏn ... Couldn't someone at least grant her that? If she was willing to give up her travel cost, then perhaps someone could at least sponsor her meal stipend ... When she went to sleep and woke up, ten *wŏn* was left over to cover only her meals. On the seventh day, Tabuk'o finally paid a visit to the innkeeper's wife's room.

Tabuk'o said to the innkeeper's wife, 'There aren't that many guests at the resort this year.' The sharp woman immediately understood what Tabuk'o meant by this.

'Why do you say that? It's because schools are still in session. Once school is out, more people show. Even the XX Motel (the filthiest inn) down there fills up.'

'When is school out?'

'Ah, on the twenty-first. Soon.'

Guests who awaited the summer break were either those who came with their families or students. Although they were welcome guests to the innkeeper, they were useless folk to Tabuk'o. But simple Tabuk'o didn't discriminate against such clientele. She banked her hopes on the 'summer break' guests.

But it wasn't summer break yet. Tabuk'o's pockets now contained four days' worth of meals. Should she wait for the break or should she head back home while there was still a couple of *wŏn* left? Or should she wait until she ran out of money? When she thought about taking off, the potential of catching a client that night entered her thoughts and stopped her in her tracks. Then again, the thought of waiting till she spent the twenty *wŏn* that she'd worked herself to the bone to gather, and returning without a single *chŏn*, embittered her.

Ah, what to do? A day went by while she contemplated back and forth, then another. If she settled the bill on her meals, she'd barely be able to make it back home with just a train ticket left.

The rainy season came. It rained the day before. It rained again that day. Tabuk'o, who always crumpled that ugly face into a frown, looked up at the sky. She settled the bill with the innkeeper. Afterwards, she had two *wŏn* and thirteen *chŏn* – just enough for the train ticket, a transfer bus and a little left over. After she settled the bill, the innkeeper asked, 'Why don't you try waiting till the summer break?'

The innkeeper spoke to her frankly so Tabuk'o responded just as frankly, 'I don't have any money left for meals.'

'You can work for your meals while you stay.'

Tabuk'o just smiled in response to this. But there were some things that just didn't go as planned. It just kept on raining. The transfer bus arrived a little past eleven, dropped off passengers, then picked up new passengers before leaving. The rain kept falling.

Eleven o'clock ...

'Forget it. I can't leave with all this rain. Let's leave at noon.'

There was another bus at four thirty. *That's when I'll leave*, she thought. Her excuse was the rain. But if we were to look into Tabuk'o's actual thoughts, the rain had nothing to do with her not leaving. Between eleven and four – five hours – wouldn't a nice catch find its way towards her? With her dream of turning the twenty *wŏn* she'd brought into a hundred *wŏn* now turned to ash, the thought of losing everything and returning empty-handed made her feel not only shame but also deep regret. There were no rules that said that she couldn't make a catch within five hours. Ah, Tabuk'o, who said she hated the rain and refused to take the bus, wandered from this inn and that and back while getting soaked. Her face, body, arms and legs – not a single part of her body had the opportunity to be graced with beauty. She accepted this appearance with the one defense she had – 'womanhood' – and gave up on the hundred *wŏn*, but at least tried to make up the twenty *wŏn* she'd lost with the hope of finding a man ... But the heartless men were ignorant of this bitter woman and simply scolded her for looking like a slutty dancer, chasing after their tails.

The four thirty bus. Tabuk'o gave up completely and brought out her things. The rain continued to fall relentlessly. There by the bus station, she sat below the corner of an inn, clutching on to her bag with both arms, staring at the vehicle. The passengers rushed onto the bus, trying to avoid the rain ... The bus eventually filled up.

'All aboard. Final call.' Even as the bus filled up, Tabuk'o continued to frown her ugly face and gaze at it without any intention of hopping on. The bus was completely packed. After filling up, it let out a *bu-u-u* sound and took off. Tabuk'o's heart sank.

'From this point on, it's debt.'

Each day going forth, she'd be one *wŏn* and fifty *chŏn* more in debt. With self-disdain and her heart full of terror at the thought of the debt that had no end in sight (a debt that would continue to grow day by day), Tabuk'o trudged back to the inn.

Tabuk'o's pathetic life began from this day forth. She was out of money, so she started begging for meals from this inn and that. Whatever a guest ate and left behind was Tabuk'o's meal. Tabuk'o had to be moved into a back room somewhere, seeing as another guest insisted on using the room she was staying in. But Tabuk'o, who was strong-willed, simply smiled with her ugly face and gave in to the request without a fuss.

'The days go by' has a particular resonance to each person, depending on who it is. For Tabuk'o, 'the days go by' simply meant a daily debt of one *wŏn* and fifty *chŏn*. Furthermore, given the innkeepers' slash-and-burn farmer backgrounds, they served breakfast at shockingly early hours, and dinner extremely late. To stave off the long fourteen hours of hunger, guests in the area used currency to their advantage and went around making all kinds of deals and pleas throughout town. It was the only way. But given Tabuk'o's empty pockets, she couldn't possibly fathom the thought of lunch. She had no choice but to clutch on to her voracious belly and stare up at the sky during the long hours of the day. Then, the summer break that all the innkeepers had long awaited finally arrived. Tabuk'o wasn't sure just how great this long-awaited summer break could even be. She assumed that perhaps some rich, mischievous young men were going to flock in, and she waited alongside the innkeepers.

Twenty-first of July.

The sky was unrelenting, and the monsoon rainstorms continued to plague the town. The innkeepers' faces grew gloomy. Even so, when the time reached half past eleven, they sent their clerks to the station. Tabuk'o also headed out and stood in the corner of a house, waiting for the bus. But the guests who unloaded from the bus amounted to just one or two. They were the only ones who had come to the countryside to bathe. The sky cleared in the afternoon, but the four thirty bus was also empty. The rain forewarned the innkeepers of their disappointment on the twenty-first. By the twenty-second, a tired sun began to dry up the drenched lands. But nothing ever goes as one planned.

Even up until the year before, young men and women came in droves and enjoyed themselves to their hearts' content, and so the innkeepers expected the same this year, but the Mukden Incident had a large impact. The flash news that followed thereafter never quite reached rural places like these. The couple of students (from a professional school) who did arrive were those whose health had deteriorated during the last year of studying. Other than those two were only families who brought their children to rehabilitate their health, taking up two or three rooms all to themselves. They scorned the innkeepers, who had no outside world encounters aside from the inns, and Tabuk'o was an even less useful being in their minds. Then there were a couple of well-to-do girls who came with their mothers, but there were no guests that would be of use to Tabuk'o. Meanwhile, students were caught up volunteering in the labour force and unable to break away.

Now what to do? The long-awaited summer break brought disappointment to the innkeepers and despair to Tabuk'o. What was she thinking when she came back to the hotel after she'd paid off her meal tab and walked out to the station with her bags packed? On that day, her loss amounted to twenty *wŏn*, but her body was now stuck here due to the debt she'd incurred. Women who had arrived with the same motive as Tabuk'o were at inns all over with their webs lying in wait. Were they doing any better than she? Tabuk'o was extremely curious of their situation, and she scanned them thoroughly. The economic depression must've reached this field of work as well. At night, the women went to bed alone and in the morning, they awoke alone. But were they like Tabuk'o and coolly but calmly hanging in there despite not having any money for meals? Or did they bring plenty of money to cover that? Or were they just pretending not to be broke? In any case, Tabuk'o had told the innkeepers with her own mouth that she was broke (she wasn't getting cash, and the leftovers for beggars wasn't even food). They treated her like a parasite and humiliated her to no end.

'Tabuk'o-*sang*. It's a bit slow around here. Why don't you take the kid out by the stream?' The innkeeper's wife would call Tabuk'o over whenever she was a bit busy and sent Tabuk'o away with her child on her back.

'Tabuk'o-*sang*, the guests in room number five are drinking beer. Why don't you go in and pour it for them?' Even the innkeeper himself treated Tabuk'o as though she were a hotel maid. At times like this, Tabuk'o wondered angrily to herself if she was indeed eating free meals, but she maintained a leathery smile on her face and did whatever they asked her to do. She was shackled to the establishment.

Of course, Tabuk'o didn't spend all her time here in the hot springs district like a pure widow. She did have relations with a few men. But Tabuk'o's appearance was what it was, and on top of that, her circumstances were the talk of the town. The patrons who visited her only did so knowing that her services were free. Others who stopped in did so out of filthy curiosity. They barely exchanged proper greetings with her. If she did well, she made one or two *wŏn*. Otherwise, they'd leave behind their leftover cigarettes in an open carton and sneak away without paying at all. Even in her poor state, when one *wŏn* just barely made it into her hands, Tabuk'o would go to the store and buy caramels, soda, cigarettes and candy, and spend her entire earnings just to make it seem like she wasn't broke. She lived her life in a state of complete self-abandonment. Out of desperation, she even fantasized about running away and heading back home to Sunch'ŏn, but the thought of carrying her heavy body down ten *li* in the hot summer was unbearable.

The daily debt of one *wŏn* and sixty *chŏn* she incurred continued to bloat. The prospect of paying it back was nowhere in sight. Her favours had dried up all around her, and she had no choice but to carry other women's babies around for them on her back, pacing the *maru* back and forth, crumpling that ugly face of hers and sneaking glances at the family members. It was a truly pitiful sight. Her mind, which had retreated deep into its own ravine, was in search of all kinds of plans to get out despite her dim-wittedness. Whenever a guest left and a new one entered, she'd tighten her grip around her pockets and sit on the floor outside the guestroom's door and sing a pop song in her melodic (?) voice, even tossing out a few words to engage him. However, what prevented folks from taking her bait was, of course, her looks, but even more so the rumours that surrounded her. Whenever a guest entered a hot tub to entertain himself with a little bit of gossip, he feared the possibility of becoming associated with such an infamous story that he avoided her at all costs.

The old Taet'angji lady. She was no longer Tabuk'o or Butako. She earned herself a new name out here. The truth was that of all the guests at the inn, Tabuk'o was the most senior patron. The guests who'd arrived before Tabuk'o were, of course, gone already, and the ones that arrived after Tabuk'o had also left. Tabuk'o was the longest staying patron. Thus she became known as the old Taet'angji lady.

There were two men who the old Taet'angji lady, Tabuk'o (with her massively thick face), went after. These two men made Tabuk'o's name so infamous that it wasn't just the hot springs that knew of her but all of Yangdŏk county. The guests who came to the hot springs would first ask about her at Yangdŏk station, where the transfer bus arrived. It was enough to irritate the bus driver himself. One of the men was a coal miner who was known around town as Flat-face. One day, Flat-face was playing *hwat'u* with a friend. Tabuk'o, who'd been actively looking for a catch (if she didn't make a catch then she would've at least looked for some cigarette money), went over to the *hwat'u* table and looked over the players' shoulders.

'Why don't you join us, lady?'

'I'm not sure ...'

This is how the relationship blossomed.

Tabuk'o, who'd come to the *hwat'u* table without a single *chŏn* on her, joined the game without giving it another thought. Tabuk'o ultimately won eighteen *chŏn* that day. But one man's loss is another's win; Flat-face lost eighteen *chŏn*. Flat-face was settling his eighteen *chŏn* with Tabuk'o when he said, 'So, lady, you think you'll put my money to good use?'

'I'm not sure ...'

'Eighteen *chŏn* ... It's just money. Unfortunately, money can't be eaten.'

'Never mind that.'

And so they met.

He was a miner, so he was good with money. He had a flat face and so he was generous. Nevertheless, the only money that she was able to earn from him was just the eighteen *chŏn* she won at the *hwat'u* table – so the story goes. From Tabuk'o's point of view, she had no way to figure out what went on inside Flat-face's head. Flat-face would not hide these facts from his friends.

'I'm gonna have to marry that lady over there.'

And he called Tabuk'o '*Manura*, honey, *manura*.'[4] Even so, he gave her no signs, asking her to come over at night. Tabuk'o was surprised to find herself feeling slightly vulnerable to him. When he called her *manura*, she felt a touch of joy. During the day he'd call her *manura* and then order her to pour him a drink. But at night, he never came looking for her. Perhaps Tabuk'o's fat, slippery body disgusted him. Whether it was her own doing or by sheer chance, she one day decided not to wait around and paid him a visit. She did it twice. She did it three times. But whenever she visited Flat-face at his home on the second floor, he'd pretend to be asleep and shoo

[4] *manura* – wife.

her away.

After putting up with this a couple of times, Tabuk'o decided to stop being coy. She removed her nightgown and slipped into his bedding (while Flat-face pretended to be asleep). After getting a taste of a man's shrieks and Flat-face's violence, Tabuk'o came rushing out.

'I've been hearing about girls like you coming into people's territory, and I suppose they were right. These pinchers are here to catch your kind.' After getting her thigh pinched by the man's strong fingers, Tabuk'o let out a scream and came tumbling down the stairs before running away. She didn't even have time to grab her nightgown. After this incident, Tabuk'o became just a tad more famous, and Flat-face earned a new nickname: 'Strong Pincher'. Whenever Tabuk'o roamed the streets with her dark expression, she heard people mutter 'pincher, pincher' all around her. Just a couple of days before the pinching incident, a new connection had begun.

At four thirty in the afternoon, a young man with a kind face, dressed in a suit, stepped into her guestroom. Tabuk'o, the small-town bar *nakai*, couldn't tell a suit's quality from high, standard, or low. She simply assumed that, given his youth, handsome looks, and suit, he came from money. She began to put her moves on the young man. Despite her clumsy seduction, she was able to get him to surrender relatively easily. Two people slept in her room that night. A lonely bed spent the night in his room, untouched. The next morning, the two lovers shared a hot tub together, went over to the canned goods store to eat, then took a walk alongside the brook. The astonishment in the eyes of onlookers ... At any other time, Tabuk'o would've felt shy, but because this was something she'd been waiting for so long, she didn't even sense humiliation. She walked with her head held high. They spent that evening together as well.

Early next morning, Tabuk'o woke from her sleep to the sounds of bustling in the courtyard. She saw the young man hurriedly putting his clothes on. Both doors burst open and a young woman holding a child on her back entered.

'Honey, what is this?' It was his wife. It goes without saying that a huge fight erupted between the two. They say that a married couple's fight is impossible to tame, but even so, they made up afterwards.

'While you're here, why don't we have breakfast and then go for a dip in the hot springs?' he asked his wife.

'All right.'

When breakfast arrived, the woman spoke to Tabuk'o just as the innkeeper's wife used to address her. 'While we eat breakfast, why don't you take the child with you and wash this diaper for us down by the brook?'

Babysitting again ... Her insides boiled with rage and disgust, but nice Tabuk'o – more idiotic than nice – took the child onto her back, accepted the dirty diaper and headed towards the brook.

'Whose kid you got there today?' The innkeeper that Tabuk'o stayed with was a native to the town. He had a huge family in the area. Whenever his relatives needed a babysitter, they called upon her to do the job. And so Tabuk'o had carried quite a few children on her back. Even though all the women in town knew that it was a stranger's baby, they teased her anyway with this question just to jab at her. Tabuk'o responded, 'It's a relative's baby,' and trudged down to the brook, clutching a diaper.

The handsome suit appeared to be living under his wife's thumb. Even so, he promised to sneak away and meet Tabuk'o. Tabuk'o overlooked his wife's ragged clothing and the child's dirty clothes and diapers. Instead, she continued to focus on the man's suit and thought, *This handsome suit must have some money*, and awaited a message confirming a time and place to meet. Her debt had now snowballed to fifty or sixty *wŏn*. No amount of change could possibly make this debt go away, and it weighed heavily on Tabuk'o's shoulders.

The Mukden Incident's air defense exercise began here in the village hidden deep inside the mountain. Four days of blackout. A Japanese police officer and three firefighters arrived in the hot springs district to conduct the blackout. Around eight in the evening, a blackout air-raid warning would begin. After thirty minutes, it'd be air raid control. Everything would be clear by eleven. Then the Japanese officer and the firefighters would take the bus and head back into town.

On the first day, the blackout lasted till eleven, then the restrictions were finally lifted. Brightness returned to the lands. In the darkness, she heard, 'Shall I rest here a while?' A man spoke as he entered Tabuk'o's room. It was a firefighter. The firefighter was the well-dressed suit from the other day. The man she assumed to be of a decent background turned out to be a measly wage-earning firefighter. Although she did lie beside him, Tabuk'o couldn't help but cry inside due to this sudden realization – the soft-skinned suit turning out to be an idiotic firefighter.

Tabuk'o mistakenly lit a match and caused a fire. As she ran up and down trying to put it out, the men gave her a new nickname: 'the firefighter's missus'. After enduring many similar incidents, Tabuk'o stopped luring men. She walked down to the brook daily and squatted beside it, staring at the stream while crumpling her thick leathery face into a frown. Perhaps she envied that water, for it might flow all the way down to her hometown in Sunch'ŏn.

I (the writer) came to the springs to recover my health for a month, and I was ready to depart. A massive transfer bus arrived and filled up with people. It gave off a loud noise before taking off immediately. Just then, I caught a glimpse of

Tabuk'o, who looked on from the corner of the inn towards this direction.

There's no way for me to know what's happened to her since then. But unless a kind philanthropist appeared and paid off her meal tab, or wrote off her meals, gave her money for the train and sent her on her way, there's no way she could've used her 'femininity' to her advantage given the size of her body and that face. It's quite possible that she is still there, incurring a daily debt of one *wŏn* and sixty *chŏn*, watching the town's children while crouched beside the brook, staring at the water flow by.

October–November 1938

MOTHER BEAR

Her official title was Komne.[1] The name her parents gave her was Kil-nyŏ. Her surname was Pak. Legally her name was Pak Kil-nyŏ, but the parents who gave her the name Kil-nyŏ never called her by her actual name. Ever since she was five or six years old, her parents were already calling her Komne. When she was young, her mother held her close and called her 'Komne, Komne,' so often that the adults who went to that house found themselves calling her by that as well. Komne also referred to herself as Komne, so she never even knew that her actual name was Kil-nyŏ. She only knew of herself as Komne.

When she was eight or nine years old, a distant elderly relative called out to her, 'Kil-nyŏ.' Komne had no idea who she was referring to, so she continued to go on playing her games. Then the relative stretched her hand out towards her and said, 'Kil-nyŏ, Kil-nyŏ, come here.' It was at this moment

[1] *kom* – bear.

that Komne understood that the call was for her. She did not go to that relative but went straight to her mother.

'Mom, mom, that person keeps calling me Kil-nyŏ. What's a Kil-nyŏ? She doesn't even know my name. It's scary ...'

Komne's mother explained: 'Little girl! How dare you speak of your elder this way. When you were young you used to roll around like a big round bear so we decided to call you Komne. Now go back out and play, child.'

'Hmph! I'm cuddly and adorable like a bear, which is why I'm Komne, not big and round. If I were big and round, I'd be called Komt'ong!'

'Go out and play!'

'Wah! Hmph!'

The truth was that, for a girl, her moves were incredibly slow and awkward, much like a bear. Hence the name Komne. The skin on her face was thick and coarse. Not only were her hands and arms big and strong, but she was big and barrel-chested, which gave her a dopey appearance. Her voice was rough. Even the hair on her head was thick and stiff. If one were to painstakingly search for a feminine quality in her, it would be her sleep talk. Whenever she sleep-talked, she made tender little sounds which expressed an instinctive desire to hold a baby on her back.

Aside from this, there wasn't the slightest trace of womanliness about her. Her name was Kil-nyŏ as in fortune, *kil*, and female, *nyŏ*, but neither fortune nor stability could be found in this child. She wasn't *kom* for being soft and cuddly. She was *kom* for being dim and slow like a bear.

The minute she came off her mother's breast she was sent to the fields. The family had a tiny bit of land. During a good crop year, the family of three (father, mother, Komne) just barely escaped hunger. As soon as Komne entered the fields, her mother's workload lightened substantially. Komne's father was a lazy man, which was quite unlikely for a farmer. He lacked both stamina and substance. He was the town lout.

He wandered around looking for booze or gambling dens. If not, he climbed over other people's walls to peek at strangers' wives. During farming season, the work had to be done by both him and his wife, so he went to the fields out of duty, but he hated getting dirt on his hands. On top of this, he lacked physical strength. He couldn't handle hard labour because it made him short of breath. All he ever did was think about how to get out of working. Aside from light and easy tasks, he never did any work. Even if he was asked to do something, he was an unreliable person for it. At age five, Komne went to help her mother in the fields. Her sturdy body was so much more of an asset compared to her father's. Her strength and vigour tripled his. Meanwhile, she retained the passion and earnestness of a young child. And so it went. By the time she was seven or eight years old, she was already bringing in her share of the harvest as a farmer. Her farming sensibility was as sharp as an adult's.

Her lazy father died when Komne was about twelve or thirteen. Although the head of the family was now gone, this had absolutely no impact on the family's financial situation. To put it frankly, now that the size of the family had dwindled, the mother and daughter had a little more room to stretch their legs. When the father was alive, all he did was waste food. He was a being of no help or contribution whatsoever. Nonetheless, having spent a little over ten years with the man, Komne's mother couldn't deny the attachment she'd developed for him. She wore a white ribbon to mourn his death and would occasionally stare blankly up at the sky with pity. But aside from this, there really wasn't any change. He was the head of the household but the kind who only lay around, ate, and stirred trouble. When it came to their day-to-day living, he was of no help. But now that Komne was here to pick up the slack, her mother felt a whole lot more at ease, and she found herself needing to put in less work. Komne's mother often took a moment to simply gaze at her daughter, who had the integrity to take on the workload herself. When Komne turned fourteen, her mother, too, passed away. It was the kind of event that would disorient any fourteen-year-old girl.

There was no one around to incur debt, so there wasn't any debt to repay, but the only things left behind for her were an iron cauldron, two or three pieces of kitchenware and a couple of pieces of worn-down clothing. This poverty-stricken household had nothing. On top of that, the pillar of the household – Komne's mother – had now toppled. But Komne, who'd grown up without the taste of luxury or leisure, didn't cave during times like this. The small scrap of land that they had was insignificant, but it was what had helped her and her mother live from hand to mouth. Losing the land would be a disaster. In autumn, when Komne brought her light harvest over to the landowner ('landowner' meaning a poor, independent farmer), he said, 'With your father and mother both gone, there probably isn't anyone around to work the land.'

'When Father was around, what did he contribute?' Komne tried countering.

'Sure – your father was no help, but your mother was, wasn't she?'

'And what did Mother contribute? I did all the work.'

'Even so. How could a single girl such as yourself handle all that farm work?'

'I can do it. I brought the harvest to you as promised, so I did my part. I can handle it.' Since Komne had been doing the farm work herself all along, she didn't consider other thoughts or opinions on the matter. Because she didn't think twice about it, she had no backup plans. But during the brief exchange with the farmer, she grew suspicious. She sensed that the farmer was about to pull the land. Sensing the oncoming threat, Komne first insisted on working the land on her own. Then she began to plead. Towards the end, she was begging. But the landowner wouldn't have any of it. He ignored her requests.

'How's a single girl like you going to look after the land by yourself?' In short, regardless of her skills and strength, his rationale was that he couldn't leave the farm work up to a girl.

Komne eventually lost the land.

But Komne didn't succumb to fear. Because she was born into poverty and raised in poverty, she didn't know how to fear it. She inherited a tiny shack from her parents, so she dwelled there. In that tiny village, everyone knew one another. She began to pay visits from house to house. Come autumn, shortly after the harvest, farmers twisted straw rope and wove straw bags. Komne went around and helped out with these tasks. When she went to these houses, there were folks who paid her a wage for the day's labour or simply fed her a meal in return for the work. Whether it was just a meal or a bit of money, Komne had no complaints about the manner of payment. So long as they fed her, she was glad. If they gave her a bit of money on top of that, she was grateful. She was characteristically honest and without greed. She didn't know how to be cunning, and so she didn't know how to tell apart her work from that of others. If she began something with her hands, it became her task to complete. Regardless of whether anyone was watching over her or not, she always maintained a steady mode of work, putting all her efforts and attention to the task. Young men smoked cigarettes and chatted leisurely, whiling away precious time, but Komne never participated in any of that. When she began something in the morning, she worked till lunch. During lunch, she worked while eating, and repeated the same for dinner. She worked till it grew dark, and continued through the night. Since she didn't have a wholesome family waiting for her back home, she would typically eat skimpy meals alone in a corner. She became the village's precious worker who would work extremely hard at whatever she was assigned in return for a cheap wage.

'Komne must be working this hard to raise seed money in preparation to get married.' The women around town would tease her in this way.

Komne, who didn't quite understand what they meant, would reply, 'What? Ha!' and laugh it off.

'Hey, Komne, what kind of husband would you like to take home?' When folks asked her questions like this in jest, Komne didn't know whether to react with embarrassment or joy. A husband and marriage were foreign concepts that she couldn't even fathom at this point.

When she twisted straws or wove bags, her hands would brush up against young men's hands frequently. Other times they would be held together. But during these times, she never thought to pull away. She always remained composed in such moments, as though it were a natural interaction between men and women. Her looks, her manners and behaviour all seemed so much like a boy's. The young men who worked with Komne didn't appear to see her as a girl. There were occasions when Komne would be held up by her arms and moved over, or times when they would come very close, face to face, but no one would so much as flinch during these times. They would all treat one another as they would a fellow man. Komne shared the same feeling.

They say that when a single girl turns seventeen, she gives off a pungent scent. Komne, too, was a person. She began to think ahead of her years. If it had been any other young lady, this was the age when she would look at herself in the mirror, paint her fingernails, brush her hair and rush towards the door at the mere sound of a man's voice. Komne, however, had no such sweet moments in her life. But she did notice one change. When she went to another person's house to work till late at night, she didn't want to return to an empty house.

She occasionally felt envious of the sight of a wife bringing lunch to the fields where her husband worked while her child trailed behind her. *Someone had gotten married. Someone had lost their wife.* These kinds of rumours entered Komne's ears more and more frequently. Then there were the town's women:

'Komne, you ought to get married too, now. Don't you think?'

'You might die a virgin at that rate.'

'She doesn't have parents. There's no one to guide her on the marriage procedures.'

'Since you're strong, even if you do get married, you'll still be able to work real hard.'

Comments like these erupted all around her. Furthermore, if she were a married woman, the excuse, 'How can a single girl like you work the land herself?' would no longer apply, and she wouldn't be turned away when she sought a plot of sharecropping land. Come to think of it, if she found a husband, she would no longer be a 'single girl making a living alone', but she could own land and work on the straw ropes and bags as well. She could be so much wealthier than working for a wage in other people's homes.

Should I find a husband? When it came to a husband's qualities, she had no particular expectations or demands. Since this was a farmland, it was a given that he'd be a farmer. Komne had no understanding of how to even consider a man's education or personality. She didn't know how to tell apart a handsome man from an ugly one. All she needed was a man that she could label 'husband'. Beyond this, she had no other wants. She felt neither envy nor greed about the situation. She needed a husband in order to gain a plot of land, and some help with the labour. And so, the year Komne turned fifteen, she found a partner to wed through an arrangement by a town elder.

The husband-to-be was also a waif. He was an uneducated

twenty-four-year-old bachelor. He had no savings. He had no land. His background was a mystery, but around three or four years ago he'd found himself in the town. He had no home of his own, so he worked from house to house in return for meals and a place to sleep. He was that sort of bachelor.

'He probably lived that way because he had no home of his own. Once he has a wife, he'll probably be able to bring his portion to the house.'

'The boy's a farmer. At least he won't let his wife go hungry.'

The matchmaker and women who married at an early age all said the same thing. Komne shared a similar sentiment. Once a man was around, the workload would double up, and their living could become a little more plentiful. She collected three months of pay to buy herself a new outfit. And on one auspicious day in January, they held a marriage ceremony.

———————————

The honeymoon phase was sweet. But when it came to Komne's lifestyle and emotions, there were no changes. A man had simply entered the room and shared the covers she once used alone. On the first night of their marriage, the town's women stopped by to make dinner and the bedding. For the first time in her life, Komne ate a meal and slept in a bed that was made for her by someone else. Not only that but the women adamantly refused to let Komne help out.

'You think the new bride does any work?' Everyone hurried around Komne as though she were the master. But after that night, Komne's life went back to the way it was before. The next morning, just as she always had, she wrapped a towel around her head and went over to Mister Lee's house to weave straw bags.

When she stepped into the kitchen, she was told, 'You think a newly wedded woman comes to a place like this?' and was kicked out. When she asked what she was supposed to do then, she was told, 'Find some materials and go back to your house. Sit with your husband and do the work together. Why would you leave your husband back at the house and come to a place like this? So, did you at least have breakfast?'

And so she hauled a stack of rice straws and returned home. From that day forth, if there was any work that could be done at home, Komne did it at her house. Through someone's arrangement, she was also able to take on a small plot of land.

After the nuptials, her new husband didn't have any reason to step out of the front gate of the house for a while. The front gate was surrounded by sorghum plants and he never once set foot beyond them. He didn't even step out into the yard or through the back door. He simply stayed put. All he did was lie back and grab handfuls of Komne all day. When Komne got disgusted and annoyed by him, she would say, 'What are you doing?' and shove him aside. He would then coyly remove his hands, but soon pick right back up from where he started.

One day, when Komne asked another woman about this, she gave her a sly grin and said, 'It's because he finds you so precious. Don't say a word and do as he says. What's not to like?'

Some time passed and her husband's advances no longer disgusted or annoyed her. She eventually began to miss them, and when he didn't make any moves, she found herself longing for them. She began to grow fond of him. Komne, just like her name, had a round bear-like face that seemed dim and slow. There wasn't an ounce of femininity in her. Even when she felt incredible joy and laughed out loud, it was hard to tell from her face whether she was angry or happy. And with that face, whenever she interacted with her husband, a smile came over her effortlessly. That smile, however, appeared awkward on her.

'Honey,' she learned to call her husband. 'Would you like some scorched rice water? Or some cold water?'

'Ah, when I'm this thirsty, some *makkŏlli* would be real nice.'

'Then let me go fetch some.' And the wife would hurry out.

'My my. Is it the dust? Why do I keep coughing? I can hardly breathe.'

'Sŏndal's father got himself a calf. Should we go and put down a share for it?'

'Don't know ...' And the wife would hurry over to put down a deposit.

'The heat wave's gone down. Not sure why my leg keeps going to sleep.'

'Then let me go get some pork loin for you.'

The young man, who was a complete stranger to her up until half a year ago, was now the object of all of her affections. The care and effort that she couldn't show her parents now poured onto this young man, who was taken in by her from the streets. Now that Komne was married, the landowners who never would have given her the time of day otherwise, offered her plots of land. Komne, who knew no greed, never took on more than what she could handle. And she put all of her heart and soul into the plot of land she took on. She was generous with the fertilizer, and worked the soil harder than anyone else. When autumn came and the rice harvest turned gold, Komne's field looked a lot more plentiful compared to the others. When she was single, they wouldn't give her a plot of land the size of her palm because she was alone, but now that she was married, she realized taking on a whole field by herself was completely manageable. Genuine and hardworking, Komne thought that this was all thanks to her beloved husband. But it wasn't as if her husband worked the fields or weeded the paddy. He was a man of weak constitution who couldn't handle farm labour. He was lazy and never bothered working the fields. On top of this, Komne devoted a great deal of her time and efforts into protecting his physical health.

What if he gets sick? What if he gets hurt? While these thoughts plagued her, if there was the slightest bit of heavy lifting to do, she never let her husband shoulder it. Her lazy husband never even bothered to shoulder it. All he did was look back at his wife from time to time. The 'work' that her husband did take on were small tasks that needed tending to because Komne ran out of hands to do them herself.

'Please throw that over here,' or 'While I work on this, please press down on this firmly.' Such were the simple chores her husband took on.

Komne's face wasn't just ugly. It was hideous. It was so foul that a normal fellow wouldn't so much as come near it. Since Komne's husband had eyes that could see, it's very likely that he thought this way about her, too. But he could not leave his wife. If he ever left her, he'd live the rest of his life alone. The chances of finding another wife were little to none.

He was a gambler (and not the jolly, vivacious kind of gambler, either; rather, he was the type who would languidly look over at another's game or go and take a free cut of another's winnings). He would fall vastly short of the title 'a good man'. This man, who'd lived twenty-four years as a waif (wait, no – a *bachelor*), had met Komne out of sheer chance, and Komne was a blessing from the heavens. She was a rare and precious golden calf. He had no right to judge her by her looks. Regardless of her looks, a woman is a woman. She fed him, clothed him and was the sole breadwinner of the household (on top of working the fields, she even wove straw bags). All he lived on was his title as husband, which gave him food to eat, clothes to wear, an occasional allowance and the nightly bedding she spread out for him. He even got to be called 'honey'. There was no better deal than this.

Her body was strong, so she never got sick. Her face was ugly, so there was no reason to worry about another man eyeing her over. Her personality was so honest that she easily fell for his lies. She was the perfect wife. She'd grown up in poverty, so she didn't know how to hate it. When she got angry, there was no aftermath following her fit. She was born and raised in this town so if there was anything they ever needed, there were plenty of people to rely on. She was the jackpot. There was no end to the benefits she brought. The first year of their marriage was a bumper year thanks to Komne's hard work. She'd made enough to get them through the winter months with simple side jobs. There were enough savings to go around.

Komne's domestic life moved steadily and peacefully for a year. The husband, who spent his year being scorned by the town, mostly stayed confined to the house. He ate what she made, wore what she gave, drank only the *makkŏlli* that Komne brought him and did as he was told without complaint. Within the twenty or thirty households in town, Komne's home was viewed as a happy one. Due to the year's hard work, they made a profit of about three or four hundred *nyang*. They even bore a son.

'It's hard to know a person until you start living with them.'

'A man needs a woman in order to make his earnings.'

'It's a match made in heaven, no? Who knew that a street rat like him could become a person? Now that he has a wife, he's always on duty as a husband. He pants all the way home to play the father role, too.'

'Well, it's all because he has a good wife. His wife is the one who brings them luck.'

'Nah. His wife is just the same. It's not exactly a match made in heaven. Imagine those two together in one place. Sitting in a room, nose-to-nose ... Ick. If it was me, I don't think I could stand a single day. Up close it's even worse. Each of her nostrils is the size of the East Gate. Yikes. What a sight.'

'Even so, they're living together because they're happy. There's a saying, isn't there? After falling for a pockmarked person, one finds luck in every pore. It's in the eyes of the beholder.'

'Without a doubt. Ah – *hyŏngnim*. You lived with that old whiskery moustachioed man for thirty years, didn't you? Ick! Wasn't his beard itchy?'

'You wenches. Why are you picking on someone else's old man?'

'If he blows his nose, his snot probably gets caught in his whiskers. He probably drinks salty water that touches the snot on his moustache – agh, gross! Ick! Ick!'

'Shut up.'

'But when you were young did you at least kiss him?'

'Why you little ...!'

He was the talk of the town. Komne's husband, who once wandered the streets, was rumoured to have become a changed man after marriage. After Komne the ugly old maiden found a husband, she walked around town, sticking close to him, without any concern for all the eyes that followed them, and became an even bigger topic of gossip. No one could've imagined the shy and quiet Komne to suddenly become such a talkative (always about her husband) woman. It was as though a naive seventeen-year-old bachelor and a virgin had suddenly found each other. It was an unseemly sight to the elderly, but neither of them paid attention to what others thought of them.

A year passed. Another six months went by. It was mid-January. Komne's husband went into town to sell off the year's harvest. That year was another bountiful year. His plan was to sell off the excess product they had. Komne was quick to work out arrangements to find more land to produce added surplus harvest that was a lot better in quality than the previous year. The price of the grain was slightly higher in town, so after selling the surplus, the plan was to get a small plot of land of their own. During the off season, they planned to weave straw bags and raise silkworms to add to the land fund. She sold everything that was harvested from the fields. It was a slight risk, but considering the odds, this would bring in a lot more money than any other option. If they just waited a few years this way, they'd be able to make a modest living without worrying about who to pay their rent to. In the meantime, their son would grow up, making things a little more manageable. If they worked as both independent farmers and tenant farmers, they'd be able to reach their goal in no time. With this plan in mind, Komne gave all of her assets to her husband and sent him off to town. Komne smiled in her dreams. She calculated the amount of grain her husband had taken to the market in her head. She thought about the land that was available for purchase nearby and compared it to the amount she calculated, smiling to herself.

'Child,' she said to her infant son, who didn't know a thing, 'we're going to buy land. When you grow up, I'll give it all to you. You like that? You can go to your own land, do your own farming and make your own harvest. Hurry up. Grow, my child.' She held her son and swayed from right to left, dancing around the room. She wandered over to the plot of land available for sale and silently roamed about with her son on her back. From here to the town was about a hundred and twenty *li*. A two-day walk. After two days of getting there, spending a night to rest and walking back – that would take five days to complete the trip. If for some reason another night needed to be spent, it would take six days. Komne spent the first couple of days, then three to four days, restlessly. Time wasn't up yet so there was no reason for him to return, but her mind was ceaselessly restless. If her husband had gone there in a real hurry, spent the day there accomplishing his task and by some good fortune made negotiations that very night in order to leave first thing the next morning, it would still take two whole days. She even imagined impossible scenarios. She knew it was all in vain, but she carried her son twenty *li* down the road through the gusty wind and waited half a day there for his return. Komne, who was completely penniless and starving, held her son and patted her aching back while waiting the whole time. As she turned and made her way back she realized that she'd wasted the day away when she could've spent it twisting straw rope instead. After a couple of days' rest ('rest' meaning twisting straw rope) she headed out again. She felt like now was about the time of his return if he had made an effort to make it back fast. Indeed, that was another wasted day. After a couple more days, it was actually the right time for his return. Komne headed out to greet him again. She bought some *yŏt* at the crack of dawn from the market to go and greet her husband.

There's nothing harder than waiting for another person. Before that day, she knew he wasn't going to make it back but she waited for him earnestly regardless. Today was the day. She waited and waited till she was blue in the face.

'Child, your father is coming home today.' A girl carrying a water jug over her head took a break in front of Komne to readjust its position. Komne immediately struck up a conversation with her. The girl carrying the water jug side-eyed Komne then walked right on past her without a word. There must've been a well nearby. Women carrying water jugs over their heads walked to and fro before Komne. Komne wanted to tell all the girls that today was the day her husband was coming home. The indifferent sun made its way gradually from the east to the west. As it began to set, a gusty wind began to pick up. The baby on her back began to scream as though reacting to the chill.

'There, there, sleep now, my brave boy. Your father's probably making it over that last hill. When your father comes, he'll bring you candy and *ttŏk*. There, there, go to sleep, my brave boy.' She paced back and forth, coaxing the child on her back. He cried and cried until he eventually fell asleep as though he'd gone into shock. But now it was Komne who wanted to wail her lungs out. No matter how short the day-light is, it was incredulous to find the sun already set halfway over the hill. While she wandered to and fro with the baby on her back, her body never fixed itself to either side and her eyes were constantly looking north. They never left that spot. If her husband were to return, he was definitely coming from that direction. There weren't any shortcuts. There wasn't an alternate route. It was the closest and the only path in the vicinity. She never looked elsewhere, but her husband still had not returned.

'I'll try ten more steps.' The distance from the well to the market was about twenty or so houses. She must've walked that path to and fro about a hundred times. If he hadn't returned by now, there was no hope of his return any time soon. There was no other choice but to turn back around and head home. But as she turned to leave, her heart decided to circle back to the well again another ten times.

'Let's go a little more. Ten more times.' She completed her ten rounds. She still didn't find any results. She suppressed her wails, covered her face and turned to walk back to the house.

————————

The next day, Komne's husband still had not returned. Yet another day went by without his return. He returned after four whole days. The coat string around his jacket was torn, and he was covered in mud. It was a pathetic sight.

'Oh my goodness. What on earth happened?'

'On my way back I ran into some hooligans in the hills.'

'Are you hurt?'

'I'm not hurt but I've been robbed down to the last penny.'

Komne felt the wind knock out of her body. 'It's a good thing you aren't hurt. So, when did this happen?'

'... The day before yesterday.'

'Then where were you this whole time?'

'Oh wait, no. Was it the day before that?'

'Where were you, then?'

'Well, I was in town that day, of course.'

'What were you doing in town for three to four days straight?'

'Gee, it's cold.' Komne's husband didn't reply. He stretched his legs to lie down.

'If you ran into trouble why didn't you come straight home?'

'Ahem. I need to get some sleep.' Komne's husband didn't bother getting undressed or spreading out some bedding. He simply shoved his head deep beneath the covers.

'Aren't you hungry? There isn't any food other than some cold rice ...' Komne couldn't tell whether he could hear her or not. He simply stayed beneath the covers and didn't reply. Komne was at a loss for words. She was glad that her husband wasn't physically harmed, but thinking about the year's worth of hard work, devotion and hope turned into ash made her dizzy. Komne held her baby close and rocked back and forth beside her husband, who stayed beneath the covers. She stared off into space. In order to make back what they'd lost, she needed to put in another year's worth of labour. She also needed to count on another bumper year of crops and for no other trouble to come her way. It was unbelievable how all the sweat, hard effort and credit she'd built up could break apart so easily. The sight before her was pitch black. She couldn't muster the courage again. All she could do was let out a long sigh.

———————————

A strange rumour began to spread around town. It was that Komne had entrusted all of her assets to her husband to bring to town, but he gambled them all away. He then couldn't find any other way to return so he tore up his clothes and lied that he'd been attached by thieves on his way back. He even pretended to be ill for several days.

Rumours stirred. But it was a small town where, although word travelled fast, it didn't go very far. The gossips were quick to hush one another about it so the rumours ultimately did not reach Komne's ears. Regardless of these rumours, Komne headed back out into the fields and pushed her husband to prepare for the spring and the upcoming year. It was still a shock to her that the spring would be spent in impoverishment and that her goal now was to work so they could raise a little bit of money. She thought about how she could raise back what she had lost the previous year, and mustered the courage to step back out. The plot of land that she used to gaze at and mutter, 'I shall buy this land,' while holding her baby on her back and braving out the gusty winds, now brought a bitterness to her mouth whenever she looked at it. She promised herself that she would buy a better plot of land within the year, and worked with all her might. But since the spring, she noticed something different about her husband. While working the field, he would find a gap in between to sneak away. He would then sneak back after a while. When he did return, he would avoid her. But whenever she got close, she detected a hint of booze on his breath.

'Where were you?' she would ask him.

He'd respond, 'I was so tired I went over to the sorghum field to nap.' He would then stretch his arms out in the air to feign sleepiness. This happened on a number of occasions. Komne, who wasn't used to being suspicious of anyone, could not ignore his strange behavior any longer. She became determined to catch him in the act and kept a watchful eye on him. Without fail, her husband looked about him then slowly crept away, hiding himself inside the field. Komne watched her husband hide inside the furrow, then followed him while keeping a long distance behind him. Komne's husband crept all the way through the furrow, then stood upright when he reached the path. He glanced around behind him once then went into a bar. Komne followed him in. Around the fence and at the back was a yard. Komne went around and hid behind stacks of dried straw to eavesdrop. She overheard a table being set inside the room. Then she heard alcohol being poured into a glass.

Pour. Drink. The festivities seemed to have begun. Amongst those sounds, she also heard a woman's voice. Komne got closer to the bar to get a better grasp of the conversation. Just then she heard a man's voice, 'Did you know that a *ttŏkdol* could have a face?'[2]

A woman's voice replied, 'Quit it. Your wife will get mad.'

The man's voice chastised himself, 'You *idiot*. What made you want to have a baby with her?'

The woman's voice replied, 'When you screw, do you do it with your eyes open? If you screw with your eyes shut, how are you supposed to know if what you're screwing is pretty or ugly? That's all it takes to make a baby.'

Komne couldn't take it anymore. The righteous have a ferocious anger. She put her sleeping baby gently down on top of the straw stacks. She gathered up both of her sleeves, kicked the door open and ran inside. Right below her feet was the woman. Komne grabbed her hair with her left hand. She saw her husband next to her. She grabbed her husband by the throat with her right hand. Another man kicked down the door and scurried away.

'You little wench! What did you just say?' Komne yanked the girl by the hair and bashed her head against her husband's forehead. She then grabbed her husband by the hair and forced him to look at the girl's face.

'That's right. Look at that stone.' Just like her name, she turned into an angry bear, bashing everything in sight. Her weakling husband. The barmaid. No one could tame this angry bear.

'Honey. *Manura, manura* ...'

'I thought I was a *ttŏkdol*. Since when am I your *manura*?'

[2] *ttŏkdol* – a large stone base where rice cakes are laid for pounding.

'When did I say such a thing, honey? *Manura*?'

This was the first time Komne had ever been called 'honey' and '*manura*'. Even in her state of anger, she was glad to hear it. 'If I'm the *ttŏkdol*, does that make you the *ttŏkme*?'[3]

'Honey. *Manura*. When did I ever say such a thing? Why would I speak harshly of my own wife?'

'Then what was all that before?' The bear's fury had already calmed down.

'*Manura*, listen. I was so thirsty that I came here to have a bit of *makkŏlli*, but those worthless bastards started talking that way. I got worked up about it and was going to fix them up anyhow. I'm glad you came, *manura*. Boy, am I glad.'

'*Hŭng*. Are you sorry to see this wench take a beating?'

'What are you talking about? Come on. Let's get going. Where's our little Tangson?' And so the couple left the bar. They ended things calmly that day, but her husband's nasty habit was hard to break. It was a habit that had been deeply rooted long before he met Komne. After meeting Komne, he must've felt self-conscious. Or perhaps upon meeting his new wife, he felt afraid of her and didn't let it show. For a while there, his bad behaviour didn't quite show. Then he went to town to sell and coincidentally, his old habits began to surface right around this time. After his return, he kept disappearing from his wife's sight in order to head in that direction. On the very day that he got caught, there was an outburst from his wife which he was able to calm, but immediately thereafter he insisted that there was somebody he needed to meet, so he sent his wife home alone then turned to head straight back to the bar. From that day forth, whenever any money came into his hands, or after stealing some from his wife's pockets, he always headed in that direction. Because of this, the fights with his wife became a lot more frequent. Whenever they did fight, he would beg his wife for forgiveness and swear up and down that he would never go back there again, but all he ever

---

[3] *ttŏkme* – a wooden rod used to pound rice cakes against the *ttŏkdol*.

did was think about when the opportunity to get away again would show.

Their living situation became more and more unstable and impoverished as the days passed. As the trips to the bar became frequent, Komne stopped grabbing on to her husband's hand to stop him. As his trips became more expensive, he would do everything in his power to coax his wife, or steal from her, or fight her in order to get away. Meanwhile his wife worked herself down to the bone out in the fields. Because her husband had stopped going out to the fields, she was taking on his load of the work, too. There were occasions when a bit of money did get saved. If it wasn't for her husband, it'd be possible to always live with some savings. But with her husband around, who seemed to have a financial demon on his back, it was impossible. Hot-tempered and righteous Komne would swear never to listen to her hateful husband again, but as soon as he came home and rubbed her back, calling her 'honey, my *manura*', her hardened heart would melt away like snow on a spring day. Then her husband would dig deep into her pockets to find some cash to waste away.

'I'm sorry ...' After her husband took off again, Komne would feel her empty pockets, lament, then swear never to fall for his tricks again. But she could never keep that promise to herself in the end.

One day, Komne took a trip to the town market. Whenever she went to the market, she made some *chottŏk* to bring with her to eat.[4] On that day, just like all the other days, her husband begged her for some cash, so she gave him two *wŏn* before leaving the house. Even though it was she who'd given it to him, by the time she got to the market, she regretted it again. She was too thrifty to even spend fifteen *chŏn* on *ttŏk* at the market, so she made *chottŏk* at home to bring

4 *chottŏk* – millet dough cake.

with her. She could barely swallow the stiff cakes without water. Meanwhile, her husband was off somewhere drinking merrily. She felt ashamed to have given him the money. She opened up her bag and took out the *chottŏk*. Her throat was dry and in her perturbed state she lost her appetite. In spite of this, she took a couple of bites. Then she heard a babbling beside her. She turned and found a nine-year-old boy asking her for something.

'What do you want?'

'*Ttŏk.*' The child asked for one of her *chottŏk*. Komne didn't feel like eating it anyhow and the boy looked so hungry that she picked up two large pieces and handed them to him. As soon as she did so, the boy gobbled them right up.

'You want another?' The child nodded his head. Komne gave him two more. The child began to gobble them up again but left about half of a piece and stopped eating.

'Go on and have some more.'

'Ah. So full.'

'You've never eaten *chottŏk* before?'

The boy shook his head.

'Why not? Doesn't your mother make you any?'

'Mother's dead.'

'You poor thing. You don't have a father, either?'

'Father used to drink all the time. He left one day and now I don't know where he is. I'm alone.' Komne felt her heart ache. She turned the baby who'd been sleeping soundly on her back over and held him close to her chest. She lowered her head. She stroked her son's cheek with her hair lovingly.

I suppose his father is a stranger to this child.

Her husband was the kind of fellow who found spending a single *chŏn* on his only child's sweets wasteful compared to his drink that cost him one *wŏn*.

I need to live. I need to live in order for this child to live. No matter what happens or what trouble arises, I must never fall down. If I fall, this baby falls down with me!

'Hey, Tangson. What would you like? What would you like to eat? Tell me whatever your little heart desires,' she said to her sleeping baby. She woke her baby and rubbed his cheek as she spoke. The child opened his eyes and looked at his mother's face which was right beside his. He must've felt secure at the sight. He lifted up both his arms and let out a long stretch.

'Child,' Komne said to the homeless boy, 'you don't have a mother or a father. You must be hungry and tired. Come with me. I'll buy you whatever you like – whatever you want to eat. Come along.' As she held her son close to her chest and rubbed her cheek against his, she walked towards the market with the homeless boy at her side.

April 1941

THE TRAITOR

He was born into a completely unknown household – a
P'yŏng'an Province *sŏnbi*'s home. No matter how skilled one
may be at flying or crawling, this nation treated the P'yŏng'an
people as if their dusty hard work would always be for naught.
But O I-bae was born with the useless gift of 'vast talent'.[1]
Rumours of his 'prodigy' had spread around town. Useless
talent, talent that can't feed you, talent that merely brings you
a countryside's scent or helps you pass the state examination,
talent that causes rage inside the body if mishandled – but
that talent was granted by the heavens, and so it could not be
discarded, nor could it be handed down to another. Generation after generation, his family played the role of the *sŏnbi*.
Due to this, they were a refined family out in the countryside. However, they did not pay close attention to credits and
industry, which caused their fortunes to dwindle each year.
During I-bae's father's lifetime, bankruptcy could not be

---

[1] "O I-bae" is modeled after modernist Yi Kwang-su.

avoided. Each generation managed to wield authority by just barely maintaining a respectable position; however, without any assets or a clue about industry, upholding that cool and collected attitude made life more than just bizarre.

In order to challenge the misfortunate prodigy I-bae, the heavens sent him many trials and tribulations. The year I-bae turned ten, the prodigy's parents passed away all at once. They succumbed to cholera that had swept away everything beneath the sky. He lived all over the neighbourhood, but because the family did not boast a great number of descendants, there weren't too many relatives. Even if he'd become this lonely, if there were at least some relatives around, he could at least find support and have someone to rely on. But the O family had no relatives to speak of after having vanished all at once, which left I-bae all alone in this vast world. A boy who'd barely turned ten, with his nose still runny.

But the family did not lose the good graces of their neighbours over the years. Their sympathies naturally poured onto I-bae. They may not have forgotten their generosity, but even so, these folks were nameless village farmers. He was a *sŏnbi*. Of course, there was no real relationship to speak of. So they could hardly express their sympathies without feeling hesitation. The villagers got together and held a funeral for his parents. But the chief mourner carrying the casket was a young boy. Three or four villagers did go with him, but the bleakness of that casket brought tears to the boy's eyes that rose like the spring.

I-bae was left all alone in this world. After his parents' burial, the only being who came out to greet him from the shack was a dog. Now that the shack that he'd been living in with his parents was barren, I-bae felt like the only person left on this earth – the only human alive. There were times when people walked by his house, but to I-bae this felt like a meaningless daydream. He felt like he was the only living person in this vast world. He felt so pathetic and stunned that he didn't cook any meals for three or four days. He didn't eat. He simply lay indoors. The shack was so lacking any signs of human life that an elderly village woman stopped in out of curiosity. Had she not found I-bae lying there, unconscious from starvation, the boy would've joined his parents in the next world.

'*Aigu.* What is this? What happened? Wake up.'

I-bae came back to life thanks to the elderly woman's dedicated nursing. A few days after his recovery, I-bae chose a school that was a hundred and fifty *li* away and left his hometown. T School was located deep in the mountains but had a good reputation that dated far back. The school's founder was a renowned patriot. The school was founded to plant an ideology that blended divinity with patriotism in the hearts of young boys. I-bae arrived at the school carrying just two changes of clothes. But by the time he got there, he didn't know how to take the first step, considering he was just a boy without anyone to turn to. The school's headmaster found him loitering outside. The headmaster was also a highly respected leader and patriot. He carried out the founder's wishes to educate the young minds of the future properly, and stayed behind as a headmaster in the countryside. He sensed I-bae's sharpness. In order to make him a great leader of this country, the headmaster took I-bae into his home, gave him minor chores and took responsibility over his education.

I-bae, who showed a brilliance in classical studies, also displayed a natural disposition in modern sciences as well. Even though this school attracted the nation's most brilliant minds, I-bae's records stood out as the highest among them. Born into a countryside *sŏnbi*'s home as a prodigy, he had a full grasp of traditional Eastern ethics. Not only that but I-bae displayed a shockingly wide array of understanding across his studies.

'China' is the land of the Manchurian people. It originally belonged to King Wu of Zhou. His direct line of descent has authority over the land. I-bae knew only up to this part, and heard for the first time that the nation Korea originally came from Chosŏn. Through the country known as Japan, which he only knew as *'wae'*, Korea absorbed a surprising amount of new culture in order to take over the entire East. He became astonished by how Japan treated Korea, what kind of intentions it held for it, and what kind of path Koreans must take moving forward. The headmaster concluded that I-bae's exceptional intelligence was his greatest asset. He educated I-bae according to his large expectation that his talent and nationalism would do great things for the country.

After entrusting himself to this school for a year, I-bae's grasp of his studies equalled that of the instructors. It might've been limited to patriotic intelligence, but at this school he became a thinker who came close to the headmaster's level. He graduated without any trouble. Upon graduation, he wished to continue his studies into the next phase, but the headmaster, who loved I-bae dearly and praised him, would not let him go.

'Typically, I would encourage you to go to graduate school and get another degree, but our nation's circumstances are such that what we need is a leader who can do more than just graduate from a great school. And it's urgent. Stay at this school and become a teacher to the students here. Do it for your country, for yourself. If a person as bright as you can support your country by achieving greatness through scholarship, sure—it'd be wonderful. But stay here as a teacher for a little while. Our nation's history is in jeopardy. Think about your future long term. Take care of urgent matters first ...'

The current state of things was indeed in disarray. Japan displayed its evil in plain sight by taking possession over Tonghakdang. Its manoeuvres to swallow up Korea became worse with each day. The traitor faction Tonghakdang collaborated with the Japanese to give up its own nation to their evils, and worked vehemently to achieve this. This propensity was expected and the Korean people's activism to denounce Japan's authority spread like wildfire. In these circumstances, there were still many Korean civilians locked in the dreamy past of the Yo-sun era just like I-bae had been not too long ago. Such were the majority – those who did not know what 'my country' was or what significance this had. Pouring this concept into the nation's people was an extremely urgent matter. In order to do this, a leader who could take on many people at once was more urgent than a leader who could become the future's greatness. This was more important.

I-bae, who was about to leave the headmaster's care and deep graces in order to become a better scholar, took the headmaster's word to heart and instead plopped down at the school, swearing that he would lead and educate the Korean people.

The power of fate can't be stopped. Korea could not avoid signing the protectorate treaty. Korea's diplomatic rights now belonged to the Japanese government in Tokyo. It was a contract stating that all of Korea's functions were now to be supervised by the Japanese. While all of Korea jostled over the protectorate treaty, Japan took another step forward and annexed the nation. Japan's foreign propaganda stated that the Korean emperor must hand over his sovereign power to the Japanese emperor, declaring it a 'merger' between the two states. And so it was. They disbanded the Korean military and all its weaponry. Without any weapons, Korea couldn't put up a fight. However, throughout the country, soldiers stood up. The hot-blooded patriots who organized as soldiers brought their hidden rifles and rusty guns together to express their resistance against the merger. But it was impossible to take on the Japanese military with just boiling blood and clenched fists as their weaponry. The soldiers knew this full well. They knew it but they couldn't bear the rage. They couldn't just sit back and take it without a fight. This was the *minjok*'s belief.[2]

The young instructor I-bae was completely absorbed in the process of teaching the national ideology to his pupils, who were much older than he. Working under the headmaster for several years, learning the meaning of *minjok* and the love for one's own people, his mind and heart went through some changes. Through his pupils he learned how to love his people, and became someone who strived to live for his people wholeheartedly. During the pursuit of this precious service, the love for his own people grew rapidly. At this point, all he had was the *minjok*. The *minjok* issue was of utmost priority. If it didn't concern the *minjok*, scholarship had no value. It was passion, it was deep affection – everything he felt and thought about was the *minjok*. Beyond this, nothing else existed. I-bae was immersed in patriotism. All that flowed out of him was patriotism. He was so deeply into it that it earned him the nickname 'Patriot Nut'. This young instructor's sincere education led to the transformation of his pupils into genuine patriots.

Down the line, the students who graduated from this school became the Japanese government's most detested *yobo*.[3] Whenever something occurred, the innocent graduates of this school took on the punishment that the Japanese government brought upon them. The reason for this began here. It was a school known throughout the nation. Students gathered from all over. After they graduated, they each

[2] *minjok* – the ethnic Korean identity or Korean people as a collective.
[3] *yobo* – a derogatory term used by the Japanese against Koreans.

returned to their respective hometowns and so the school's ideology spread all over the country. At the same time, the young instructor I-bae's reputation also became well-known throughout the country. Admiration for his passion and patriotism spread widely. The school's name and I-bae's name became clear markers of the nation's patriotism. Just then, after Japan swallowed Korea, the school was ordered to shut down. The school of long-standing honour and tradition eventually closed.

Once the school shut down, a patron stepped up to support I-bae. I-bae took off to Tokyo to study abroad with the aid of this patron. It was a long-waited opportunity. But teaching his pupils felt so urgent that he hadn't been able to take it on until now.

I shall bring you down with your own sword. I shall learn from you and make you topple over. With this ambition in mind, he went to his enemy's state and set out for Tokyo. For the next ten years, I-bae studied there with the intent to bring down his enemy with the enemy's sword. I-bae, who was once a middle school instructor, arrived in Tokyo and sat shoulder to shoulder with runny-nosed middle-school Japanese children and learned alongside them. After completing his studies, he attended a private university and majored in political science. His love for the *minjok* continued to burn brightly inside and he retained his ideological vision devotedly throughout his studies, but what he sensed the most was endless disappointment. Followed by the disappointment was heartache.

Japan was growing day by day. Meanwhile, his homeland Chosŏn withered away progressively beneath Japanese policy and education. Even if one were to say that Chosŏn was growing, it would be difficult to catch up to Japan, hence its gradual decline. The gap between Japan and Chosŏn grew. The homeland's revitalization? There was no room for such hope at this point. This caused I-bae infinite grief. Unless Japan voluntarily let go of Chosŏn, there could never be a day when Chosŏn didn't rely on Japan. While studying at the boarding house, this thought would suddenly occur, causing him to throw his book across the room. Then he would sit and stare out into space, not knowing where the time goes.

The First World War erupted then ended. President Wilson raised a sign of 'the principle of national self-determination'. Korea could not restore its national democracy on its own as Japan had annexed the country and would not let it go. In this state, what President Wilson advocated was an opportunity that might not return for the Chosŏn *minjok* ever again. All of Chosŏn wanted to break free from Japan's shackles by ceasing this moment of opportunity, and they directed their cries to the world: 'Chosŏn Independence *manse*!' This opportunity arose completely out of I-bae's own purview. He led the chants and shouted for the *kungmin* and incited rebellion. But Japan's strategies were too strong. Humans have no choice but to succumb to the stronger one. Chosŏn the weakling had a go at the independence movement, but Japan, the stronger nation, did not permit such activities causing it to fizzle out. All of Chosŏn's prisons were full of *manse* criminals. President Wilson's declaration had no impact on the stronger nation.

I-bae sat before this sickening realization with great disappointment and then thought to himself: *Japan is a giant nation that the world can't do anything about. The Chosŏn* minjok *can't break free from Japan's fetters any more. Does this mean that the* minjok *needs to always remain a Japanese colony and suffer through its days as such?* I-bae, who loved the *minjok* like his own flesh and blood, couldn't bear the thought.

Must one nationality eternally service another nationality? Of all things, the thing I love most – our minjok *... Isn't there a way to break free from this suffering and become a joyful* minjok?

I-bae completed his studies and returned to Korea. I-bae, who returned to this homeland in sorrow, was greeted by Chosŏn with joy. Every one of Chosŏn's highest ranking positions were occupied by T School alumni, and they all welcomed their passionate teacher I-bae. A major newspaper press had an editor-in-chief and vice president position awaiting him. I-bae took on the important leadership position. But what was he to lead? Korea wasn't able to free itself from Japan's fetters. To revolt against Japan would needlessly result in people's imprisonment. This was the *minjok*'s adversity. In order to achieve *minjok* happiness within Chosŏn, the *minjok* needed to enhance its cultural improvement first. There was no way to catch up to Japan through material means. The *minjok* would be able to catch up to Japan if it put all its efforts into cultural elevation while Japan focused on exerting growth through its material culture. I-bae, who occupied a sturdy position, wielded his command over the Chosŏn *minjok*, and the *minjok* followed the leadership of their honourable commander.

Japan started yet another war. It took on China as its opponent. China, which seemed like it could be taken down by a single blow, resisted with all its might, counter to Japan's assumption. Japan narrowed its military attacks to land, air and sea but the nation did not budge. Japan underestimated this attack. They sweated bullets throughout the fighting process. At long last, they resorted to seeking aid from the Koreans. I-bae wasted no time using this opportunity to bring the Chosŏn *minjok* happiness. If Chosŏn rose against Japan, even with what little military resources it had, while Japan desperately struggled in the fight, there was at least the possibility of freedom. But Chosŏn's present condition was such that it had only focused on elevating its culture. In terms of military power, one Japanese soldier's cry alone would shock the thirty million Chosŏn people to pieces. Counter to that, if Chosŏn supported Japan and succeeded, the impact of that success would transfer over to Chosŏn history as well. *Let's not lose the opportunity to bring happiness to Chosŏn and join forces with Japan.* He raised his co-operative flag high. He shouted the command to co-operate loudly.

Chosŏn's *minjok* was baffled. I-bae, who had been deeply committed to nationalism up until this point, was now shouting for co-operation with the Japanese – something no one could have ever expected. But I-bae, who believed that this was a unique opportunity to bring happiness to the Chosŏn *minjok*, put his whole heart into this cry.

Japan declared war against the United States and Great Britain. If they won this war, Japan would become the world's hegemon. If Chosŏn joined forces with Japan, and won the war as one with them, the share of that victory credited to Chosŏn would be enormous. Rather than be a scanty independent state that could barely endure on its own, there was much more to be gained by taking part in Japan's victory by supporting its war effort. I-bae gradually changed manoeuvres in his activism towards collaboration. I-bae always had a lot of influential power. When he used it to call upon the public, that impact was not insignificant. Gradually, the crowd among the Chosŏn people who stood in support of Japan's war cause began to rise. During all this, I-bae only looked straight ahead towards success. He believed wholeheartedly that they would succeed. He expected Chosŏn to be credited and achieve glory the day that Japan won. But how on earth would Japan win? He had his own answer to that question. It was not Japan's fate to understand defeat. On top of that, it was destiny that the West now faced decline as it was the East's turn to progress and unfold a new world order.

When the war had reached its peak, the three nations' (USA, Britain, and China) representatives met at Cairo and made a single declaration. The details of this conference reached I-bae somehow, and initially knocked the wind right out of him. It was a recommendation that Japan surrender. On top of that, it advised that Japan relinquish Chosŏn. They'd initially joined Japan believing that gaining independence on their own was impossible – this was all for the sake of Chosŏn's happiness. But according to the Cairo Conference, it appeared that Japan had lost it all. And there was the Chosŏn independence. He'd devoted fifty years of his life to the Chosŏn *minjok*'s happiness. To realize this happiness, he'd supported Japan, ah – ah ... Everything that had been prioritized for the sake of Chosŏn's happiness resulted in the opposite outcome. If the Cairo Conference did in fact lead to Japan's surrender and Chosŏn was relinquished, he would be deemed a traitor from that day forth.

The Chosŏn that I'd loved and valued so – me? A traitor? Never have I held the slightest contempt against Chosŏn. Chosŏn, my homeland, is more precious to me than my own life. How on earth do I become the traitor? On the day that Chosŏn gains independence, will I lose the right to even rejoice due to my traitor status?

On the fifteenth of August 1945, when the Japanese emperor Hirohito announced in a tearful voice to the Japanese people of their surrender, I-bae sat before the radio and cried as he listened to the broadcast.

October 1946

A NOTE ON THE ILLUSTRATION

The cover illustration was commissioned by Honford Star and is by South Korean illustrator Jee-ook Choi. Jee-ook's muted, yet evocative artwork has been gaining a large following both in Korea and internationally. She was the head illustrator for the 5th Diaspora Film Festival and contributed to the 2016 Bucheon International Fantastic Film festival. Her work has also appeared in the *The New Yorker* and *The New York Times Book Review*.

honfordstar.com

Lightning Source UK Ltd.
Milton Keynes UK
UKHW011421150922
408921UK00003B/1054